THE
FAMILY
STRING

DENISE PICTON

THE
FAMILY
STRING

ultimo
press

Published in 2022 by Ultimo Press,
an imprint of Hardie Grant Publishing

Ultimo Press
Gadigal Country
7, 45 Jones Street
Ultimo, NSW 2007
ultimopress.com.au

Ultimo Press (London)
5th & 6th Floors
52–54 Southwark Street
London SE1 1UN

The Family String
ISBN 978 1 76115 108 8 (paperback)

10 9 8 7 6 5 4 3 2 1

Cover design Christabella Designs
Cover images Dachshund by Asia Kravchuk / Shutterstock; girl by Maria Ion / Shutterstock; stripe pattern by CSA Images / Getty Images
Typesetting Kirby Jones | Typeset in 13/18 pt Adobe Garamond Pro
Copyeditor Deonie Fiford
Proofreader Ronnie Scott

Printed and bound in Great Britain by Clays Ltd, Elcograf S.p.A.

Ultimo Press acknowledges the Traditional Owners of the country on which we work, the Gadigal people of the Eora nation and the Wurundjeri people of the Kulin nation, and recognises their continuing connection to the land, waters and culture. We pay our respects to their Elders past and present.

For Roslyn Johnson.
Singular. Sparkling. Missed.

CHAPTER 1

It was me who heard Mum calling first. It was Saturday morning, so Mum had still been in bed when we'd headed for the tree house at the bottom of the garden.

'Shhhh,' I said to the other two. 'We must have missed the first call.'

We had been singing 'April Love' by Pat Boone in the tree house loud enough to drown out a World War I warning claxon, never mind my mother calling from the back door. We froze, and I heard Caleb take in a deep breath so he could hold it until otherwise instructed. Ruthy quietly opened her notebook, pen ready.

'What kind of day will it be, Dorcas?' she whispered after a moment. 'Can you tell yet?'

'Caleb! Ruth! Dorcas! Where are you? I'm warning you. Don't make me come down there to find you,' we heard Mum shout, insistent.

I could just see her through the branches of the enormous old olive that held up our tree house in an upturned leafy hand. You had to see what she was wearing, as well as hear her voice, to be sure what kind of day it would be. She was standing in the doorframe in her stained pink candlewick dressing-gown, one of the two pockets torn and flapping sadly at her side, already looking tired at eight in the morning. Untamed auburn waves exploded around her pale face. My dad described her complexion as 'peaches and cream', but there was no sign of colour this morning. If it was a good day, she would have been wearing her gold quilted housecoat and her matching gold Jiffies. The cowlick at the crown of her head would already be forced into submission by a whoosh of Taft hairspray.

'Cross,' I said. 'It's a cross day, Ruthy.'

Ruthy immediately leaned over her book and wrote the date and the word 'cross' by it. She used a gum leaf as a bookmark and snapped it closed. Ruthy never questioned my assessment. As the oldest living at home, and now on the way to my twelfth birthday, I had the most experience of Mum's moods, and was pretty much always right, particularly as it

2

could be said I was often the cause of the bad ones. Besides, our older brother Daniel had anointed me as the mood-sayer before he left, and none of us disagreed with Daniel.

He was now boarding with a church family in New South Wales and doing God's work with his local youth group. At seventeen, he wasn't old enough yet to be a member of the Arranging Brethren of the Christadelphian Ecclesia, which was our church, and more important than almost any job, even school principal or the premier of South Australia. In his new youth group, he led a team of doorknockers on weekends, a merry band who cheerfully received each inevitable refusal to discuss the relevance of the Bible to their lives.

I often wondered why Jesus would choose 1969 to come back, given all the exciting times in history He could have chosen. If I were Jesus, I'd have returned in time to see the Knights of the Round Table, or the beheading of Anne Boleyn, or the opening of the Sydney Harbour Bridge. Ruthy said He could see all these things anyway at the right hand of God in Heaven, but if I was Him, I'd rather be walking around with everyone else seeing them close up and eating ice-cream or a pie than watching from what must be a pretty big distance away, given not even scientists with powerful telescopes could spot Him where he lived.

Daniel had been gone since just before school started this year and we missed him sorely. Ruthy made notes in her notebook for him every night so she could tell him what was happening when he came home for a visit because she knew he wouldn't want to miss anything. All three of us knew that you had to love your mum and dad the most of anyone, but we all agreed we secretly loved Daniel just as much. Ruthy wasn't sure whether this was allowed. She looked it up in Dad's Bible concordance, where you can try out topics to see if the scriptures have rules about them. She couldn't spot anything that said loving your brother as much as your mum and dad was wrong, so we decided to stick with it.

'How many cross days is that in a row now, Ruthy?' asked Caleb.

Ruthy reopened her notebook and flicked through the pages, counting.

'That's fourteen cross days in a row,' she said. 'It's not a record, but it's getting up there. Before that she had eleven head days and one Jesus day, and before that it was twenty cross days one after the other.'

Caleb nodded, accepting and considering. Head days referred to terrible headaches that made her stay in bed all day until just before Dad came home from work. We all liked the Jesus days best, because they were the ones where Mum seemed happy and hummed hymns quite a bit.

Ruthy kept her notebooks in two Arnott's Christmas Selection biscuit tins under a board in the floor of our tree house. She was on to her seventh book now and had saved up her pocket money so she always had at least one fresh one ready to go. She was about halfway through the current journal and she was hoping Mum and Dad would gift her a big pile of blank books for Christmas so she didn't have to use her pocket money for them anymore. Then she could buy lolly teeth and sherbets at the local shop with us on Saturday mornings instead. I was sometimes prepared to share my teeth with her but only after I'd sucked them for a while first.

Caleb usually shared his lollies with her, but I didn't because I wasn't always friends with Ruthy, and besides, as Mum would say, you have to learn you can't have everything you want in this world. Mum heard me say this to Ruthy one Friday night and smacked me for having a smart mouth. She said I didn't share because I was greedy, not because it was my job to teach Ruthy anything. Teaching Ruthy was her job, she said, and not to forget it. Ruthy poked her tongue out at me behind Mum's back, but I didn't tell on her because I knew Mum would take her side.

Besides, I was still in the bad books for going down to the shop one night after school and buying ten cents' worth of mixed lollies and putting them on the tick under Mum's name. Mum was furious when she found out I'd charged them to her account and yelled at Mrs Abrahams in the shop as much as she yelled at me. I'd already eaten all the sweets though, so in a way it didn't matter too much, except that Ruthy said she'd written a note about it in her book to tell Daniel, and that always made me feel sorry. I scratched the sores on my head more that night, and Mum had a cross day the next day when she saw bits of blood and scabs on my pillow in the morning.

I don't know why I scratched my head. I did it a lot when I got into bed at night, and sometimes during the day. It often hurt, because I would take the top off scabs again and again just as they were healing up, but for some reason I just couldn't stop it. Because of the blood and sores on the pillow, Mum returned to tying my hair in ringlet rags at night. I hated, hated, hated ringlet rags. She tied them so tight they hurt my head and made it difficult to go to sleep. The long, hard, hair-filled ropes kept getting in the way when I tried to get comfortable, and the knots she made to secure them stuck into my face. And as if that wasn't bad enough, the kids at school teased me and called me Sausage Head, which made me mad as Hell, even though Mum says you shouldn't say Hell like I do because I make it like a swear word. She said if I didn't stop scratching the sores in my head, she would shave it like a collaborator during the war, and the whole family would be shamed. I didn't actually mind that idea – hair was a bit of a nuisance really – but I knew to say so would make her madder than ever. She often said all she wanted when I was born was a pretty girly girl to dress and show off, and instead she got a tall, skinny tomboy with a scabby head and knock-knees.

Caleb was Mum's first favourite ('the light of my life'), Ruthy was the second favourite ('my little writer'), Daniel was the third ('my darling firstborn'), and I was the last ('Miss Crabby'). We agreed we should still call me a favourite, because Mum loved me and I loved her, but we all knew I was at the end of the line.

To record our views about the order of Mum's love, Caleb used six wooden beads he got from Mr Driver next door. Caleb nominated the best gold one as Mum and put her bead at the top of a piece of string that was thick enough to hold the beads exactly where he put them on the thread. The Dad bead, a silver one with little blue dots on it, was right next to the gold Mum bead, because they'd chosen each other and made vows in the sight of God at the Christadelphian Temple in Halifax Street.

Caleb left quite a bit of string after the Mum and Dad beads before positioning ours though, and when Mum and Dad did a lot of fighting and Mum threatened to go back to her mother in Scotland, and Dad said he'd happily drive her to the plane because she'd driven him to the madhouse, Caleb pushed the Dad bead further away from the top to reflect the current state of affairs.

Caleb's bead was next after Dad's. He chose a blue one because it was his preferred colour, and it had been his idea to put the family on the string. Ruthy's bead was fairly close behind his and, because she was next loved, she got the next choice and selected a bright red bead with little white dots on it. That would have been the one I'd have chosen, because I was mad for anything with polka dots on it. Dad called me Dotty Dorcas once. I quite liked that name and thought it was a friendly kind of message between Dad and me.

Caleb chose the green bead for Daniel because we agreed boys should choose for boys if one was away. Daniel's was a fair way down the string from Ruthy's because, although he was Mum's beloved firstborn, something had happened to result in him going away to board, and we sensed it pushed him well past Ruthy for the time being. All that was left for me was an orange bead, which is the colour I liked the least in the whole world. Mum says I shouldn't say I don't like orange because God made all the colours of the rainbow, but I was pretty sure it was not His favourite colour either. I didn't even like orange polka dots, and that's saying something.

We argued for a while about how far away my bead should be from Daniel's bead on the string. Finally we decided it wasn't at the very end of the string but it was a fair way away from Daniel's. Caleb patted my hand kindly and reminded me that just being on the string at all meant I was still beloved of God and Mum. We left quite a lot of string after my bead to allow for movement down on those days where I scratched my scabs and committed other offences, so that even then I would still have a place.

We hung the string up in the tree house, with Mum's gold bead proud at the top end, and mine hanging a bit sadly right near the bottom. We agreed Caleb could be in charge of moving the beads, but only after we had all discussed any change together first.

We heard Mum yell again. It was even louder this time. After a moment's frozen response to hearing her call, we scrambled out of the tree house and walked across the thick, springy green couch lawn to the back door, which was up six grey cement steps to a little platform. We speed-walked in a line side by side, even though Caleb was a very good runner

9

and could have easily beaten us there, but when Mum was cross, running was one of the things that could really set her off. We did not allow ourselves to be distracted by the flapping clothes on the line, which I normally felt a big need to yank as I walked past them, or by the magpie that threatened to swoop from the top of Dad's shed, or by the swarm of bees that rushed past us buzzing a spring song in unison.

Once at the foot of the steps there was an unspoken agreement that I should go first because most things were my fault, and also because of the fourth-favourite situation. We all kept our heads down as we passed Mum into the kitchen, knowing we were in for a clip around the ears, and that it seemed to hurt less if you had your head down. Also, Ruthy said it looked as though we were more contrite, which she explained meant sorry, so it seemed like the best plan. Mum had her hands on her hips and was looking scowly, which I thought was a good word, but which my teacher Miss Thompson said wasn't a word at all.

As expected, I got a clip, but she also pushed me into the kitchen as I passed her, and she yelled at me to stop pouting or the wind might change and I'd look sulky forever. She gave Ruthy just a little smack on the back as she passed, and she just touched Caleb on the head, so he got away with it as usual.

'How many times do I have to tell you children there's to be no playing until your jobs are done?' she said. 'It doesn't matter what I say; I just waste my breath.'

She tried to stomp out of the kitchen across the worn green and cream checkerboard lino tiles, but Dad's big floppy slippers slowed her down and softened the thuds. I let out a little giggle, but Ruthy grabbed my arm to warn me this was not a good idea, and I gulped the laugh down and hiccupped instead, just in time because Mum had turned to look at me. She left us to it, which was a relief because she usually stayed and yelled at us for a while, telling us we were going too slow or weren't drying the dishes properly.

On bad days she would tell us she would take us to the children's home in Klemzig. I had nightmares about it sometimes, even though when we passed the scary fenced perimeter of the home on the way to Sunday school one week, Dad laughed when I asked him if he'd been there. He told me it was the Peter's ice-cream factory, not a children's home, and not to worry.

Mum swung around the doorway for a last instruction. 'And don't use too much Sunlight in the dishwater, Dorcas, or I'll take it out of your pocket money.'

It was my job to fill the sink ready to do the dishes. Caleb's job was to take the dishes from the table to the sink, and to put away the cornflakes packet, sugar bowl and milk jug. Ruthy had the job of washing the dishes, which she did atop a little step Dad had made for her so she could reach. I liked washing, but Mum said there was more water on the floor than in the sink by the time I'd finished. My other jobs were to dry the dishes and put them away, and to sweep the floor and use the dustpan to put all the bits of fluff and flakes and dirt into the outside bin 'without stopping to examine ever dirty particle, Dorcas'.

Ruthy and I had a list of other jobs too, but Caleb's only other job was to clean Dad's shoes on a newspaper on the laundry floor, which he quite liked doing. Dad was always happy with them and thanked Caleb every morning, which was nice, but Mum said, 'Careful, Harry, or you'll make him spoilt.' The main reason for Caleb only getting a couple of jobs was that he was a boy and in our church men were always the head of the family and didn't do women's work. Boys were also the most loved.

Ruthy had to put all the week's towels into the outside copper room for washing on Saturdays and to tidy up her toys. I had to spread all three beds, wipe out the bath once we'd all had our three-times-a-week wash, run the hoover around the lounge and bedroom carpets, help Mum push the clothes through the mangle in the laundry and, because

I was nearly as tall as Mum, help her to hang out the washing on the Hills Hoist, 'Without leaving peg marks I can't iron out please, Dorcas.' I also had to iron the tea towels, sheets and anything else flat. Luckily, she didn't trust me with clothes yet.

If we did our chores, Dad would give us pocket money on Friday nights. This was also our best night because Dad came home before we went to bed and watched the tellie with us for half an hour while we all shared a family-sized block of Cadbury's milk chocolate. Even though every Friday I told myself to savour my share and keep it for as long as possible, I always chewed and swallowed it straight away.

Caleb would eat his a square at a time and wait until each one had melted in his cheek, so it lasted longer. Ruthy wrapped half of hers in any silver paper that was left on the table and then put it in the fridge so she could eat it on Saturday when Caleb and I were gobbling the mixed lollies we bought from Mrs Abrahams. Dad said the way we each ate chocolate was a metaphor for the way we lived our lives, that Cadbury's told the whole story. I asked Ruthy to explain metaphor, and she tried, but her explanation left me none the wiser.

We always wanted to watch tellie for longer than we were allowed, but when we nagged, Mum would remind us that the only reason we had a television at all was because we went to the progressive ecclesia in Halifax Street in the city – we call our churches 'ecclesias' – and that if we'd been members of a suburban ecclesia we probably wouldn't have been permitted to have a tellie in the house at all. We knew this was true, because if we ever had visitors from what Dad called 'the suburbs', the kids seemed a bit nervous about talking to us because of our worldliness, and several told us they had no television in their house. So that did make us think.

Because it was Saturday, once the chores were completed we could go and play for the rest of the day. Mum usually packed us some sandwiches and encouraged us to go exploring in the foothills so she could have a bit of peace and quiet. But because it was early September, and therefore almost time for the Christadelphian Church's union exams, we were told to be home to study by 2 pm. Because Caleb was eight, his exams were pretty easy. He just had to colour in some pictures and write the names of the key people in the drawings. But Mum still made him sit with her and tell her the Bible stories he had been learning that year to make sure he knew what he was doing.

Ruthy, at ten, would have a more grown-up exam and would have to sit in the middle hall for an hour to write out answers. Ruthy had won a union prize already. That meant she was in the top three Christadelphian students across Australia for her age group. Mum and Dad were very proud of this, and Dad framed her certificate and hung it on our bedroom wall. Mum and Dad put more store in results in the annual church exams than school exams, and when Ruthy had won her prize last December, Caleb had pushed Ruthy's bead right up to his on the string until well after Christmas. He also pushed her, pinched her, called her a girly swot and a suck-up, but the bead told the real story.

Because I would be twelve just after Christmas, I had to sit the first of the senior exams this year, which meant a two-hour stint in the rear hall of the Halifax Street temple. I wasn't looking forward to it and was hoping for an illness that would mean I couldn't sit up straight or move my right hand for a week or two around exam time. I had considered praying for a relevant disease, but Ruthy said that was selfish because it wasn't about God or someone else's welfare, so I said I wouldn't do it, even though I did sneak a little one in a couple of times. I explained to God that it would benefit Mum and Dad not to have me get yet another second-class certificate, and I couldn't see any way to get a first-class certificate this year given I hadn't done any homework between one Sunday and the next. Besides, Stephen Worth would win the prize for our year, as he did every year, so it was pretty much wasted effort.

We finished our jobs and pushed each other to be first out of the back door. We agreed to stay together until we had visited Mr Driver over the fence, and then go our separate ways for a couple of hours before study time. Mr Driver was our great friend, even though he was an old, old man. We had even considered giving him a bead, because his wife Mona was dead and he was almost like a member of our family, but we decided the beads should just be for Wilsons.

Mr Driver kept his house pretty clean and tidy but spent most of his time in his garden and shed. He had a son who lived in Brisbane and didn't get home much. He cooked for himself. His specialties, as he called them, were tuna and sweet corn mornay, baked-bean toasties, eggs with soldiers, and self-saucing chocolate pudding he made from a packet. I was a great fan of his pudding and had asked if he would make it for my birthday this year, and he'd said he would. Sometimes if he had some of his bowling friends in for tea, he made three times the usual packet size in a big tray, and everyone clapped and told him it was the best ever. I whipped the cream for him to serve with it, which he said was a very big help. I tested it because you have to check how much sugar it needs. He never complained about my testing, and didn't point out you probably didn't need to try it out by the dessertspoonful.

Dad said we shouldn't bother Mr Driver too much because he had been in the war and became tired easily, but we could usually tell how tired he was by his limp. He had a wooden leg, which was just about the best thing you could have if you were going to get hurt in a war without dying, and some days he would roll up his trousers and take it off and show us the stump. Mum said not to ask him to do it, but sometimes Caleb couldn't stop himself. Mr Driver didn't seem to mind. He was quite good at saying, 'Not today,' if it really didn't suit him, so Caleb would regularly try his luck.

We found Mr Driver in his shed, which is where he was most of the time. He lifted Caleb up to sit on the bench he was working on, and Ruthy and I perched on old oil drums that had nothing in them, but which Mr Driver said he liked to have around. He didn't ever ask us not to touch anything, or to watch what we were doing, or not to get dirty, or to stop asking questions, and these were, of course, some of the reasons we loved him rather a lot.

'We have to study for the Sunday school exams today, worst luck,' said Caleb. 'Did you have to study for Sunday school when you were little and still had two legs?'

Mr Driver stopped planing the wood he was working on for a moment. 'No, I didn't have to do exams for church,' he said. 'Never met another family that did, come to that,' he added, muttering.

'No, we are the only ones in our school,' said Ruthy. 'But our Sunday school friends all have to, even though some of them get teased.'

'What kind of teasing do they get?' asked Mr Driver.

'They get called Mormons, heathens, sect members and Ku Klux Klan. We don't know what that means, but luckily we don't get that at Rostrevor Primary School,' said Ruthy.

'Dorcas gets called Sausage Head a lot, but that's because of her scabs and sausage curl rags, not because of Sunday school exams,' Caleb helpfully added.

Mr Driver turned to look at me. 'They tease you, Dorcas?' he asked.

'Yeah. But it's okay. It's mainly Maynard's older brother Rufus and I kick him a fair bit if it gets out of hand.' I showed him how I kick. Mr Driver nodded in a fairly impressed way. 'Or I tell the girls in his class that he wets his bed, and that gets him really riled. I've got strategies,' I offered confidently.

'I bet you have. I bet you have,' said Mr Driver, and smiled and tapped my head, but gently because he knew about my scabs. Usually when old people did that I hated it and twisted away from them, but when Mr Driver did it, it felt friendly and I didn't mind.

A visit to Mr Driver always helped set Saturdays up to be the best day of the week, and after we'd chattered away with him for a while, asked for and been refused a look at his stump, and each had a Scotch Finger biscuit from his kitchen canister, we headed off to play with our friends before the dreaded study time at two o'clock.

I'd thought it was just an ordinary day up until then. I thought things would just keep rolling on until I was big enough to get a job and a house and a dog. I never guessed what was going to happen: grown-ups shouting in our street, boxes full of bad news, people I loved going all over the place. And the most terrible, terrible loss of all, which I can't think of without the pain still making it hard to breathe.

CHAPTER 2

After our visit to Mr Driver, we walked together to Mrs Abrahams's shop for our lollies, and then we took our sweets and sandwiches into the vacant block across the road from our house. It was full of ancient olive trees. Dad said it had been part of a large commercial grove before we moved to Rostrevor. The big grey trees weren't looked after by anyone anymore, so there were branches at different heights, which made them great for climbing. There were ten kids there when we arrived, and for a while we all stayed together playing. Caleb, Ruthy and I climbed our favourite tree as high as we could to eat our lunch. My jam sandwiches fell out of the paper onto the ground, but I climbed down to fetch them, dusted them off, picked out a few twigs and a bug of some kind that had been trapped by the separated jammy bread, and ate them anyway. The two Phillips boys yelled out, 'Gross!' but I didn't care.

I had a fight with Ruthy who stormed away with Caleb in tow, after I called him a flat-nosed rude. It was a Wilson rule that we weren't allowed to swear, so we had made up our own cussing, and flat-nosed rude was right up there with the best of the real obscenities. Caleb deserved it. I had finished all my lollies and asked him nicely for one of his. When he refused, I asked him again in my very friendly voice and also reminded him that in the Bible there was a story that said if someone asked you for a shirt, you should give him your coat, or something like that, and so he was lucky he only had to give me one set of lolly teeth and not the whole bag. He said he was pretty sure that wasn't a rule. He twisted the top of his white paper bag tight, as though that was the end of the matter, and put his sweets in the waistband of his shorts. So I pinched him. He told me I would be in 'tremenjous' trouble with Mum. I started laughing and called out to the other children that Caleb couldn't say tremendous. Ruthy said that just because I was too lazy to learn new words didn't mean Caleb couldn't, and she put her arms around his shoulders and led him away

Those who saw a chance to be closer friends with Ruthy, which seemed to be everyone's goal, followed her and Caleb to a clearing amongst the trees on the other side of the block. Only Teddy Edwards stayed with me.

Teddy Edwards was just a straight-up strange boy. He asked me to marry him most Saturdays. I explained to him over and over that I would never get married unless it was to a Knight of the Round Table, and there weren't that many of them in Australia as far as I could tell. Teddy persisted. I didn't understand why he kept choosing me, because I wasn't particularly nice to him, although I did make up roles for him in my plays, whereas the others often left him out of games and activities because he was a bit weird and quite smelly.

After a while of huffy silent treatment from me, even Teddy gave up and joined the other kids. I hung around in the tree for a bit longer, pretending I didn't care that everyone always liked Ruthy better, and talking loudly to a person I made up so the others would think I had a new friend, but eventually I dropped to the ground, softened by old olives and leaf litter, and decided to visit Mrs Johnson and Sixpence.

I wanted a dog more than anything in the world. And not a dog I had to share with Ruthy and Caleb, but a dog that loved me alone and belonged to me and slept on my bed and walked with me to school and then waited for me to come home. I would call her Raspberry, because that was a good name for a dog, whereas Fido and Rusty and Max had no imagination to them. But we were not allowed to have any pets. Mum said it was because of Caleb's asthma, but I think it was because she didn't like any kind of dirt, and if you have dogs, well, you have dirt too.

I pleaded and promised and prayed and protested but nothing made any difference. Mum was firm. No dog. If I couldn't have a dog, my next greatest wish was for a guinea pig, but Mum said they were really just rats with long hair and cowlicks, and there was no way she was having a rat in her home. I tried to explain I was pretty sure I would be a vet when I grew up, and I needed animals to practise caring for, but Mum said there was no way I'd get to vet school with my school marks, and I was more likely to be a mum than a vet, if anyone would have me, which she said she doubted if I kept scratching the sores on my head.

Mrs Johnson lived across the road from us and four houses down. I liked her for lots of reasons, but the main one related to the animals she kept in her backyard, and in particular a guinea pig called Sixpence.

Mum didn't like Mrs Johnson or her family. We lived in a street where all the houses had been built at the same time by the government and all looked like each other. People changed the colour of the paintwork or the cement steps leading up to the front door, or the plants they put in the garden beds, but that's about all. Our mum was very houseproud and had a reputation for being a bit of a style queen around the neighbourhood. She always looked tiptop herself before she left the house, although we saw the other side of her of course.

She didn't much care what happened in our backyard – she said backyards were for men and front yards were for women – so she threw her heart and soul into making sure we had what she called 'street appeal'. She repainted the cement steps dark grey each spring, once the worst of winter was over, and swept them clean every day. She said she held no truck with people who let the paint on their steps blister and flake. Caleb asked Ruthy what a truck had to do with the steps, but even Ruthy just shrugged.

Most of our neighbours had low front fences made of crisscrossed wire. Some people grew ivy over the fence, although if you didn't keep it clipped it grew too heavy and often made the fence line dip towards the pavement. Others left it wiry and you could see the plants they put in their garden beds. Mum grew roses along our wire fence line. She loved her roses and clipped them and sprayed them and picked bugs off them so she could have flowers to put in a vase come the summer. She grew seasonal flowers beneath them, only in white to show off the colour of the roses. She mowed the little square of grass between the wire fence and the front of the house with an old push mower because Dad wasn't home enough to do it for her. She had a large terracotta pot on the doorstep that she kept filled with whatever was flowering at the time. She refused to have stone gnomes or fairies or plastic anythings because she said they were common. And she hated, hated, hated Mrs Johnson's front garden.

Mrs Johnson had removed her fence altogether, which everyone in the street agreed was a strange thing to do. She'd filled the whole front yard with native plants, except for the crushed gravel driveway where Mr Johnson parked his Holden station wagon. Her front yard was almost like a forest and disguised much of the house from the street. She'd made a crooked sort of path from the pavement to her front door, so you couldn't see the door until you had gone around a couple of little bends. She had taught me the names of many of the trees and shrubs; my favourites were the little bells on the correa and the flowers like tiny bunches of purple grapes on the hardenbergia. She believed we should all plant things that grew naturally in the area we lived in. Mum said the only good gardens were the English ones, that Australian plants were ugly and attracted wildlife, and that Mrs Johnson had no style.

Mrs Johnson's back garden was a wonderland. It was full of windy paths where you had to turn and twist to find surprises around bends. She had built little grottos you would come across suddenly, with stone fairies or gnomes or cement animals in little frozen scenes from plays she called tableaux. These were regularly changed so that every visit offered fresh discoveries. She had a rabbit hutch, and a huge guinea-pig enclosure that used to be an enormous aviary so you could actually walk inside it. In her shed, she kept mice of several colours in a special mouse house so their little hearts wouldn't die from the cold, and blue tongue lizards that had been attacked by cats and needed to be looked after because they couldn't slither away quickly anymore. She had a magpie that wasn't in a cage but had a sore wing and used to stay near her back door to talk to her. She fed it mincemeat and scraps of toast. It tried to talk to her in return, and sometimes you would swear they really were having a good old chat. For a while she had a sick baby kangaroo that lived in a sack tied to the back of her chair in her kitchen, and that she had to feed with a bottle every four hours, even in the night-time.

Mrs Johnson also unfortunately had two girls and a husband called Athol. I say unfortunately because I didn't like them nearly as much, and they tended to need her attention, even when I badly needed to talk to her about something important. I particularly didn't like Mr Johnson, who was a big man with tiny eyes and fleshy red lips that rested on a bushy beard. He had bad breath, and often leaned right into my face and sort of grinned at me, but in a way that didn't seem that friendly. Ruthy said it was more of a leer than a smile, which felt right to me when she explained what leering meant.

Mum called the Johnsons tree-huggers and hippies. I didn't know what that meant, but hugging a tree seemed like a rather nice thing to do, and Mrs Johnson was a seriously interesting person. She knew so many things. She was a very unusual adult because she spent a lot of time playing with us, or setting up interesting activities for us, and looked carefully at all the things we made. I often bossed her children, and any of the other local kids visiting, into participating in a play I would make up, and she would sit on an old metal seat Mr Johnson found in the tip and watch the play all the way through and then clap when we finished. She would then tell me what she had liked about the story, and often encouraged me to write the words down, which I wasn't that keen to do because I was better at just directing the kids to say what I needed at the time.

But best of all, she let me help with looking after the animals. I loved, loved, loved sitting in the guinea-pig enclosure with her, and one day she let me name one of the latest litter. She taught me that the Latin name for guinea pig was *Cavia porcellus*, and that Mum was right in a way when she called them rats because they are not pigs but rodents, although I decided not to tell Mum about that. Apparently they used to be worshipped by people in a place called Peru, and some people believed they could cure diseases. She also mentioned that there were people in the world who ate them, but I think it would have been better if she hadn't shared that bit with me.

At first I wanted to name a little black and white one, but she gave that to her oldest girl River. I resented this because River didn't care that much for animals, and I knew she wouldn't spend time with the cute black and whitey, which she called Smudge. I was a bit jealous of that name though, because I had to admit it was quite good, and generally speaking I am the one who is excellent at making up names for things. Mrs Johnson's other daughter, Sunshine, was just three and didn't care too much about which guinea pig she named, so Mrs Johnson let me have the second choice. I pointed to a dear little baby that was mainly white but with coffee-coloured polka dots. I named her Sixpence, and I instantly loved her very much. When Mrs Johnson wasn't too busy, she let me sit on her metal chair in the enclosure, and I nursed Sixpence and stroked her and fed her greens.

One day, Mrs Johnson had said about the most wonderful thing I had ever heard. She told me that if my mum and dad gave permission, I could have Sixpence as my very own as soon as my dad made a safe enclosure in our garden. I was so excited I ran straight home and nearly knocked Mum over when I hurtled into the kitchen with the news. Her answer was a very firm no.

After she'd smacked me for nagging, she stormed over to Mrs Johnson and told her off for offering me Sixpence without speaking to her first. I heard her tell Dad that Mrs Johnson was determined to put a rift between me and my mum, but Dad said he thought she was just being kind. This infuriated Mum, who yelled at him that he always took everyone else's side and never hers, and it started one of their bad arguments, where she threatened to go back to Grandma. She stomped out of the house, which happened quite a bit when they had a fight. She would march away and say she was never coming back, and we would huddle together on my bed and I would comfort the little ones.

After a while, depending on how cross Dad was, he would sigh and look for his keys and go driving to find her. She always agreed to get in the car and return home, but sometimes they wouldn't speak to each other for a day or more. After this particular fight, I was banned from visiting Mrs Johnson for two weeks, which felt like a lifetime, and also unfair because I was just reporting the offer. I picked the sores in my head often during that time. Mum said this was to make her angry, but it wasn't. Like I said, I don't always know I'm doing it.

Dad came and sat on my bed one night, which was always special because he didn't do it much. He said that I had to understand a guinea pig might make Caleb sick, and he was sure I wouldn't want that, but that if I really pulled my socks up in the Sunday school exams and at school, and didn't cause Mum too much grief or pick my head, he would think about making me a hutch for Sixpence over the Christmas school holidays. I shrieked with happiness and gave him loads and loads of baby kisses all over this face, but he pushed me back into the bed and reminded me of all the things that would have to happen first, and that he was making no promises. He suggested that I only talked to him about the guinea pig, because Mum would worry about Caleb. I understood, and I agreed.

When he left the room, Ruthy, who shared the room with me, sat up and spoke into my happy darkness.

'It won't happen, Dorcas. There's no way you will behave until Sunday this week, never mind until Christmas. And there's no way Mum will agree to having an animal in the garden. And if she did, there's no way Caleb wouldn't have another asthma attack if he touched it. He gets sick every time he plays with animals. Dad was just being kind so you will stop picking your head.'

I jumped out of bed and dragged her out of hers over to the stain in the carpet we called 'the wee patch'. The big brown stain on the carpet was there when we moved to Fisher Street, and Ruthy was the one who imagined that three dirty boys had lived in the room before us and had urinated a little bit each into the centre of the room every night like puppies marking their territory. Caleb and I believed her story instantly and always jumped over the stain. The thought of touching it even in our shoes would cause terror. I pushed Ruthy over and rubbed her cheek into the patch. She let out a long piercing scream that resulted in Mum racing in to see what had happened.

'She pushed me into the wee patch,' hollered Ruthy.

'But Mum, it was fair enough because ...' And then I realised I couldn't justify myself because I had promised Dad not to tell Mum about the plan to bring Sixpence home.

'I don't care why you did it, you dreadful child. I am sick to death of having to come into this room after I've put you to bed because of your nonsense.' She pulled back the

31

covers of my bed and smacked me hard twice on the legs. I flinched but didn't say a word. 'No chocolate for you on Friday night, my girl,' she said, and slammed the door shut behind her as she left.

'Well, that's not going to help you get Sixpence, is it?' said Ruthy. 'See what I mean, Dorcas? There's just no way.' She said it in a kindly explaining voice, not a mean hurting voice, but it made me furious anyway. I wished I had a sister who took my side. My friend Venita at school had an older sister who always looked out for her, and I dreamt about having one who would always be kind to me and help me with projects and somehow stop Mum from getting so cross with me. But Ruthy said she had to call it as she saw it, which was what my Aunty Maisie used to say, particularly if she was being critical. Any time Ruthy quoted the dreaded Aunty Maisie, it made me doubly mad, so I crept over and pretended to smother her with my pillow.

I remained angry with Ruthy, so it wasn't surprising we had another fight that Saturday morning, and that she took Caleb away to play with the others. She didn't understand that I needed a pet. It didn't seem fair because she loved her notebooks and got to have them, and Caleb loved bugs and got kits where you could catch them and kill them and stick pins in them to put them on a board, but I didn't get to have a dog or even a *Cavia porcellus*.

Caleb got the bug and science kits he wanted because of the light-of-Mum's-life situation, and because he suffered badly with asthma and was often pretty sick but wasn't allergic to bugs. It's not fun when you can't breathe, and it's not much fun watching your brother struggle for breath either. But Mum was pretty sure he was allergic to lots of things and was always fussing about what he might eat or play with and whether it would give him an attack.

So now that I had rushed out of the olive grove in a temper, Mrs Johnson's was the obvious place to go. She didn't answer when I knocked on the front door but I was pretty sure she was home because I saw Mr Johnson's car in the drive. I squeezed down the side path, walking sideways because of how thick the grevilleas had grown, and called out at the back door. Again no one answered, and I decided to let myself into Sixpence's pen for a visit.

There were two wire doors. The first one let you into a space just big enough for a grown-up to stand in. We called this the safe room. You had to make sure the first door was closed before you opened the next one, to make sure none of the furry family could escape. Mrs Johnson trusted me to go into the pen alone sometimes, because she knew I loved every one of them and wouldn't allow them to sneak out. I carefully let myself in, sat on the metal chair and stroked Sixpence, and told her about the other children taking sides with Ruthy. I'm pretty sure she understood. She snuggled right under my cardigan. I cried a little bit, which I didn't like to do, but it didn't matter that Sixpence saw me crying because she was my true friend.

It was because I was bending over Sixpence and telling her things that I didn't hear Mr Johnson creep into the pen. And he must have been creeping, because normally the door was quite squeaky when you opened it. He stood behind me and called out, 'Boo!' and frightened me half to death. I screamed and accidentally jumped about a bit, causing Sixpence to leap from my lap and scamper into the little shelter with all the others.

'What are you doing here, Dorcas? Does your mother know you are over here with the reprobates and morally bankrupt?'

'Sorry, Mr Johnson. I don't think Mum has said anything about how much money you've got. Mrs Johnson said it's okay to visit Sixpence, given she is sort of my pet anyway. Where is she?' I asked.

'She's taken the girls to her mother's,' he said. 'Come on inside, Dorcas, and I'll make us a cup of tea. There's something I want to show you.'

'Aw. No thanks, Mr Johnson. That's okay. I don't really like tea and I should be getting home. I have to study for the Sunday school exam anyway. Thanks very much though,' I said, remembering my manners.

'Rubbish. Everyone likes tea. Obviously your perfect mother doesn't know how to make it. I said I want to show you something, Dorcas, so in you come. Now.'

I hesitated. The 'now' was said in that way grown-ups use when there's to be no debate. Still, I hesitated, although I wasn't sure why.

'If you want to visit that guinea pig again any time soon, in you come now,' he said.

He opened the inside door and held it open for me. I worried a furry baby would escape into the little halfway room and then maybe get out, so I reluctantly followed him. I called out to Sixpence once we were in the safe room and gave her a wave. She looked up. I'm pretty sure she understood. We would have a conversation about Mr Johnson next time I visited, and I suspected we'd reach the same conclusions about him. I trudged behind the man with hands as big as a Sunday roast.

It was dark inside. All of our houses were pretty dark. Dad said this was because they faced east–west, but the Johnsons' place was darker than most because of all the trees crowding round the doors and windows. I wasn't sure what to do, so I just stood by the door, tapping on the lintel, wondering what Mr Johnson wanted to show me. He put the kettle on the gas ring, and I tried again to tell him I would be late home for study, but he just waved away my worry with two swipes of his meaty fist, and then pointed to a chair at the end of the green formica table. I sat down. I could see a bit of the metal edging on the tabletop was coming loose, and pulled at it to see what would happen. He told me to stop fidgeting.

He left the room. I seriously considered making a run for it, but I was worried I wouldn't be allowed to see Sixpence again, so I stayed put. There was spilled sugar on the tabletop, so I drew some circles in it while I waited. After an hour that was probably a minute, he returned with a magazine in his hand. He sat on the chair next to me. I could smell him – a combination of sweat, tinned tuna, car oil and the breath of someone who was a stranger to a toothbrush.

He opened the magazine to a page about halfway through and pushed the page under my nose. I was so surprised when I looked at it I made a little 'O' noise, which made him laugh. On the page was a very naked lady. I don't think I'd seen a grown-up naked person before so it was a bit of a shock. I quickly turned away, but he grabbed my face in his huge paw and made me turn back to it.

'What do you think of that?' he said.

'I'm not sure Jesus would want me to look at that, Mr Johnson, so it's probably best if I just close my eyes.'

'Not if you want to see your little furry friend again, it isn't,' he said.

I opened my eyes but did a sort of squint so I couldn't really see much.

'Why do you want me to look at this, Mr Johnson?' I asked.

'Because you'll look like that soon,' he said. 'Let's just say it's part of your education. You'll have hooters that size, I reckon, given your mum's stack. Not like my Janet. She may as well be a boy.' He snorted in a dismissive way. It made me feel even sorrier for Mrs Johnson.

'In fact, while you're here, Dorcas, let's see how those baby hooters of yours are going.'

The whistle on the stove started to scream that it was time to take it off. He stood up and reached over to the hot plates. At that very moment Mrs Johnson walked into the kitchen, back from taking her girls to stay with their grandma overnight. She stepped towards the kitchen table and saw the picture lying open near the empty mug. She turned to Mr Johnson and said in a scary sort of whisper: 'What have you done this time?'

I made a dive for the back door and ran home as fast as I could. I ran down to the tree house and climbed my favourite branch. I knew I should be in the kitchen ready to study, but I couldn't go inside yet.

I tried to think happily of nursing Sixpence, but every time I thought of her, I saw Mr Johnson's red face and set of big yellow teeth, and so I had to stop and think of my friend Maynard's dog Rastus, which helped a bit. I heard Mum calling my name after a while, and decided I'd better go in.

'What a nice surprise,' said Mum, in a voice that didn't match the words. 'You're late.' She was standing with her hands on her hips, looking at me with her head turned to the right, favouring her left eye, which was not a good sign.

'Sorry, Mum,' I said. Ruthy and Caleb were smiling at me in a not-very-nice way.

'Did you call your brother a bad name?' she asked.

'Don't remember doing that, Mum,' I said. 'What was the bad name I called him?' I spoke innocently, knowing the others would never disclose a single word from our swearing vocabulary.

'They wouldn't tell me, but it had better not be a swear word, my girl,' she warned. She leaned over and peered into my face, as though she would be able to see a lie in my eye.

'Nope. I can promise you I never cussed,' I said confidently, because of course this was true.

'Well, I should hope not. Now get your books out and open to your revision chapter.'

I went into my room and took out my Sunday school busy bag from under my bed. It was blue with big spots on it; Aunty Maisie had made it for my last birthday. I decided to put one of Ruthy's dolls, Milly Molly Mandy, right into the middle of the wee patch. Mum called out for me to hurry up. I sat at the table and sighed as I opened my book, which made Mum crabby again.

I had four questions to review: Who is the chief cornerstone in the temple God is building today? What had David done as a boy that helped him to be a good king? When David became king in Jerusalem, what did he want to do for God? and What sort of man was Nehemiah?

I had no idea about the answers to any of those questions. I thought of answering the one about Nehemiah and making up a picture of him. I thought he might be tall, good-looking and obedient if he was an important character, but then a lot of stories were about people who had been bad and then come good in some way, so I thought that might be too risky.

So I decided I'd have a stab at David as a boy. I started to write down all the things I could do that would make Mum and Dad happy, and hoped I'd 'cornered the market', as my Aunty Maisie used to say all the time.

I took a long time to sharpen my pencil, until I could tell Mum's patience was running out again. With a nice point ready to go, and my tongue sticking out in its thinking hard and writing position, I made a start.

David did a lot of things to make him a good king when he grew up. What you do when you are a kid shows a lot about what you will be like when you are grown up. My mum is always telling me I am limiting my choices because I don't do as I'm told, and I'm pretty sure David knew about this from his own dad when he was small. So to be a good king he did all the family washing on Saturdays, never argued with his brothers and sisters, which I think would have been hard because he might have been Catholic and they have quite a big number of children. And he did very well in Ye Olde Worldy Union Exams ever year.

I was actually pretty pleased with myself about this answer. It made me forget about Mr Johnson for a minute, but then I saw him in my thinking and my guts went all squirmy again. Mum finished helping Caleb colour in the story of Joseph and the coat of many colours. I would quite like to have helped with that because I enjoy colouring in and I am very good at it. She then checked Ruthy's work and told her it was outstanding. I was actually looking forward to her reading mine, because I thought I might have nailed it.

When Mum read my work, her face changed colour to a bright red that clashed with her auburn hair. She grabbed me by the ear and dragged me outside. She smacked me on the backside and pushed me into the laundry and told me to stay there until my dad came home. She turned the key and took it out of the lock from the outside, so I was trapped. I sat on the stool in the corner, worried about what Dad would say. I also hoped Ruthy wouldn't write about this in her notebook for Daniel to read. I think he would be particularly sad if I'd made a mistake that concerned the Bible.

After a while Caleb came out and spoke to me through the hole under the handle of the wooden door.

'Are you or-right, Dorcas?' he whispered.

'Yeah. It's really good in here. Better than being out there. There's a kitten and a little green and white bird here to play with. It's the best really.'

'Aw. No there isn't, Dorcas … is there?' he asked, and I saw his eye through the hole in the door, trying to check out the animal story. 'Anyway, I'm sorry you got into trouble. Ruthy read your answer and she said it was quite well-written for you. Here's an orange snake you can have. I'm sorry it's an orange one but I ate all the others.'

I watched the long springy lolly as he fed it through the hole. 'Thanks, Caleb,' I said. 'It doesn't seem to have a head though.'

'Yeah. Sorry about that. I did eat the head, but I left the rest for you. Will you be or-right? If they leave you out here all night, Ruthy and I will bring you a candle and pillow and rug so you don't die of frostbite.'

'That's nice, Caleb, but how will you get all that through that hole?' I asked, interested.

'Good question.' He went quiet as he thought of a strategy. 'I might go in next door and ask Mr Driver about that.'

'Better not, Caleb. I think Mum might put you in here with me if she finds out you told Mr Driver.'

'Aw. No she won't, Dorcas. You know where I am on the string. Besides, Mum doesn't like me going into the laundry because she says the cold and damp is bad for my chest.' He went quiet again for a moment. 'I wouldn't worry anyway, Dorcas, I think Mum is getting over it now.'

Then we heard a scream like a banshee. I think that is actually the right word to describe it, because my teacher Miss Thompson said a banshee is a female spirit who cries out to warn that someone's going to die, and given it was Ruthy screaming, I was pretty sure I was going to be the one to die.

'Muuuuuum. Dorcas put Milly Molly Mandy into the wee patch. She's ruined for life. Muuuuuum.'

I hoped Caleb would work out a way to get supplies through the hole in the door, because now I knew I'd need them.

CHAPTER 3

Generally speaking, I didn't like boys all that much, except for Daniel. And Caleb. And Mr Driver. And, of course, Dad. But one of my two best friends at school was a boy called Maynard.

He wasn't like the other boys. He didn't play rough and tumble and he didn't play sport. He didn't call me names like Sausage Head. His clothes were different. He wore white shirts with waistcoats and a tie. He wore his hair long, despite the fact this was the fashion and he usually had no time for fashion. I suggested he say he had 'no truck' with fashion, and he was quite impressed with that idea. He had too much hair on the top of his head, resulting in a thick brown wave always falling over half his face.

His voice was different from most of ours. At first, I thought he was English, because some of them can sound a bit la-di-da, but he wasn't. He said it was just the way they spoke in his family. He lived in quite a flash two-storied house with trees that were clipped – he said tortured – into neat round shapes. They had a woman to clean for them every week, and a gardener who made the front yard look like a bit of the botanic gardens on North Terrace.

And the year after next, when we were all ready to go to high school, he was going to a place called Princes, which he said was a school in the city his dad had gone to. Apparently four of his older brothers and sisters all went to Princes right from kindy, but his dad said they couldn't afford the fees for him until high school, so we got his brother Rufus and him. I was very glad about Maynard, but I was not at all happy about Rufus. It didn't seem right that two brothers could be as different as salt and pepper, but as Mum would say, God moves in mysterious ways. And some would say Mum also got a pair that didn't match in Ruthy and me.

Maynard read a lot of books, which I didn't, and he told me that Ruthy was very talented, which I already knew. He would often talk to her about things, which was unusual, because most kids knew that anyone in the year lower than you was beneath you. He liked the plays I made up, and said

I was just as creative as Ruthy but in a different way. I said I knew that wasn't true because I didn't like to write them down and all it meant was that I was good at making things up, which Mum said was most of my trouble. I quite liked him saying this anyway, but I knew it was just because he was a mate.

He would often help me organise a group to be part of one my plays in the lunch breaks. When we weren't doing that, we just ate our sandwiches and hung around and talked about stuff. We had a bench we considered our own under a big gum tree in the corner of the school grounds, and met there most lunch times. The tree was grey-and-cream-coloured, with a smooth strong trunk that forked into two main branches above our heads.

My archenemy, his brother Rufus, said it looked like an upside-down lady with naked private parts. He pointed up to the fork where a bird had left a nest and said that's exactly what grown-up girls looked like with no underpants on. I punched him and said I'd tell on him, and he laughed and called me Miss Prissy Sausage Head but left us alone. I don't think he wanted any of the teachers to know he knew what girls looked like with no clothes on.

It spoilt the tree for me a bit, because if I accidentally looked up, I felt I was doing something filthy. Although I didn't understand exactly what yet, I knew anything rude was somehow against God. I'd asked Mum one day if I could watch tellie when I got home from school because the girls in my class were talking about something called *Days of Our Lives*. Mum said it wasn't appropriate. I said I wouldn't watch the sex bits, and Mum slapped me.

'Don't let me hear you use that word in my house,' she said. So if the word sex was so bad, I'd hate to think what happened if you actually did anything.

Maynard and I weren't in the same class. He was streamed A and I was streamed B, because he was clever and I was classified as 'has some potential'. He told me if I applied myself, I could be in his class but I wasn't that interested. As long as we could meet at lunchtime that was fine with me.

My other very good friend was Venita, who was in my class and sat next to me, but she was mad about netball, so often it was just Maynard and me with a sandwich. He had quite interesting ones and let me have a bite if I was of a mind. I'd tried smoked salmon and sardines as a result. In our house you had jam, cheese slices or peanut paste. I quite liked tomato and onion sandwiches, but Mum was right when she said that by lunchtime they were all soggy, so I usually settled for peanut paste.

Maynard's mother – he didn't call her Mum – often gave him money to spend at the tuckshop, and he was pretty generous about sharing. I would strongly recommend Kitchener buns to him even though vanilla slices were his favourite, and he would buy a bun quite a lot of the time and break it pretty much in half. He was even good at wiping the cream with his finger so we had about the same amount each, although he usually kept the bit with most of the jam on, which we agreed was fair given it was his bun.

Worrying about Sixpence and whether Mr Johnson would let me see her again – and if he did, whether I'd have to look at the awful magazines – I'd finally tried to confide in Venita. But she just interrupted me and said that a photo of a rudey woman was nothing. Her mum couldn't wear underpants for some reason and had to be careful her skirts didn't blow up in the wind. Normally I'd be quite interested in this and ask many questions about what strange disease her mum had, partly to check I didn't have the symptoms myself, but I was too worried to ask. So I gave up on her.

I decided to tell Maynard about it, even though I was a bit embarrassed to tell a boy about the picture and what Mr Johnson had said. But I shouldn't have worried. Maynard stayed very calm and listened carefully until I had completely finished. He was probably the next best listener I knew behind Mr Driver. He asked if Mr Johnson had hurt me, or done anything else, and I said no, except that he wanted me to drink his awful tea, but Maynard waved that misdemeanour away. We discussed whom I might tell about this. We agreed there was no point in telling my mum, who would just cut me off from the Johnsons altogether, and probably even think I was making it up to cause trouble.

We agreed that Dad wasn't around enough to talk to about it, and that I wouldn't get a chance to tell him by myself anyway. And in any case he would probably feel he had to tell Mum about it, which would just lead back to the problem of being banned. We considered telling my teacher, but Maynard cautioned against this. He had heard of children who made complaints about things to do with nudey or rudey things who had been taken away from home by a social worker, so that pretty well axed that idea. I didn't really know what a social worker did, but I gathered they just drove around listening to children's stories and taking them away in a van if they didn't like what they heard. My guess was that they were all women, because they seemed a bit like witches from what I could tell, and therefore were probably a bit warty with pointy chins and missing teeth.

Mr Driver was a possibility for advice. He had been to the war, so he was probably used to terrible things and big problems. Also, he listened and didn't say too much, so he wouldn't go off like a cracker and I didn't think he'd do anything about it without telling me. We weren't sure though, so we decided to keep thinking about it at lunchtimes until we had a solution.

That night Dad wasn't home. He was in Mount Gambier for work again. Mum was very upset, claiming that his boss, Mr Henry Bednarski, took advantage of Dad and that Dad wouldn't stand up for himself. When he was away, she had a lot of cross days, and would often stay in bed with 'one of her heads'. When this happened, she would stay in her room with the curtains tightly closed, and we would all have to tiptoe and talk in whispers so as not to upset her. We would get ourselves ready for school, and I would make everyone eat cornflakes before we left. Mum made the sandwiches for school on Sunday nights, so we just took our share from the fridge and let ourselves out. On many of these days if she wasn't up to get tea by six, she would call out to me to bring her purse and then give me money to take the three of us to the main road to buy our dinner.

Although we did not enjoy her head days, we did love buying our own tea, because we could choose whatever we wanted, and would just tell Mum we had sandwiches and fruit when we got home, even if we had bought cakes and lollies and ice-creams. Before we set out, we would meet in the tree house and divide out the money. I used to try to keep a few cents extra for myself, but Ruthy was too good a counter and I couldn't get away with it. We usually had a council of war before we left so we could plan where to go. Most times we agreed to buying a medium serve of chips from Mr Conjunctivitis, which we would share. We didn't know the fish shop owner's real name, but Mum called him that one day when his eyes had been red and oozy for weeks and weeks, and it had sort of stuck. Ruthy and Caleb added a potato cake each to the order, and I chose dim sims, not really because I loved them, but because I wasn't allowed to have them if Dad was buying fish and chips for a Saturday night treat. I usually made the other two buy at least one piece of fruit each, because I liked to be somewhat responsible, and because then I could honestly describe the fruit to Mum if she asked. What was left was free choice. It was usually enough for one cake or ice-cream or a White Knight or a large bag of mixed lollies. I tended to buy a White Knight because it had the word knight in it, although I did really like peppermint anyway.

The Thursday I told Maynard about Mr Johnson was one of Mum's head days, and she felt so bad she could only whisper when I went into her room for her to give me the money for our dinner. She didn't even insist we buy fruit or a sandwich, so I took that as permission to buy a Kitchener bun if there was one left at the bakery.

The day itself was in a temper. There was stuff flying around in the wind like a nasty boy throwing sand at the beach. I said this to Ruthy who was quite impressed and said I should put that in my homework, which was an essay about the weather.

Ruthy was good at describing the weather. I was not. I hated writing about it, but it seemed to be a favourite topic for essays. I think teachers ran out of ideas, and when they did, out of the drawer came the good old weather essay, and here we go again. I particularly didn't like it when grown-ups would say 'You can see the weather coming in', because there's always weather, and it doesn't come in. But that's grown-ups for you.

My teacher often wrote comments on my essays such as 'Surely you can say more than "it was hot"', and 'Dorcas, this time try for more than "very hot" when you revise your work'. Ruthy, on the other hand, would describe a day as 'blustery with the wind playing "catch me" down the road to school', or 'the sky was like a bright blue blind pulled down low on the otherwise dull spring day'. Teachers raved about Ruthy's descriptions and called her a protégé. I asked Ruthy to write descriptions for my essays, but she said the contrast would be too obvious. When Caleb asked what she meant, she said it would be like plopping a diamond into a lump of fresh dog's poo, and I said, 'Thanks for saying it would be *fresh* dog's poo', to try to be smart, but it didn't really work.

We had to walk past Mrs Johnson's house to go up to St Bernards Road to buy our tea, and I noticed Mr Johnson doing something down the side to the backyard. When I realised he was there, I walked faster, and Ruthy asked me what was wrong, because usually I went into the Johnsons' for any reason. I told her I was worried all the Kitchener buns would be sold if we didn't hurry, and that got Caleb and Ruthy talking about what they'd buy, so they left me alone.

* * *

The next day was Friday, and I was planning to go to see Sixpence as soon as I returned from school and before Mr Johnson got home. That left a small window of time because he was usually home by four. He was a teacher at the South Australian Museum on North Terrace and took classes of kids sent there for excursions. Little bits of pictures about Mr Johnson kept popping into my brain during the day. I must have tried literally shaking them away, because

Maynard asked me twice if I had a bee in my hair or something. I badly wanted to see Sixpence but I almost as badly didn't want to see Mr J. I started to call him that in my head so I could pretend he had nothing to do with his nice wife and all the animals at their place. But my plan to get to the Johnsons' and back again early went down the toilet when I walked in to find Mum making happy-clappy hands over yet another Ruthy triumph.

I hadn't walked home with Ruthy because we had been fighting a lot lately on the way home from school, and Mum had given me trouble for it. I also needed the walking-home time to think about my Sixpence strategy and to worry quietly about her. So I didn't know Ruthy's news. Apparently, she had won a writing prize, and Mum was over the moon. It had been sponsored by Adelaide University, and there would be a special ceremony where they would give her a framed certificate and a token to buy some books from a big bookshop in the city. Even though it wasn't the Sunday school prize night, Mum loved a ceremony, so she was in a very good mood. Apparently, Ruthy had already written 'happy' in her notebook for the day, which broke the run of cross and head days we had been managing.

When Dad came home, Mum rushed to tell him the news, and he was all smiles, although I think that was as much because Mum was having a happy day as about the prize. He sat in his big corner chair in the lounge and let Ruthy sit on his knee to tell him all about it. Dad was a pretty good listener. The problem we had was that he wasn't home to listen all that often. Mr Bednarski, Dad's boss, was a hard man. He squeezed as much time from Dad as he could, always promising him that if he just worked a little harder and a little longer, he would make Dad a senior manager and give him a pay rise. Mum was always nice to Mr Bednarski when we met him at the annual work picnic or if she visited Dad at the office but she didn't like him and made that very plain to Dad on a regular basis.

Mr Bednarski made all the men go to the Cremorne Hotel on Unley Road to drink alcohol with the other men after work on Friday nights. He paid for the drinks. But because Dad didn't drink, his boss let him off, and it meant he was home by five thirty instead of six thirty or seven like most of the other nights when he worked back to get everything done. From Monday to Thursday, we pretty much always had already finished our dinner and were reading in bed by the time he came home, and he would just come in for a few minutes before we switched out the light. On Friday nights, because there was time to talk to him before tea and television and Cadbury's, it always felt a bit like a holiday.

I sensed there was something going on with Ruthy that night. I could always tell, just as she could tell when something was up with me, which was another reason I had been avoiding her since what Maynard and I now referred to as 'the picture incident'. And sure enough, it all finally came out. Mum always referred to Ruthy as bright, but I personally think she was more sly than clever, and her little plan became clear after Dad had heard the story about winning the prize, and Mum had left us for a bit to go and finish getting tea.

'And Dad,' said Ruthy, 'the other wonderful thing is that I can have a place in a special school for young writers over the Christmas holidays at the University of Adelaide.' She clapped her hands as she made this exclamation, in a way that invited Dad to say 'hip hooray' and clap too, before he'd realised what he'd agreed to.

Dad just looked at her with a funny, sad kind of look. He ran his hands through his black curly hair, and then made a sort of washing motion with dry hands over his face as though he was using a flannel.

'Have you told your mum about this, Ruthy?' he asked.

'Not really. I thought I'd save a lovely surprise until you got home,' she said. 'I don't want you to always get the good news second-hand.'

'That's not why,' I said, before I knew the words were coming out of my mouth. This happened a lot to me, words just turning up and pouring out before I'd even really thought them. 'You didn't tell Mum because she would be cross, and we have had almost twenty cross or head days in a row, and you didn't want to go back to the pattern.'

Dad's mouth started to open, I was guessing to ask me what I meant, but he must have worked it out because he stopped.

'Ruthy, you know we don't do worldly things except go to school or to work,' he said. 'Not only would it be hard for Mum to take you into town every day, but you know most of the school holidays are taken up with Sunday school camp, summer Bible retreats and catching up with your Sunday school friends.' He started to give her a little knee bounce, which is something we all liked him to do. 'It just wouldn't work.'

'But Dad,' she said, with a beseeching look on her face, 'it's only nine 'til twelve weekdays for two weeks, and there will be really special people there – proper published poets and novelists. And they will teach me all sorts of things and read my writing and give me feedback. I will work really hard. Please. Please. Please. Please. Please?' Ruthy held Dad's face between her hands, pleading inches away from his nose.

'I'm sorry, Ruthy, the answer is no. And if I were you, I wouldn't even tell your mother about it. It might make her cross and even stop her from going to the ceremony to get your certificate,' said Dad.

'Why, Dad?' asked Caleb. 'Why would it stop Mum from going to the Sunday school prize night? It's her favourite night in the year almost. She's made a new dress for it and everything. She's made the girls matching yellow dresses with polka dots on them for Dorcas and I'm getting new shorts.'

'It's not Sunday school prize night, you dummy,' I explained. 'It's a special one at the university for kids who won writing prizes.' There goes that mouth again. Dad gave me a warning look.

'That's enough, Dorcas,' said Dad. 'Don't speak to your brother like that.' And Caleb turned so Dad couldn't see him and poked out his tongue at me.

'Dad, Caleb just poked out his tongue,' I said. Caleb could just be so dumb sometimes I lost my patience. Besides, he was taking Dad's attention away from Ruthy, and I was now on her side. If Dad agreed to her going to writing school at the university, then it was possible making a hutch for Sixpence was in the frame too, so her win might be my triumph. Dad was always pretty fair, and if he did something for one of us, he tried to balance it out with the others. It seemed to me making a guinea-pig hutch was a good equivalent for taking Ruthy on a bus every day for two weeks. I felt a bit of hope jump around in my heart.

Dad just looked at me. 'How old are you, Dorcas?' That was a thing he said when what he really meant was: 'You are supposed to be a grown-up girl and a model to your siblings so act like it'. Given I had promised to be good until Christmas, it wasn't in my favour to give Dad too many opportunities to ask me this. I backed away and sat next to Dad's chair, waiting to see how Ruthy's request played out. I sat up very straight and stayed quiet.

'But, Dad,' she said, her little pale oval face crumpling in a sad pouty expression. This often worked with Dad when it came to Ruthy. She had a pretty face with a tiny girly rosebud mouth, and soft pale white hair like a halo around her head. People were always stopping Mum in the street to tickle Ruthy under the chin and to remark on what a dear little angel she was. Given we had strict views on angels at our church, and they didn't include looking like ten-year-old girls from Rostrevor Primary School, this sometimes made Mum pause for a moment to decide if this was a good time to spread the good news of the word of God, but usually she just gave in and thanked them and agreed Ruthy was as cute as a button. This pouty look at Dad would often make him all soft-hearted and sometimes she would get her way.

I had tried this a few times, but Ruthy said I looked like an angry Hush Puppy dog, and it didn't really work for me. Besides, somehow Ruthy could look all forlorn and sad and still keep her eyes wide open and big as plates, whereas if I tried to look sad my eyes shut into squinty slits you could hardly see. If Mum saw it, she would tell me to stop it at once or I'd have deep wrinkles on my face before my years. I was not that worried about deep wrinkles, but Mum, being a hairdresser and therefore meant to always look fine, seemed sure it would stop me from having a husband. Telling her I didn't think a Knight of the Round Table would care, particularly as I planned to go with him on expeditions in a suit of armour, and you could really only see eyes out of armour if you're lucky, didn't make much difference to her position.

Caleb sometimes just didn't know when enough was enough. 'Dad, why wouldn't Mum go to the special prize night?' he asked again.

But Dad just stood up, gently putting Ruthy down on the carpet as he did so, and walked to the door. 'Let Mum have a good night, kids. She's happy. Try to behave when we come back in for the tellie.' And he joined Mum in the kitchen.

'Dorcas, why wouldn't Mum go to the prize night if she knew about the special writing course?' Caleb asked me, even though I'd tried to get him into bother.

'Because she might not think it's right to take a certificate if I don't do the course,' said Ruthy, huffy.

I thought about that for a moment. 'No, I think it's because someone might ask her why you couldn't go, Ruthy, and she might not want to be a witness to the truth and explain why we have to be in the world but not of the world when we are all dressed up and at a kind of party,' I said.

'But why not?' asked Caleb. 'Aren't we always meant to be ready to tell people about the love of God and His purpose for us?'

'Yes, but sometimes it's just damn inconvenient,' I said.

'Dorcas!' cried Ruthy and Caleb in unison. 'You said the D word!'

Mum came to the door with a warning look. 'What's going on in here?' she asked. We all froze. We didn't want a happy day to change to a head day, not just for our sakes, but for Dad's too.

'Nothing,' we all called out in perfect unison.

Luckily, she only stopped for a second to give us a piercing, checking look, and then turned away. We all started to breathe again.

What happened during tellie-watching and Cadbury's-chocolate time after tea was just typical of Caleb. As Ruthy says, 'He just doesn't understand family politics.'

We had been having a great time. Our usual half an hour of tellie with Mum and Dad included *The Bugs Bunny Show*, but we held our breath when Mum changed it to *Gilligan's Island* and didn't ask us to go to bed. We looked at each other very carefully, trying not to draw attention to the fact we were still upright, and watched it right through almost to the end. We couldn't believe our luck. And then blow me down, Caleb dropped a bomb.

We were only allowed to speak in the advertisement breaks. When Coke was telling us it was the refreshingest, Caleb piped up.

'Mum, I forgot to tell you I would need a new footy jumper,' he said, as though he was just asking her to pass the salt at the kitchen table.

'Really? And why is that, might I ask? There's nothing wrong with yours unless you're going to tell me you've lost it.'

Ruthy and I looked at each other with fright faces on. This might not be good. Caleb hadn't told us he'd lost his jumper. There was a good chance we'd be blamed for it if he had. There was an even better chance I'd be blamed for it.

I hadn't been walking home with them from school that week, so it might end up being my responsibility.

'No, I've still got that one,' Caleb said, 'but I need one to play in the Rostrevor under elevens on Saturday mornings. I'm on the team now.' He was sitting cross-legged on the carpet as though he hadn't just taken a big knife and cut a gaping hole in Mum's good mood.

'What are you talking about, Caleb?' asked Mum. 'You don't belong to the Rostrevor under elevens. I don't know anything about this.'

'Mr Parkinson choosed me this week. Brian Wentworth has moved to another school, so I'm in his spot now,' he said, sucking quietly on a square of chocolate still sitting in his cheek.

'Oh no, you're not,' said Mum. 'You know we don't join outside clubs. You're not on any footy squad so you can forget that right away.'

'But, Mum. It's like an honour. And if Ruthy can go to writing school at Adelaide Uminersity, I should go to footy.' He didn't even turn his head. His eyes stayed glued on the ads. He had no idea what he'd just done. This is what Mr Driver would call 'a real Hiroshima'.

Ruthy and I were still sitting stock-still. No one spoke for a moment, and I hoped against hope that Mum hadn't really paid attention. Minutes that were really seconds passed by in the quiet, as The Skipper and Mrs Thurston Howell the Third continued chatting, unaware that a big tidal wave was about to hit our island, never mind theirs. Or would we be lucky and find the storm had passed us by? We waited.

'Harry, do you know anything about this?' Mum asked.

'Know anything about what, Agnes?' he asked. I had a feeling he was hoping the wave would pass us too.

'Aren't you listening?' she said. 'Do you know anything about a course at university?'

Dad gave up, sighed and turned to Mum. 'Yes I do, but I've already said no so there's nothing to worry about. Caleb, you aren't playing footy on Saturday mornings, and there's an end to it. Now, if you kids can't watch quietly, you can go to bed now.' He slumped back in his chair like he was all relaxed and it was all decided, but I knew he was bluffing. I could see his right foot was crossed over his left knee, and it was jiggling.

I am an expert when it comes to Dad's jiggling. I can tell when it is a tired jiggle, when it's an angry jiggle, and when it's a jiggle to warn that something big is about to happen. This was a warning jiggle if ever I saw one.

My chances of a hutch and a guinea pig were pretty finely balanced at that moment. And I knew, as though sitting on a family see-saw, that depending on what happened over the next few days, I'd either soar into the blue sky, or come down to earth on my bum with a painful bump.

CHAPTER 4

Although we could get ready for school and work in no time flat during the week, it was usually chaos on Sunday mornings, even though we had more time than usual. This was in part due to the fact we had to put on our best clothes and all have breakfast together, and because as well as getting all of us ready, Mum had to get herself ready too. She cared what we looked like on Sundays and would make us sit in front of her kitchen chair as she brushed and tugged and plaited hair. Caleb had cowlicks, which drove Mum mad, and she would try to tame them with sugar and water, which often just made them stick up worse in little stiff peaks.

Dad would come out two or three times before Mum would be happy about which tie he was wearing. He had a big tie collection because he had inherited his brother's ties when he died, and because Mum bought him a silk one every Christmas from money she saved from the housekeeping. She liked his tie to go with her dress. Sometimes it was good fun watching them negotiate about the tie. Dad would come in sort of dancing like a model in his socks and twirl around the table with his chin in the air and his wrists dangling down from the end of his hands and Mum would laugh and laugh and tell him to stop being an idiot, when she really meant she thought he was very funny.

We would leave home at ten thirty in order to be at the Memorial Meeting in Halifax Street by 11 am. After the meeting, which Mum said finished later and later every week because the Exhorting Brothers loved the sound of their own voices, we either stayed for a family lunch, or came home and had fresh white bread sandwiches together before driving back for Sunday school at three o'clock. We bought the bread from an Italian shop on the way home and I loved, loved, loved it. It was often still warm, and sometimes the three of us had a fight in the back seat about who would hold it. Occasionally Caleb hugged it too hard, and it was a bit flat when we got it home, which made the sandwiches squishy, small and out of shape. I sometimes couldn't help it and dug little holes in the end to eat the soft white heaven, and then tried to pinch it together so Mum wouldn't notice, but she always did. And that meant I wouldn't be allowed to have a crust, which every person in my family agreed was definitely the best bit of the whole loaf.

And then Dad would go back to the evening meeting at 7 pm and I would often go with him because Mum said it was too much for the little ones to stay out until after 8 pm. This was true but I think it was also that Mum didn't enjoy church nearly as much as Dad did and she was glad to have an excuse not to go. I liked Sunday nights because Mum made my favourite tea quite often which was cold roast lamb, baked beans and mashed potato. I think it was her way of saying thank you for going with Dad to church. The other two got to watch *Walt Disney's Disneyland* with Mum before they went to bed, and I was a bit disappointed about missing that, but if I had to choose, I'd rather go with Dad into town.

Going to the Sunday night meeting with Dad was great. Sometimes we talked, but sometimes we didn't, and even if we were quiet, it was a kind of cosy, friendly quiet, and he smiled at me a lot. When we did talk, it was about all sorts of things. Sometimes he asked my views on world events if I'd heard about them. Because of this I tried to remember to look at the *Sunday Mail* before the Memorial Meeting to see if I could think of something intelligent to say about what was happening. Sometimes he told me about his work, which I always found interesting. And sometimes he told me about how to be a good person, which I paid a lot of attention to and tried to remember. He told me that life was like a game of snakes and ladders and I had to enjoy going up the ladders, but be just as joyful when I slid down a snake because it would teach me how to be a stronger person. He said all experts had to practise and fail many times over, and I had to develop persistence if I was going to be good at anything. He said I should always be reliable, and that he tried hard to be reliable for Mr Bednarski even though it made Mum upset sometimes, but he believed it would work out best for the family in the end.

If I was lucky he would tell me stories about Mum. He told me once that, even though the ecclesia didn't approve of it, when he and Mum were first married they would go to dances at the local RSL, and that Mum was the most beautiful woman and the best dancer in the whole room. He said that because she didn't grow up in the Christadelphian Truth, the way we lived was hard for her sometimes, because she loved to go to parties and dances in Scotland, and never went to church. He said he was very lucky she had accepted Jesus as her saviour, but every now and then having a house and children and a routine at church could get her down a bit, and we had to be patient with her because she'd given up so much for us. I asked him if having us children felt like a punishment to her, and Dad said, 'No, no. Not at all. She loves you dearly. But every now and then she misses her old life too.'

One night I told him I knew Ruthy would be a famous writer one day, but I couldn't see what I would be famous at. I asked if he knew what it would be. He said it wasn't important to be famous, just good. I thought about that a lot but decided famous would be better. I hadn't heard about a lot of famous vets, but I bet there was one, and perhaps I could have a television show and teach people how to look after their animals. That would do the trick.

When we parked in front of the hall for the evening meeting, I was in charge of choosing our seats, and I carried Dad's Bible and hymn book in with mine and put them on the seat next to me ready for when he joined me. He used to be 'on the door', which meant he stood in the foyer in case a stranger came to the meeting, so he could say hello and welcome them and loan them a Bible and hymn book. When the meeting was due to start, Dad would close the big doors that opened onto the street and slip in next to me, which is why I always chose two seats at the end of a row.

I used to worry that perhaps a stranger was just running late, and that Dad had closed the big doors and turned them away by accident. It seemed concerning that you could lose your chance at eternal life if you left home a bit late or caught the wrong bus. I asked Dad about this, but he said if someone was seeking God, they'd find a way, and he had to close the doors because otherwise people slipped in when the service was on and rummaged through people's coats and bags in the cloakroom and stole things. I said surely it would be okay if they stole one of our loan Bibles – we always had a pile for strangers and members who forgot them for some reason – but Dad said they never stole the Bibles, only the purses.

I used to look up at the board that had the hymns we would be singing that night and put little bits of paper in the right pages to make it easy for Dad, which he always thanked me for. I didn't often listen to what was being said, but I felt quite happy sitting next to him. I loved his strong, fine singing voice, and he always smelled of Old Spice, which is what we kids gave him for Father's Day every year, along with nice cards and other things we made for him. Sometimes I would just take in lots of deep breaths to breathe him in. I felt proud sitting with my dad at the meeting. It made me feel I would start the week being the best child he could ever have. Unfortunately, by Monday morning something happened and I always seemed to mess it up.

Not too many other kids my age went to the meeting on Sunday nights. It was mainly old people and a group of over sixteens who were members of the youth group, and who were allowed to go into Rundle Street afterwards to have a milkshake at Mr Randall's shop, which was open until ten. In my opinion, from watching them closely, they didn't really come for the service. They spent most of it passing notes, looking at each other and smirking if they thought they would get away with it. I was pretty sure they just came so they could go partying afterwards, because most of the parents wouldn't let them out on a Sunday night if they didn't go to the meeting first. I used to like noticing who sat with whom, because this told me the latest on girlfriends and boyfriends, and my best Sunday school friend, Anne King, was mad for this kind of information and quizzed me every week on what the seating arrangements had been the Sunday night before. She said she was pretty sure she was going to marry a boy called Bruce Bacon, who was sixteen and who I thought was out of her league.

In our church, although no one admitted it, there were some families that were more important than others. The

Bacons were sort of church royalty and lorded it over other families a bit. Deborah Bacon wore very expensive dresses and had new ones all the time. She was always perfectly clean and tidy – Ruthy said 'groomed' – and very sweet to everyone. She was a particular favourite of the old people because she would go and say hello to them before the Memorial Meeting and peck them on the cheek and smile prettily. We Wilsons were almost royalty – sort of like dukes rather than princes – but my family was a poorer branch because Dad wasn't an Arranging Brother. And because Aunty Maisie said that sometimes Mum lowered the tone.

Bruce Bacon was sitting next to Naomi Stubbs, who was also from a royal family, so Anne would have her work cut out to break them up. But, as she pointed out, she was only twelve and had six years to organise a way to get him to the altar, so she was pretty confident. She said Naomi would look grim in six years' time, whereas her mother said girls were 'at the height of their powers' at eighteen, whatever that meant.

I couldn't wait to be sixteen and go to the youth group. I didn't want to go out with boys, but I was mad to go to Mr Randall's for a milkshake and to go to the car rallies they held on Saturdays and to youth camp without Mum and Dad. Mum said she didn't know why I was hoping to go because, as far as she was concerned, I could wait until I was baptised before I went anywhere with anyone except the family, and the way I behaved she couldn't imagine me passing the test for baptism before I was thirty, if ever.

I knew it was a very serious thing to ask to be baptised but I was pretty sure I'd learn how to behave better by the time I went to high school. That would give me plenty of time to prove I was ready for what Anne King called 'the big dip' in the huge bath that was under the stage in the rear hall, ready for the next person who asked to be put fully under the water and to be raised new and responsible. My dad was a Baptising Brother, and that meant you could ask him to dip you if you wanted, and I knew it would be my dad who would dunk me. This made it seem a bit less scary, because you had to put on a white robe and walk out in front of everyone and then get into the big bath and the Baptising Brother would say some important words and you had to answer him and then he would lower your head and shoulders in until you were all submerged.

The last baptism I went to was for Graham Walters, who is very tall and skinny, and when the Baptising Brother put his head under, his feet shot up and they struggled a bit to get him right under. Anne and I thought this was very funny but Mum pinched my leg hard and told me I could wait in the car during the next baptism. I had an almighty bruise for ten days. I didn't mind once it stopped hurting because it was very colourful and I showed quite a few people at school including Maynard, who was fiercely impressed. Anne King said she was in no hurry to be baptised because you couldn't kiss boys until you were fully married to them and she was keen on kissing quite a few before that. I couldn't see the interest in this, but Anne was a year older than me and what my Aunty Maisie called 'a bit forward'.

The Sunday night meeting was meant to be for strangers. It was also called 'The Public Address'. Strangers were people who hadn't found the Truth yet, and who might realise the error of their ways if they came to this meeting. We very rarely had strangers, and I wasn't surprised because I don't think the meeting would have felt all that friendly if you were an outsider. We all dressed in our Sunday best, just for starters, and that meant anyone who came to the door of the hall in casual clothes would have felt right out of it. Girls in our church were never allowed to wear trousers to meetings, so that would have made a lot of girls feel pretty awkward if they were strangers. And baptised women had to have their heads covered, so seeing a pile of women in dresses and hats would have felt a bit out of the ordinary to most people. And on top of that, Anne always said we probably looked pretty ugly. Women weren't meant to wear makeup or miniskirts or heels or sheer stockings or much jewellery, and boys had to wear white shirts and suits and ties, even when it was very hot.

So Anne was probably right and even if I'd been a stranger who wanted to learn the Truth, I think I'd have gone somewhere that was a bit cooler. And I meant that literally in the summer, because men were not allowed to remove their jackets until it was over one hundred degrees, and the Presiding Member on the stage invited them to remove their coats. We had a few big fans hanging on the side of the wall in the temple, but every summer at least a few old men and a couple of younger ones passed out with the heat. Girls weren't allowed to go barelegged or wear sleeveless dresses, but at least we could wear short sleeves and that was a blessing.

I hated, hated, hated wearing stockings, and made Mum cross by asking where it said in the Bible we had to do it. I also pointed out that Mr Driver told me that women couldn't find or afford stockings during the war and had to go barelegged with a line drawn up the back of their leg to pretend they had a stocking seam on, and as I said to Mum, surely God didn't stop loving them then because it wasn't their fault about the nylon situation.

Mum said God wanted us to always do the best we could in the situation we found ourselves in and that meant dressing up for church. Mum didn't mind dressing up. Aunty Maisie regularly said she 'went to the edge of what was decent', but she got lots of admiring looks from people and she looked very fetching in hats, which not that many people can do.

Ruthy looked sweet in hats and liked wearing them, but I seemed to have a small head and they always sat too low over my eyes and bugged me. I tilted them up to get them out of the way, but Mum always tugged them down again and said you should always wear a hat level with your eyes unless it was a pillbox or a beret, neither of which she would buy me. I always seemed to get my straw hats dirty or a bit torn or straggly, which also drove her nuts. She kept hers in lovely hatboxes she covered in flowery wallpaper in the top of her cupboard. Ruthy also put hers away on the top shelf of our wardrobe, but mine always seemed to find their way to the floor of the wardrobe under jumpers and shoes.

Once I found a little fieldmouse in our room and made it a nest in my upside-down summer straw hat. It did lots of little mousey poos and wees in it and the hat smelled quite bad after a while, but Mum just smacked my legs and hung it on the Hills Hoist with a peg to air it. She said I would just have to smell like a rodent and no one would want to sit next to me. I didn't care too much, and after a while it only smelled bad if you put it up to your nose and took in a deep breath.

Aunty Maisie cornered Mum in the ladies' toilets after the Memorial Meeting on the Sunday morning after the Caleb-football-jumper fiasco, as Ruthy called it. I was in a cubicle. Mum had just asked me to hurry up because she was insisting I sit next to her for the community lunch in the rear hall as a punishment, partly for making Caleb laugh in the meeting, and partly because of the Gary Johns incident. The Memorial Meeting was the most serious of all the church activities because it was where the grown-ups who had been baptised took the wine and the bread to symbolise the death of Jesus. Ruthy had the right word for it – solemn.

We had to sit in rows in very uncomfortable brown wooden chairs with no arms and no padding. When it was time for the bread and wine, the front row of men in dark suits all stood up at the same time, walked solemnly down the aisles to the back of the room, and then walked to the end of each row in turn to pass along the little dish of bread or the little glasses of wine. I had pinched a bit of bread when I passed it along to Mum, and then rolled it between my fingers and stuck it up my nose. This made Caleb giggle quite loudly, and Mum pinched me so hard I knew I'd have another bruise on my leg.

It wasn't fair because I wasn't the only one behaving out of line. When we all stood to sing a hymn, Gary Johns, a thirteen-year-old boy with a reputation for being a bit of a black sheep, had passed me a note saying the Serving Brethren in their dark suits and white shirts and plain ties were really mafia men sent to infiltrate the church and steal the collection money for their Sicilian masters. I didn't laugh but I made a snorting noise and then pretended I was coughing when Mum's head snapped to the right to check on me. She wasn't fooled. I was sentenced to lunch beside her with just a look.

Aunty Maisie was my dad's sister-in-law. She was really old. Dad had been born twenty years after the brother before him. My grandma, who I didn't really remember, had some kind of mental breakdown and the doctor suggested to Grandpa that another baby might help. Grandma was very old by the time she had Dad, and I didn't like to ask if it cured her of being mad, but I hoped it did, because now that I know how you actually have babies, it's not something you'd do for the fun of it. My source for this knowledge was Venita, who had described both conception and childbirth in such graphic detail, I was a bit surprised there wasn't a law against both, or at least books in the torture section of every library to warn you to stay away.

When Grandma died, Aunty Maisie sort of took over as a mother to my dad, who was fond of her, but I think, like all of us, quite frightened of her too. She was very tall and very square. Her thick steel-grey hair formed a helmet of frozen waves. She wore waisted floral dresses with skinny belts that were almost entirely lost in the folds between the enormous rolls of her chest and belly. She wore black orthopaedic shoes well shone but always worn down on the outside edges, contributing to the rocking motion of her stride.

On her fingers was a collection of old diamond rings Mum said she bullied Uncle Rob into buying her, even though they didn't really have the money. Uncle Rob had died fairly young. Dad said it was from asbestos dust from between the floors of a department store in Rundle Street. The gaps between the floors were used as storage, where they kept all the spare racks and the stuff to choose from to dress the floors, and Uncle Rob spent a lot of time in them.

Mum said he died from sheer desperation.

Aunty Maisie was famous amongst the kids in our family for saying 'Self-praise is no recommendation', and 'If I want your opinion, I'll give it to you'.

She had a very scary dark bathroom that had pink and black tiles, and we were all especially scared of the black bath, which Mum said was the height of fashion, but which we thought was like a big coffin. Her toilet seat was very high off the ground too, which meant you had to climb up a bit to get on it. Caleb tended to miss whether he climbed on or stood up, which made Aunty Maisie cross. As a result, he wet his pants quite a few times at her house because that seemed less scary.

Two things were nice about visiting her though. She had a lovely dog called Fudge who was a collie with a beautiful copper and white coat. And Grandpa lived in the sunroom out the back, and although he didn't talk to us much, we all loved him and used to hang around his door hoping he would invite us in and give us a butterscotch lolly or even let us sit on his knee. Even though I'm not one for people touching me, I liked sitting on Grandpa's knee. He was a huge old man with a white moustache, an enormous nose, ears full of white hair, and an English accent because he hailed from Bristol. That's what he used to tell us – he hailed from Bristol. I wanted to tell someone I hailed from Rostrevor, but I always forgot to say that when I had the chance.

When I heard Aunty Maisie come into the ladies' toilet, I decided it would be better to stay exactly where I was.

It was bad enough that Mum had dragged me by the ear into the lane after the service to tell me off. I didn't need Aunty Maisie having a go at me as well.

Mum had been combing her hair and reapplying lipstick when my aunt stomped in. I could tell without watching that Mum had frozen. Mum had to bear the criticism of many church members because she wore makeup, coloured her hair, wore high heels and because she was a hairdresser, which was a profession all about appearance, and therefore about vanity.

'Agnes.'

'Yes, Maisie.'

'I notice you've coloured your hair a rather jaunty shade of orange this week.'

'Auburn, Maisie. It's auburn.'

'I suppose you think it's rather fetching?'

'Well, that's why I chose it,' said Mum.

'I was wondering if you noticed a rather relevant verse in the reading of Proverbs this morning?' asked Aunty Maisie.

'Which quote was that one, Maisie?'

'"Charm is deceitful, beauty is vain, but a woman who fears the Lord is to be praised",' chanted my aunt.

Mum didn't answer at first. I sat very still. I think I was holding my breath.

'Well, that is very reassuring, isn't it?' I heard Mum answer.

'I beg your pardon?'

'A woman who fears the Lord is to be praised ... and goodness knows I fear the Lord, Maisie, nearly as much as I fear you.'

'Agnes, we all know it's been hard for you. Getting on a boat from Scotland on your own at nineteen was quite an adventure. Leaving all your family behind because there was no work to be had. And then finding the uncle here who'd sponsored you had died while you were on the way. No home to come to, and no way to get home. Well, that's just awful. And I'm sure it's one of the reasons you badger Harry to work so hard for a promotion ... so you can afford a visit to your family.'

'Are we going to go through my entire history in this toilet, Maisie? And surely if you thought that was all it would take to get me to leave him, the entire ecclesia would have banded together to sell enough homemade cakes by now to buy me a plane ticket home.'

I knew one of the reasons Mum had said 'toilet' was because she knew Aunty Maisie hated that word. My aunt insisted we refer to it as either 'lavatory' or 'water closet'.

'And there we have it, Agnes. You just referred to Scotland as "home". I'm just saying, dear, that we all understand what you've been through. It must have been so hard. And I'm sure you feel lucky that our darling Harry walked into the hairdresser who'd apprenticed you that day ...'

'And I'm just as sure you all wish he'd never stepped inside that salon,' said my mum. The tap was still running, but I was sure Mum's hands couldn't have been that dirty. I wasn't breathing because there were things Aunty Maisie was saying that I didn't know about, and I didn't want to miss a word. My bottom was getting pretty chilly with my pants around my knees, but sometimes gathering family intelligence takes sacrifice.

'Well, it must have been God's will for Harry to find you and bring you to the Truth,' said Aunt Maisie, who sounded as though she said it through clenched teeth.

'It must be hard for you to accept that a heathen like me caught his heart when there were rows and rows of mousey girls in brown skirts and brown cardies and brown lace-up shoes just waiting for him to choose them so they could set up their beige households and sit with him, reading their Bibles on their brown cord sofas,' said Mum.

'There's no need to be rude about God-fearing women, Agnes,' said Aunty Maisie.

I could hear a noise that sounded like my mum swivelling on her heels. I guessed she was looking my aunt in the eye.

'Are you saying I'm not God-fearing, Maisie? I married him and I accepted the Truth and I was baptised. I've tried my best. I am so worried about being considered a poor Christadelphian mother that I am stricter on my children than almost anyone else. I've given you nearly all of me. There's very little of the old Agnes left. The only thing I haven't done is transform myself into a little brown mouse. For the sake of my marriage and my sanity, I need to keep a part of that girl Harry first met. And if God is the God of anything useful, surely he doesn't judge women on what they choose to wear. Quote me the psalm that says we have to be dowdy.'

I could hear my aunt breathing now. It was faster and wheezier than usual. And after quite a long minute, I heard my mother say: 'I Samuel 16:7, Maisie. "For God sees not as man sees: for man looks at the outward appearance, but the Lord looks at the heart."'

I heard my mother's heels click quickly across the old terrazzo as she escaped.

I must have accidentally said, 'Yes!' out loud.

'Who's there?' I heard Aunty Maisie command. 'Is that you, Dorcas? Come out here now.'

I remained motionless, with my breath held.

'I know you're there, you naughty girl. Come out here at once or I'll tell your father.'

Darn. She had me now. I wouldn't want Dad to have another lecture from her about me. I slowly pulled up my witches britches and opened the creaky door into the basin area. We stared at each other for a moment, and then without a word, she grabbed me by the ear and yanked me out into the side lane and off to find my father.

CHAPTER 5

Maynard told me that Caleb had been teased for not turning up to footy on Saturday morning, and that the sports teacher had made a comment about religious nuts in the hearing of most of his class.

I wasn't surprised then when Caleb didn't come home from school when expected, and that by four thirty Mum was beside herself with worry about him. She decided he must have had an asthma attack and would be lying in a ditch not able to breathe. Ruthy and I were pretty sure he'd just done a runner again.

We looked for him in all the usual places: the tree house, the skinny bit between the shed and Mr Driver's house, Mr Driver's backyard and the laundry, but he'd obviously gone a bit farther afield this time. I wasn't personally too worried about him. Caleb had a habit of finding a spot to sit in when he was unhappy, and we usually found him within a few hours. He would curl up in a ball with his forehead on his knees and talk quietly to himself, making up stories and acting them out in whispers until he felt better. If I'd been the one to go wandering, I'd have had the strap when they found me, but Caleb was treated as the treasure he was, and just got hugs and kisses and cuddles when they finally dragged him out of whatever cupboard or neighbour's shed they found him in.

I asked for permission to go and look for him, and Mum said okay, as long as I didn't go near the Johnsons', which is of course exactly where I headed straight away. I was desperate to see Sixpence again. I started to skip down the drive toward their house when I thought about seeing Mr J, and it took the skip right out from under me. And in any case, I realised Mum was looking out the window and that it would be a good idea to walk slowly with my head down as though I was really worried about Caleb until I had crossed the road and couldn't be seen from the lounge room window anymore.

I felt so happy at the thought of cuddling my little friend again that I could feel my heart beating quite fast, and it seemed to me that spring smelled more springy than usual, and that the flowers in the Johnsons' front garden were larger and brighter than I remembered them.

I pushed my way past the thickets of native shrubs to the path down the side of the house. And was then stopped in my tracks. In front of me was a tall gate I had never seen before. And when I gave it a little push, it was clearly locked. I walked back a few steps, thinking that perhaps this wasn't the right house, although I knew it was. It didn't make sense that this gate had suddenly appeared. I felt I would have known about this kind of change somehow. After a minute I looked around it to see if there was a way to open it or even to climb over it, but it was a big, solid gate that was making sure I couldn't get to my friend.

I slowly walked back to the front door and knocked. It took a long time for Mrs Johnson to answer, and she didn't have her usual friendly face on. I asked why she had a gate now, and if I could visit Sixpence. She just looked at me, uncomfortably I felt. She wrapped her stained pink cardigan around her even though it wasn't cold. She told me Sixpence wasn't living with them at the moment. Mr Johnson had taken her to work in a cage for the children who visited the museum to look at, and she wasn't sure when she would be coming home again.

I asked her if Sixpence was okay, and she assured me she was fine – just having an adventure for a while. I asked if I could visit the other guinea pigs but Mrs Johnson said she thought it would be better if I waited until Sixpence came home, and we could talk about it then. I noticed she kept putting her hand up to her cheek, and I wondered how she got the yellow bruise on it. I heard Mr J's mother calling out from the kitchen behind her.

'Hasn't that girl caused you enough grief? Tell her to go back to her saintly mother.'

I didn't know what kind of trouble I could have caused, but it didn't seem to be the time to ask. I just stood and looked at her for a moment, and then remembered my manners and said, 'Thank you very much for your time,' and turned around. I felt my heart race again but in a very bad way this time, and I started to run. I ran and ran and ran, crying a bit as I did, making little unhappy groaning sort of noises to fill up the quiet which was too sad. I ran right around the block and back to our olive grove. I climbed my favourite branch and just moaned because I didn't know where Sixpence was and I wasn't sure I believed Mrs Johnson.

I was pretty sure I would never be happy again, so I just let myself cry and whimper for a very long time. Teddy Edwards turned up under the tree at one stage, and asked if

I was okay, but I just picked some olives and threw them at him to make him go away, which he did.

I couldn't quite catch my breath. My heart was aching and aching. I just kept seeing my little baby and remembering stroking her and talking to her. I remembered her little swirly coat and the cute way she sniffed at me. I remembered all the cowlicks on her back and head. I wished I hadn't waited to go to see her. This was all my fault for being afraid of Mr Johnson. If I hadn't been so cowardly, I would have been back to visit and I could have asked Mrs Johnson not to let him build that gate. They probably thought I didn't really care enough about Sixpence anyway, and that's why he decided to take my baby to the museum. If I'd been to see her, he would have taken one of the other ones that were spare. This was my fault.

I dreamed up plans to rescue Sixpence. I would take the bus into town to the museum and check she was okay, and then, when no one was looking, I would pick up the cage and run away. I wasn't sure if you could take a guinea-pig cage on the bus, but you can take seeing-eye dogs on public transport, so I could say I had to have her with me for medical reasons. I would ask Mr Driver if I could hide her in his garden until Christmas, and I would make sure I was the best-behaved child in the world so Dad would build her a cage. I didn't have any pocket money for the bus, but I knew Ruthy had money in her Savings Bank of South Australia tin, and I would ask her if I could have it. If she said no, I would just open it anyway with the key stuck on the bottom of it. Although that would mean I would be in trouble again and it would be harder to get Dad to build me a cage, but it was the best plan I could think of, and I had to hope and hope and hope she was really at the museum and not down the creek and already a cat's dinner. That made me start to cry again, so I just thought about saving her instead, so I could have a fierce rescue plan.

I must have been in the tree for a long time, because it started to get cold and dark. And then I remembered I was meant to be looking for Caleb and so I jumped out of the tree and ran home. I rushed into the kitchen and ran straight into Mum.

'And where do you think you've been?' said Mum.

'Looking for Caleb. Is he okay? Has he come home?' I asked.

'Yes, thank goodness, and no thanks to you. You've been gone for hours. I hope you weren't at the Johnsons', my girl.'

'No, Mum, I was out looking for Caleb. I looked in the olive grove and round the streets and everywhere. I went down to St Bernards Road. Where was he?' I asked.

'So you didn't go to the Johnsons'?' she asked. She had her hands on her hips, and a daggery look in her eye. I suddenly felt a bit sick.

'Well no. Well, I knocked on the door to ask if he was there, but they said he wasn't and I left straight away.' I said it without looking at her, and tried to turn away as fast as I could so she couldn't see the lie on my face.

Mum grabbed me by the arm and squeezed it hard. One of my feet lifted a bit off the ground. She picked up her wooden spoon from the table and smacked me on the legs over and over again. I pulled away from her.

'Don't you walk away from me when I'm talking to you, you dreadful child. What did I do to deserve such a beastly girl? It doesn't matter what I do for you, you still want your own wilful way. I've got a good mind to send you to the children's home tonight before your father gets home.' She was screaming now. Ruthy and Caleb were nowhere to be seen. That was smart of them, anyway.

'Sorry, Mum. I really was looking for Caleb,' I pleaded. And when I said it I really meant it, even though I had forgotten all about him. But she was in one of her furies and saying anything at all wasn't a good idea. She picked up her metal potato masher and threw it across the kitchen at me. I put out my hand to stop it, and it got me between the thumb and my fingers and really hurt. I dropped it and she screamed at me to get out of her sight. I gladly ran to the bedroom. Caleb and Ruthy were on Ruthy's bed in a little huddle. No one was safe when Mum was in a fury.

'Where were you really, Dorcas?' asked Ruthy. 'Did you go to see Sixpence?'

I was holding the potato-masher hand in my other one because it was really hurting. It was all red and throbby. I didn't want to cry in front of Caleb and Ruthy because I was the oldest one home and I was meant to be the bravest. But my hand really hurt and my heart hurt even more because I didn't know where Sixpence was and whether someone had given her a bed in her cage and some greens for her dinner. And what if no one cleaned out her cage and it started to smell and that meant the head of the museum commanded that she be thrown out with the rubbish? What if she was so stinky from lack of care that they gave her to the bloke in there who stuffed old dead things and he put her in a glass case as an exhibit? What if a little boy like Caleb went to see her at the museum and had an allergy attack and they decided to shoot her like they did old horses? What if Mr Johnson just stuck her behind a shed at the museum and no one even knew she was there?

I got under my covers so the others couldn't see me. It was better in the darkness. My hand was hurting more and more, but I could close my eyes and block out my brother and sister and think carefully about my escape plan.

I heard Dad come home, and although I couldn't hear the words, it was clear Mum was shouting about me so I decided to stay put. When Mum called us for dinner, I decided to pretend I was asleep. After a while the door opened quietly and I was pretty sure it was Dad, but I stayed perfectly still, and he went away. I could cry and cry in peace until Ruthy came to bed. And then it occurred to me this would be the perfect time to look for Ruthy's moneybox, and I crept out from under the covers. It was dark in the room, but I could see enough to realise my hand was quite swollen now, and hurt more if I put it down, so I used the other one to hold it up. I quietly opened the wardrobe to look on Ruthy's side, but I couldn't find the moneybox anywhere. I heard the chairs scraping in the kitchen and scurried back to bed to play dead.

I must have fallen asleep because the next thing I knew it was morning. It was very early according to the paleness of the light through our window, and I could hear early-morning birds rather than the breakfast-time ones. I moved and made a little yowly noise because the potato-masher hand was very sore. I held it up to the window. My thumb was about twice the usual size, and every movement hurt. I wasn't sure what to do, but I thought it might be best to hide it and go to school so Mum wouldn't be cross again. Besides, given I hadn't been able to find Ruthy's moneybox, I thought I'd asked Maynard if I could borrow some money from him. If his mother gave him lunch money that might be enough for the bus into town, even if I had to walk home afterwards.

I got ready for school but it wasn't easy because my hand was so painful, and I kept almost crying out, which might have made Mum get out of bed, and I definitely didn't want that to happen. I was hoping it was one of her head days, so she would leave us to get ourselves to school. I quietly put out all the breakfast things as well as I could. I looked in the drive – Dad hadn't gone to work yet, so I would have to be careful to hide my hand until he left. He usually only spent a few minutes in the kitchen in the morning because Mr Bednarski liked him to be at work very early. He normally made two pieces of toast with marmalade and a cup of International Roast Instant Coffee, thanked Caleb for his shiny shoes, gave everyone a cheery goodbye and headed for his car.

I was starving because I had missed dinner the night before, and the toast seemed to take forever to make. I used my elbow to hold the pieces down so I could butter them and didn't hear Dad step up behind me because he still had his slippers on.

'What on earth have you done to your hand, Dorcas?' asked Dad.

'Nothing really, Dad. I just hurt it jumping out of the olive tree yesterday,' I said.

'Let me take a look at it,' he said. 'Has your mother seen this?'

'No, I didn't show her. She was sort of mad about me coming home late. But it's not really bad, Dad. I think it will be fine once I go to school.'

'I think you need to see a doctor,' he said.

'No! Really, Dad. There's an important test at school today and I need to go for sure. Really, it's not as sore as it looks.'

'Agnes!' called Dad. 'Agnes, come and look at this.'

We waited. Mum shuffled in. 'What?' she said.

'Look at Dorcas's hand. Didn't you notice this last night? She said she hurt it jumping out of the olive tree.'

'Well, how many times do I have to ask her not to climb trees?' said Mum. She looked at me, and then at the hand, and I saw a look run across her face. She realised how it had happened but she didn't say a thing.

'Can you take her to the doctor this morning?' asked Dad.

'Yes, I suppose so. It will have to be right now though because Alice Johns is coming for a perm at eleven. Get your bag, Dorcas, and I'll walk you to school straight after. I hope they can see us straight away,' she said, in an irritated sort of voice.

'I think this is more important than Alice Johns's hair,' said Dad.

'Well if Bednarski paid you properly I wouldn't have to turn this kitchen into a hair salon,' snapped Mum, and walked into her room to get dressed.

'Are you all right, Dorcas?' asked Dad.

'Sure thing, Dad. Never better. It's no big deal,' I said, and smiled. With a bit of luck, I would get to school by recess time and could borrow the bus fare from Maynard and get straight into town.

* * *

I walked with Mum to see Dr Frayne on the main road. She had rung ahead and said she thought my hand was broken, so they agreed to see me straight away. When I say I walked with Mum, what I mean is that I walked about three steps behind her so she could ignore me and I wouldn't accidentally look the wrong way at her or hunch my shoulders or look at the ground instead of straight ahead or any of the other things I did all the time that drove her mad.

We waited for half an hour to see our doctor who was a very nice old man and always friendly and quite gentle. I had seen him many times for different things: glass in my knee from falling over while running with a milk bottle, a really big splinter Mum couldn't dig out with her tweezers, measles, and stuff to put on my head at night when I scratched the scabs too much and made them bleed.

'And how did you do this, Dorcas?' he asked, carefully turning my hand over and trying to be careful when he moved my thumb up and down.

I looked at Mum, who made her eyes into little slits as a warning, not that I would have changed my story anyway. I noticed Dr Frayne was looking at Mum's face though, not at mine.

'Fell out of a tree,' said Mum. 'She's always climbing trees when I ask her not to.'

'Is that right, Dorcas?' he asked me, peering into my face and looking into my eyes as though he could see what really happened like a television movie.

'Yep, pretty much,' I said, and looked away.

'It's a funny falling-out-of-a-tree injury,' he said, and looked at Mum again. She just sat there with a blank look on her face.

'Well, the good news is it's not broken, but it is very badly sprained, and I think it would be best if you stayed home today and rested it on some high pillows to help the swelling go down.'

'No!' I said. 'I mean, thank you for your concern and everything, Dr Frayne, but I really need to go to school today. I have a very important test and I can't miss it.'

'And it's not as though she can afford to miss school with her grades,' said Mum. 'I'm happy for her to go to school if she wants to.'

'Well, I'm not,' said Dr Frayne, a bit sternly I thought. 'I'm sure they will let you sit the test another time, Dorcas. I want you home with that hand up as high as you can, and if it's not looking a lot better in the morning, I want you back here for me to take another look and maybe take an X-ray.' He made some scratches on a yellow card with the name Wilson on the top. 'Was there anything else?'

'Well, while we're here,' said Mum, 'Dorcas has been nagging me about what she can do about enlarged pores on her nose.'

Now this was a total shock to me, and I had to stop myself quickly from asking what she was talking about.

'Enlarged pores on your face, Dorcas?' he asked me. I didn't know what to say or do, so I said nothing and tried to make my face go expressionless.

'You know what adolescents are like these days,' said Mum, 'always worrying about their appearance. I wondered if there was a good skin treatment for enlarged pores. She must get them from me.' Mum sighed. 'Goodness knows I've always suffered, but she just nags me about them all the time.'

I think the words that best described what I was thinking were astonished and confused. I had no idea what Mum was talking about. I had never asked her about pores on my face, and I didn't really know what she meant anyway.

'Dorcas, are you worried about enlarged pores?' asked Dr Frayne.

'Ah,' I said, looking at Mum, who was doing the narrow-eyes thing again. 'Ah, yes, Dr Frayne. I worry something fierce about them all the time. And the girls at school tease me about them. They call me crater face and pock skin and other awful names as well as the ones about my ringlets from having my hair tied up at night ... And I would be very glad if you had a treatment for them.' The words ran out of my mouth in a quick kind of river.

Dr Frayne looked at Mum and said, 'You still tie this girl's hair up in ringlet rags, Mrs Wilson? I thought we'd decided to stop doing that? The last thing this girl needs to worry about is enlarged pores. I would worry more about why she still picks the sores in her head at night if I were you. And I have no doubt you've searched the chemist shelves for pore cream and will do so again. Medical science can't help with vanity.'

He looked down at the yellow card and made more scratches. Mum and I sat perfectly still for a few minutes until it was clear he wasn't going to speak to us again. Mum stood up, squared her shoulders, flicked her hair out of her eyes, took her clutch bag in both hands and stomped to the door. I stood to follow.

'Thank you, Dr Frayne,' I said quietly as I turned to go. He waved me back over with the four fingers of his right hand, and I stepped back close to him.

'Take some jelly beans, Dorcas,' he said, pushing his big jar near my good hand. 'Goodness knows it's the only thing I can offer you, child.' I thought he looked very sad.

Mum clearly didn't want me to stay home from school, and neither did I, but a doctor is a doctor and we both knew we had to do what he said. When we got home, she told me to make myself scarce because she had Mrs Johns coming over and they wouldn't want a child listening to grown-up talk. She was actually a bit kind for a while and put me to bed with my sore hand on top of two pillows and brought me a Wagon Wheel from the top pantry cupboard where she kept the treats, and stroked my head for a few minutes and asked me if I'd like a book to read while she did Mrs Johns's hair. I think I slept for quite a while, because when I woke up and walked into the kitchen the stuff from Mrs Johns's perm was on the sink and Mum was asleep on her bed.

I was feeling very desperate about Sixpence again and decided to go outside and think about whether I could borrow money the next day and try to get into town to rescue her. I still hadn't worked out how to get Sixpence home on the bus with a cage though, so I thought I'd sit on Mr Driver's fence and think very fiercely about an answer.

It wasn't easy climbing the wooden fence with a very sore hand, and my balance wasn't as good as usual, so it probably wasn't a surprise that I fell sort of sideways into his garden and landed on my sore hand. I didn't want to, but this made me scream out with pain and I heard Mr Driver open his back door and run over to me.

'Dorcas, what are you doing home from school? Are you okay, child?' He helped me to sit up and then saw my hand. 'Goodness. That swelled up fast.'

'No, Mr Driver, I did this yesterday and the doctor said to stay home and rest it up on pillows, which I did, but then I had a big problem to solve and I think better on your fence.

I'm sorry.' All I seemed to do was cry lately, and here I was crying again.

Mr Driver helped me to stand up and took me into his kitchen. He sat next to me and took a careful look at my hand. He was as gentle as Dr Frayne, and just as kind. He made me a cup of instant coffee with a lot of milk and sugar. He said the sugar was good for shock. And then he asked me what the really big problem was that made me climb his fence.

I hadn't been intending to tell him but I was so worried about Sixpence that the river of words started to flow again and it all tumbled out onto his kitchen table. I told him about Mr Johnson and the nudie girl, and Mum being cross about visiting the Johnsons, about the new side gate and Sixpence living in the museum, and about the problem of getting Sixpence home on the bus if I managed to steal her back. I asked if he would let me hide Sixpence in his garage until I could be very well behaved up to Christmas and Dad would let me keep her in the garden. By the time the whole story was out there to look at, I felt quite tired and put my head on the kitchen table, which was very cool and made me feel a bit better.

Mr Driver asked me about my hand. I said I hurt it falling out of a tree. He asked me again how I hurt it, and I just looked at him and said very slowly again that I hurt it falling out of a tree. He helped me to stand up and took me into his best front room and laid me on the sofa. He put my sore hand up on pillows that were a bit dusty but smelled of roses and lavender and asked me to try to have a little rest and he would see if he could ring and find out if Sixpence was in the museum for me. I felt a bit worried about that, but I knew I could basically trust Mr Driver, and it would be good to know if she was okay. He told me to wait until he got back, and I bit off every nail down until they all hurt.

CHAPTER 6

I'm not exactly sure what happened next, and I couldn't really ask the grown-ups to tell me, but I think it went something like this.

Mr Driver went over to the Johnsons' house and spoke to Mrs Johnson. I don't know what he said, but he must have said something big because Mr Johnson came home from work straight away. I think Mr Driver rang my dad too, because my dad also came home from work. I could hear yelling in the street in front of our house when I woke up, and when I looked out of Mr Driver's best front room curtains, the three men were all standing in a kind of circle in the middle of the road. I could hear Mr Johnson's voice the loudest and then my dad's voice. Mr Driver either wasn't speaking, or was talking quietly, because I couldn't pick up the sound of his words.

Mum went out at one point but Dad must have sent her back inside. She didn't come to get me from Mr Driver's, and I was quite happy about that just then, because I didn't know how she would be.

After quite a long time, Dad came into Mr Driver's front room and sat next to me on the sofa. He asked me if Mr Johnson had hurt me, and I said no, he just made me look at some photos and tried to make me drink a cup of tea. I said I was sorry and that I know I should have been polite and stayed for the tea, and that maybe if I had, he wouldn't have taken Sixpence away and built the big fence, but Dad said not to worry it wasn't my fault, and that Mr Johnson had agreed I could have Sixpence and he was going to bring her home from the museum for me the next day. Dad didn't seem cross, but he seemed a bit 'something'. I couldn't work out what it was, and decided I'd ask Ruthy for some good words for it so I could sort it out.

Dad thanked Mr Driver, who put his hand on my shoulder for a moment as I walked past him, and we went back into our house. Mum didn't look at me, and she was a bit 'something' too, but she didn't yell and instead asked if I'd like to watch the tellie for a while until the other kids came home. Dad went back to work, and Mum left me to watch whatever I liked while she went down the street to get things for tea.

It had started out one of the worst days, but now if felt like it might be one of the best days ever because I could watch tellie and I could have Sixpence, and at the moment no one seemed to be yelling at me for anything. I was so glad I'd fallen into Mr Driver's yard, and I decided I would make him a very nice card and also write him a play we would perform in his garden for him as soon as my hand was feeling better. I was so happy my hand didn't even seem to be hurting quite so much.

When Mum came back from the shops, she came in with a packet of frozen peas and wrapped them around my hand and tied it with a tea towel and a bit of her garden string. It was almost a bit too cold, but it helped the pain and I felt I had done enough crying and being weak so I thanked her and tried to focus on the tellie rather than on my very icy hand.

When Dad came home at the proper time, I was dying to ask him where he would make the guinea-pig hutch and whether I could help and what colour we could paint the little house for Sixpence we would need for inside the hutch and where we would get all the greens from and whether I could go to the new supermarket on St Bernards Road to ask for leftover lettuces. But I didn't because, as Mum often said, I just don't know when to shut up sometimes, so I thought I'd practise, even though I didn't have to be perfect until Christmas anymore and could still have Sixpence home with me.

That night I heard Mum and Dad arguing, and I sat by the crack in the door to gather intelligence. Mum was telling Dad he could stay home from work and care for Caleb if the 'rat' caused an asthma attack, and Dad was saying don't be ridiculous, and if Caleb didn't touch the guinea pig he would be fine. Mum said it was okay for him to say that because he wasn't stuck nursing a sick child all day, and Dad said she mollycoddled him and that a bit of dirt and rough and tumble would do Caleb the world of good. Mum said don't tell me you agree with that dreadful sister-in-law of yours that it's all in Caleb's mind, and Dad said no he didn't, but it was also important to try to toughen him up so he was strong enough to cope with it. The arguing went on like that for ages, and after a while I went back to bed.

Because there had been good things about the day, I tried to just think about happy stuff. It wasn't easy because I'd start imagining what my knight's armour would look like, and then suddenly I'd see Mr J's nasty face in front of me. So then I imagined poking him a bit with a sword to keep him at a distance, but he just grabbed it and pulled it out of my hand. Then he threw it on the ground like a twig and laughed at me. I must have been trying very hard to just imagine good things, because when Ruthy walked in and looked at me, she asked why I had screwed my face up so tight.

The only thing I could think of to say was that I hoped my injury wouldn't stop me from sword fights when I became the first girl knight of the round table. Ruthy just stood and looked at me with her little hands on her hips, and I knew I wasn't fooling her. But then, fooling Ruthy for long was something I never did.

CHAPTER 7

We all agreed we had to mark the next day down as a cross day again as soon as Mum got out of bed. I didn't think I'd done anything bad in my sleep but I must have, because Ruthy and Caleb agreed there wasn't anything else happening that could have been what Ruthy called 'causal' except for me starting things rolling by falling off Mr Driver's fence. We checked my pillow but there were no scabs we could see or bits of blood on it, so it wasn't that.

We took some paper down to the tree house and decided to each make a list of why we thought Mum was unhappy again.

Caleb's list said: *sixpens is a rat and mum hats rats.*

Ruthy's list said: *Dad had to come home from work and this will make Mr Bednarski upset. Also, Mum will have to* have a guinea pig in the garden and she will be worried about mess and Caleb's asthma.

My list was the longest. *Mum doesn't like other people knowing her business and now the whole street will be asking about Mr Johnson, Dad and Mr Driver meeting in the middle of the day. Also, Mum will think Mrs Johnson won because I get Sixpence and she hates Mrs Johnson. Also, Dad will think he has to do a good thing for Caleb and Ruthy now and that might mean football and writing school and Mum will think I have won and turned us into Catholics or people of the world but not in the world. And this will mean Aunty Maisie has won because she believes Mum is full of vanity and does not love God enough. And this will make Dad very sad because Grandpa might find out and think he is not following the Ways of the Lord.*

Ruthy was very impressed with my list. She said she's never seen me choose to write so much, and I think that was actually true. She also liked it because she and Caleb started to cheer that they might get their wishes too, and I had to remind them the only thing we knew for sure was that Sixpence would come to live with us this very day, and we would have to wait to see about the other hopes and prayers. Ruthy said a prayer might be a very good idea, so we sat on the edge of the tree house platform and joined hands and closed our eyes and Ruthy prayed for us.

'Dear Heavenly Father, we come before you today, your humble servants, strong in the sure and certain resurrection of our Lord Jesus Christ. We beseech thee, Father, to hear our prayers and grant your humble servants Caleb and Ruthy their wish to be famous footballers and writers, now that you have granted our sister Dorcas her greatest wish to have her baby guinea pig come to live with us.

'Dear Heavenly Father, please make Mum continue in the way of happy and Jesus days, and make Caleb's lungs very strong so Sixpence can't cause him a mucus build-up in his bronchiole. Please ask Mr Bednarski to send Dad home for chocolate and tellie on Fridays, and bless Mr Driver's stump so it doesn't itch in the heat. Please also stop Aunty Maisie from scaring Caleb when he goes to her toilet so he doesn't wet himself instead. And if possible, make sure Grandpa has plenty of butterscotch lollies because he really likes them.

'Grant us Thy grace and mercy and hear our prayer. In the name of the Lord Jesus Christ, our Redeemer, Amen.'

Caleb and I both congratulated her on a very grown-up and fairly comprehensive prayer, and Caleb asked if she could just add a football jumper to the list, and if she could explain what a bee's itch had to do with anything.

We went in for breakfast and Mum was up with Dad, who was about to leave. What happened next occurred so quickly and in a blur that was sort of slow motion but also like a roller-coaster.

Dad asked if he could see my sore hand and did a lot of tut-tutting noises because it was still very sore and swollen. He asked Mum if I should stay home again today but she said not on your life; I'm not having her under my feet again today. Hadn't I caused enough grief yesterday?

Dad asked what grief I had caused and Mum said if I'd done as I was told and had stopped going over to the Johnsons, none of this would have happened. And if I thought deliberately hurting my hand would mean I didn't have to do the Sunday school exams, I had another think coming.

Dad turned to me and asked if I had deliberately hurt my hand, and for a minute I was quite confused because I didn't think I had but so much had gone on that I forgot for a minute how my hand got hurt.

And then Caleb said I didn't do it deliberately because Mum threw the potato masher at me and I didn't make her do that.

And then Dad asked, 'Agnes, is this true?' And Mum said Caleb wasn't even in the kitchen when that happened so how could he possibly know. And Dad turned to me and said, 'So she did throw the potato masher at you?' And I said, 'No, she didn't,' because I was worried that they would change their mind about Sixpence and then Dad told us all to leave for school right away because he had to talk to our mother and off we went.

I was furious with Caleb all the way to school and made him cry, but I didn't care. I told him he was a stupid little boy who had no idea about how families worked, and because he'd told Dad Mum hit me, I probably wouldn't get Sixpence, and he wouldn't get to go to football and Ruthy wouldn't get to go to the writing class. I called him flat-nosed rude, double bum, snot-nosed six-toes, and further selections from our swearing list. Caleb said, 'Sticks and stones will break my bones but names will never hurt me,' but I told him that was only true in the last century and that the rules had changed along with the introduction of decimal currency in 1966 and now names could actually puncture your lungs and make your poo turn to cement in your bowels and never come out and if you didn't poo, you died. I told him if it was between Mum and me, Dad would choose Mum and I would probably have to go to live in the children's home now and they would never see me again. I said Daniel would be very upset when he found out that Caleb was the reason I was now an orphan, and Ruthy said I couldn't be an orphan if I had parents and to leave him alone.

Caleb said I was just being mean and we had prayed to God and God would make sure we all got a happy thing. He asked Ruthy what she thought, but Ruthy was very quiet and stuck out her chin and walked a bit ahead of us. She usually defended Caleb more, but I think she realised what I was saying was true – Caleb might have queered all of our chances to get what we wanted. And because she wasn't looking out for him, I didn't seem to be able to stop. So much angry stuff came out that I really, really wanted to hit him too. Caleb was pretty hysterical by the time we got to the school gate, and Ruthy said she'd take him to his class and tell the teacher he wasn't feeling well, and I said good riddance to gumbies and spittlebombs and left them to it.

I had a lot of mixed feelings going on all day. Part of me was very happy about Sixpence coming home, but the other part of me was worried that Caleb's revelation might somehow wreck it all. I couldn't quite see how. Once Sixpence was home it should be okay. Mum might be cross for many days in a row, but we had managed that in the past, and at least I could stay in the garden with Sixpence now, even if it was hard in the house.

At the break I filled Maynard in on everything that had happened. He said it was sensible that I had told Mr Driver what had happened, and it would all work out for the best now, he was sure. In the lunch break he brought out paper and pencils and we did some designs for Sixpence's hutch to help Dad work out what might be the best home for her. I was starting to feel quite excited and wondered what time Sixpence would be dropped over from the Johnsons. I was hoping it was straight after Mr Johnson got home from work, which would be while it was still light and I could play with her for quite a while before teatime.

But at the end of the lunch period one of the prefects came to fetch me from our seat under the gum tree. She took me to the office of the headmistress, Miss Lillicrap, and I waited outside wondering what I'd done this time. I went through a list in my head. It could have been that I didn't finish my maths homework. It might have been that I had been asked to revise my latest English essay and had just added three words to it – 'very', 'enormously' and 'hugely'. It could have been that I was told off for talking several times that morning, because I had been desperate to tell Venita about Sixpence. I thought the best guess was about rewriting words to Gilbert and Sullivan.

Every morning we had to take out our Gilbert and Sullivan songbook and follow along while the headmistress piped in ten minutes or so of one of the operas. She was the head of the Gilbert and Sullivan Society, and thought it was an important part of our education to learn the classics. Maynard said there was nothing classic about Gilbert and Sullivan, and that his mother said the headmistress had a voice like a strangled monkey.

At the moment we were doing *HMS Pinafore*. I made up a play where we sang: 'She always swears a big, big B. So give three cheers and one cheer more for the strangled monkey on the Pinafore.' My class teacher, Miss Thompson, had heard it and asked what it referred to and I said, 'Nothing,' but I worried she might have guessed. The next day she caught us singing my version of the words to 'Little Buttercup':

'I smell like my name – that's crap –
Poor Missus Lillicrap,
Though I could never tell why,
But still I'm called Lillicrap – poor Missus Lillicrap,
Stinky old Lillicrap I.'

She pulled me aside and said she hoped she had misheard what we were singing, and that if she heard one word that didn't match the songbook, it would be down to the headmistress's office for me. Actually it was just as well she hadn't heard what I'd done with 'We sail the Ocean Blue' ...

But it wasn't that after all. Miss Lillicrap called me in and told me Caleb had been taken to the children's hospital with an asthma attack. She said it was serious. His teacher had rung Dad who had come to pick him up, and Mum and Dad had also taken Ruthy with them. I didn't know why they hadn't asked me to go too, but I guessed it might have been because Ruthy told them I was mean to him on the way to school. She said he was stable but very unwell, and that I was to go to Mr Driver's house if they were not home when school was over. Then she sent me back to class.

The bell had rung so I couldn't tell Maynard what had happened, but he was waiting for me when home time came and walked home with me even though it was in the opposite direction from his own house, which was very nice of him. I was worried Mum and Dad might have asked Mr Johnson not to bring Sixpence over today because Caleb was sick, but Maynard suggested I didn't raise this with anyone because they would think I didn't care about Caleb, which wasn't true, but in a little way was true. I was still very cross with him for telling Dad about the potato masher and now it seemed he had taken all the attention again by being sick. Aunty Maisie said he was a sensitive child and that, in her opinion, half of the asthma was in his mind. There were days I thought this might the case, although I had sat with him when he couldn't breathe, and I don't think you can make that up. Certainly when he coughed up lots of green and yellow stuff, that wasn't anyone's imagination.

When we reached our place, Maynard said he'd come in with me to make sure everything was okay. We walked down the side path to our back door. On the step was a little cardboard box. I wondered what it was and we both crouched down to take a look. Sometimes the local chemist left medicine for Caleb in a box at the back, so I thought this might be something he needed in hospital and was wondering how I could get it to him.

We lifted the lid.

And there was my Sixpence. My dear little baby. And I knew straight away she was dead. She was just lying there in that little brown box with nothing else in it. It was just a bit bigger than she was. There was no bedding or food or water or air holes or anything. I screamed out and took her out of the box and cuddled her to me. She wasn't warm and she didn't come back to life. Maynard said, 'Oh no,' and put his arm around my shoulders. I cried and cried and cried. I rocked my baby and cried. My mouth formed a wide O but I couldn't speak. My Sixpence was dead.

Maynard must have been talking to me but I didn't hear him. All I could think was, *How did this happen?* Was she alive when Mr Johnson put her in the box, and then died because she couldn't breathe? Did he kill her and put her in the box to teach me a lesson? Why would anyone do such a thing? Did she know what was happening to her? Was she frightened? Why? Why? No!

Then I realised Mr Driver was squatting down near me. Maynard must have gone in next door to fetch him. Mr Driver was talking quietly to me. He helped me stand up but he didn't try to take Sixpence away from me. He led us both into his house and sat me in his reading chair in the corner of his kitchen. He made me a cup of instant coffee with lots of sugar and even though I shook my head no thank you, he made me have a few sips.

He asked me to tell him exactly what had happened when I got home. I tried to tell him but I was hiccupping too hard. Maynard filled him in and then said he had to go because his mum would be worrying, and Mr Driver shook him by the hand and asked if he would like him to ring his mother to explain. I don't know what Maynard said. I sort of went away from the kitchen for a while in my mind, just trying to talk to Sixpence and stroking her and telling her it would be okay, even though I knew she was dead and wouldn't ever play with me again.

CHAPTER 8

Dad came in to take me home about teatime. They had brought Caleb home but he was still very sick. I heard them talking at the kitchen door, but then Mr Driver took Dad outside so I don't know what was said. When he came back in, Dad wasn't with him, and Mr Driver asked if I'd like to stay with him for tea and I said thank you I wasn't very hungry but could I stay anyway.

He didn't make me put Sixpence down, and I knew if I went home, they would take her away from me. He let me stay in his chair in the kitchen with her and went about making mashed potatoes and chops in the griller of his stove. He wasn't worried about a dead animal in his kitchen, and I guessed this was because he'd seen dead things and people in the war, so it didn't make him flip out. He put the radio on quietly and didn't make me talk to him.

After a while he sat next to me. He said Sixpence was a very pretty guinea pig, and he knew I would miss her. He said animals have a very strong sense about who cares about them, and he was sure she knew how much I loved her, and that would have made her happy at the end. He said when I was ready, he would put her back in the box, and we could bury her anywhere I liked in his garden, so I could come to visit her grave whenever I wanted to. He asked if I would like to make a bed in the box for her and I nodded. He said I could come in after school tomorrow and he would help me make a little cross for her grave. I said I didn't think our church let us have crosses or angels on graves because that was considered idolatry, and he sort of snorted and said we'd work something out. He put a pile of old socks and rags and scissors and magazines and glue on the table and asked me to help myself when I was ready. After a while I put her on the table and started to cut up some nice old soft socks to make a bed for her.

I tucked her in and put a rag with some dots on it as a cover for her. I cut up nice pictures of flowers and sunny skies from *The Women's Weekly* magazines and covered the top of the box. With a thick black packaging marker, I wrote 'Sixpence, I love you' on the top of the box in my best handwriting. I gave her a little kiss and closed the box. I tried not to cry again, but she looked so sad all tucked up that I thought I might never stop crying for the rest of my life.

Mr Driver came to have a look at my work and said he thought I had given her a very good send-off indeed. He said he doubted a guinea pig had ever had a better little bed to rest in, and he thought the decoration on the top was second to none. Even though it was getting dark outside, Mr Driver said we could still choose a spot for her and he would make her safe overnight in her new home in the garden. He took my hand and we walked around the garden. I pointed to a garden bed near the shed that had some flowers in it, and he nodded. We went back inside, and I lifted the lid and kissed her again, and then Mr Driver walked me home.

Dad met him at the door and gave me a hug and put his arm around me. We walked to Caleb's room where Mum was sitting on the bed, and Ruthy was on the floor next to her, and I said, 'Sorry for being mean to you, Caleb.' Mum didn't say anything to me and she didn't look at me. I went to my bedroom and crawled into my bed. Dad asked if I wanted some tea but I wasn't hungry. He said, 'I'm so sorry, Dorcas,' and tucked me in and kissed me on the forehead. To keep the quiet away, I made little yowly noises that no one else could hear until I went to sleep.

It must have been much later that I heard noises that woke me up. It felt like the darkest black bit of the night that you don't get to see that often. I could see a crack of light under my doorway, and realised Mum and Dad were arguing. Ruthy was making little popping mouth noises so I knew she was asleep.

I got out of bed quietly so I didn't wake her, and opened the door very gently. I stayed in our room but sat next to the crack in the door to hear what they were saying. I often did this. I had learned quite a few interesting things thanks to the crack in the door. It's how I learned about Grandma being a bit crazy and having Dad to make her well. It's how I heard about Daniel being sent to New South Wales, and that it was something to do with a girl at church, but I never found out which girl or what happened with her. It's how I knew that Mum wished she'd never left her family in Scotland, and that if our church allowed divorce, she would have been off to find a decent life for herself 'back home'. It's where I found out that Dr Frayne had suggested some tablets for Mum but Dad had said all she needed was the power of prayer and it was a shame she was so like her mother who had never been able to get out of her own way. And Mum said how would he know because he had never met her family and never would if he didn't insist he was paid properly by Henry Bednarski so they could afford to bring her mother out.

Dad said he was going over to the Johnsons in the morning to have it out with Athol Johnson. What kind of man kills a guinea pig and puts it in a box to frighten and punish a child? He thought he just might ring the police in the morning too. If he can do something like that, what else might he do? And he should have reported him for forcing Dorcas to look at that photo in any case.

Mum's voice changed somehow. It went soft and coaxing. She said it was better to just let sleeping dogs lie, and the main thing was the guinea pig couldn't make Caleb sick now, and nothing else mattered. Dad said it also mattered that I had had a nasty experience – two of them now – and what kind of mother didn't want to protect her oldest girl? Mum said what if Athol Johnson just denied that he'd killed the rat? Dad said not to call it a rat and that Mr Driver would testify to what had happened and the police would believe him given his reputation and his war record.

Mum started to beg Dad to leave the matter alone. It would all blow over. I would get over the disappointment and life would go on. It would teach me not to go to the Johnsons' when I'd been forbidden to go over there. Perhaps there would finally be some peace for a while.

Dad said, 'Give the girl a break, Agnes, for goodness' sake.' Mum didn't say anything but she went into Caleb's room and I think she slept there with him.

* * *

The next morning I decided to see if there was anything in Dad's shed I could take to Mr Driver to help build a memorial for Sixpence. I wasn't really meant to go into the shed without permission, but I had an idea when I woke up that I might try to make a little house to sit on her grave if I wasn't allowed to have a cross or an angel. I pulled the chord to switch on the light and started to poke around to see what I could find. There wasn't much that would be of any use, and I was just about to leave when I saw something pushed behind Dad's workbench near the far corner. I pulled at it and out came a small cage. I had seen that cage before. It belonged to Mrs Johnson and she used it when she had to take one of the animals to the vet. I pulled it right out and looked at it. It had some straw bedding in it, a little water tank made from a plastic bottle tied to the bars and a small dish of food. I didn't understand why it was in our shed. I took it in to the kitchen.

Dad was making his toast.

'Dad, why is this cage in your shed?' I asked.

Dad looked up, surprised. 'What were you doing in the shed, Dorcas?' I could see he was about to crossen up, but then he looked at me and changed his face. 'I don't know, Dorcas. I've never seen it before. Where exactly was it?'

'It was pushed down the back where you couldn't see it easily. Is this what Mr Johnson brought Sixpence home in? But why did he put her in a box if he had this cage? And why did he hide the cage in our shed?' I asked.

'I don't know, Dorcas. I don't know. But I think I'll ask him.' Dad walked out the door looking very determined. I thought about going with him, but I knew he would just send me home. If Mr J deliberately killed Sixpence, I would be happy if Dad told the police and if they put him in jail. We are meant to forgive other people and turn the other cheek, but I would quite like him to go away, even if it meant Mrs Johnson and the girls had to live on their own and only visit him in prison on his birthday, which I was pretty sure they would let them do even if he was a guinea-pig killer.

Ruthy was ready to go to school, but I wanted to find out what happened when Dad came home. Mum and Caleb were asleep in Caleb's room, so I told Ruthy just to go to school and I'd go by myself later. Ruthy came up to me at the kitchen table and gave me a little hug.

'I'm really sorry about Sixpence, Dorcas. I really am. It's horrible. You were mean to Caleb yesterday but you didn't deserve that to happen. Mum thinks you made him have an asthma attack, but I'm sure you didn't. His teacher said it is the spring allergy season and that lots of kids are getting asthma and hay fever, and I'm sure that's what it is because he always gets sick just before the union exams in September. Where is Sixpence now?' she asked.

'She's buried in Mr Driver's garden behind the shed. After school he's going to help me build a memorial to put on her grave. I can show you after if you like. Or you could help. You're good at making things.'

'I will be glad to help, Dorcas. I'll think about ideas at school today and we can walk home and decide what to make. We'll make something really beautiful for her.' She hugged me again. 'I'm going to make some special Sixpence pages in my journal in her honour, and you can write in them too if you want. There's a girl in my class who is a very good drawer. I'm going to ask her to go to the library with me to look for photos of guinea pigs and then I'll ask her to draw Sixpence for us. We can cut the drawing out and put it in the journal. And I am going to write to Daniel and tell him about it because he would have loved Sixpence too and I know he will be very sad for you.'

I mumbled thanks and she headed out the door.

I sat on the outside top step and waited for Dad. I let my legs swing back and forward and crash into the cement, and even though it hurt a bit I couldn't stop. I had scratched my head in the night and had to hide my pillow slip in the laundry so Mum wouldn't notice, and my head hurt a bit in one place, but somehow the leg hurting and the head hurting felt right.

Dad walked past me and he was in a fury.

'Dad. What did he say, Dad?' I asked.

'Go to school, Dorcas. Just go to school.'

'But, Dad, what did he say? Did he admit he smothered her in a box? Dad?'

'Dorcas. Don't make me cross. Go to school. We'll talk about it when you get home tonight. Not now.' He slammed the back door after him.

I put my ear to the door and I heard him call out for Mum. She came out of Caleb's room, shooshing him because Caleb was still asleep. They went into the lounge room. I decided to crouch down and go around the front to listen. As well as listening at the crack in the bedroom door, sometimes you learned things by crouching down by the lounge room windows in the spring when Mum opened them a bit for fresh air.

'He says he left her in the cage on our back doorstep, Agnes,' said Dad.

'Well, he would, wouldn't he?' she said.

'Why would he hide the cage in the garage if he had put the thing in a box on the step? It doesn't make sense. He says what happened was nothing to do with him. He says if I just think about it, two and two will make four, Agnes.'

'What on earth are you taking about?' said Mum. 'That dreadful man clearly killed the rat to upset Dorcas and you're believing his story?'

'Stop calling her pet a rat!' yelled Dad. He didn't yell at Mum that often. His voice was usually the one trying to make her voice less loud and screechy. I was glad he stood up for Sixpence and didn't want her to be called a rat.

'If I ever find out what happened, Agnes ...' said Dad.

'What? What! You'll what exactly?' cried my mum. 'You'll pray about it? You'll tell your dreadful sister-in-law? You'll work a few more hours for Henry? What exactly will you do, Harry?'

Then I didn't hear any more talking, and a few minutes later Dad got in the car and drove off. I sat quietly until I was sure Mum wouldn't see me and then snuck off to school.

I didn't understand what was happening, but I decided I would tell Maynard at lunchtime to see what he thought.

CHAPTER 9

On a Saturday night a fortnight later, Mum and Dad were going to have dinner at their friends Brother and Sister Hodges. Caleb had bounced back pretty well, and although Mum was a bit worried about taking him out in the night air, Dad said he was right as rain and that it would do them both good to have a night away from the kids. The Hodges had no children, and what Dad meant by a night away from us was that we would have to stay in the car in the Hodges' driveway for the whole night.

We, of course, argued to be allowed to come inside because it was pretty boring in the car in the dark. Mum said we were too badly behaved to be allowed to go inside when they went to dinner, and besides, they needed some time for grown-up talking. Dad put down the seats in the station wagon and laid two quilts on top of each other to make a sort of large bed. It still wasn't very comfortable though, and after a while my hips started to get sore from the metal underneath. Ruthy said to just sleep on my back then, but I couldn't seem to do that. I took turns of each of my hips hurting instead. I snatched Caleb's pillow to put under me, but this made him scream blue murder and I was worried it would bring Dad out to see what was going on, so I gave it back to him by hitting him over the head with it. He coughed a bit and Ruthy stuck his asthma spray in his mouth to keep him quiet, as well as to make sure he didn't have an attack that would be considered my fault again.

On other nights we'd spent like this in people's driveways, we weren't allowed to put the car light on, but we were allowed to use one torch in case we got frightened or Caleb needed his Ventolin, but of course we put it on the whole time we were in the back together. We were meant to lie quietly and go to sleep, but as my Aunt Maisie would say, live like a maggot in bacon, which didn't seem to mean anything sensible, but fit the situation anyway. We took turns telling stories, or sometimes singing songs.

If we were feeling brave, we would make up a reason we had to go inside, and Ruthy and I used to tell Caleb he would have to be the one to go and knock on the door, because he wouldn't get into anything like the trouble we would, and he wouldn't get a smack. We tried to convince him to say there was a robber looking in at us, or a robber looking in the windows of the house we were visiting, or a mad dog with rabies circling the car, or a big spider on the ceiling, or a police car going up and down the street possibly looking for the robbers, or even an escaped prisoner, and even once, that there was a pirate planning to steal the boat we saw in the host's driveway.

The only time Caleb actually went to the front door was when we were having a big fight, and he would get sooky and go and tell on us. We would have fights over anything really: who was over the invisible line we drew to carve up the space, whose turn it was to tell the story or choose the song, who made up the best swear words, or who had the most friends at school. When Caleb climbed out of the car in a huff, Ruthy and I would hold our breath, half in fear and half in hope. What tended to happen is that Dad would come out to the car, fling the doors open and smack us hard on the legs over and over again. Usually they let Caleb stay in the house after that, which wasn't fair. We would pretend to be fast asleep when they came out carrying him to go home, in the hope the whole thing would be forgotten in the morning.

On this particular Saturday night I might possibly have pinched Caleb quite hard, and even though his chest was still a bit wonky, his screams were very loud, and Dad came out and roughly pulled both Caleb and Ruthy out of the car, slamming it on me before I could get out. Ruthy meanly took the torch in with her, so I was in the dark by myself. Although I think I am quite brave, I was a bit scared, particularly when a strong wind started up and the car rocked a bit. I sat up and checked all the door-locking knobs were down so only Dad could get in with a key and covered my whole head with a blanket. My heart was thumping so hard I could hear it in my ears. I squeezed my eyes tight shut and imagined a new play I would put on at school. It was about knights and in particular a new character called Don Quixote the librarian had told me about she thought I'd like. He was from a picture book that had lots of good illustrations, but he was a funny sort of old knight with a pretty deadbeat horse and a fairly dim friend, so it wasn't the kind of story I usually liked. However, I did admire the fact he rode off to save people so I wrote a play with him in it but I gave him a girl to be his offsider. She was clever and even braver than he was, and of course I would play that role.

I was actually asleep when they loaded the back seat with the other two, who were also dead to the world. The next morning Caleb said they were allowed to sit in the kitchen and Mum's friend gave them hot lemon delicious pudding with cream on the top, and paper and pencils to draw with and they were allowed to stay up for ages and ages before Mum put them down on the lady's bed, which smelled of lavender and oranges. Mum had turned out the lights and closed the door, but the nice lady snuck in and turned the light on and winked at them and said it would be their secret, and brought them each two toffees. She had asked Mum if she wanted to bring me in, or if she should take something out to me, but Mum said no I had to learn. I wasn't exactly sure what I had to learn, but I think it was about my general naughtiness, because what I had already learned was that Caleb could do no wrong and people liked Ruthy better than me because she was sweet and pretty.

The next morning on the way to school, Ruthy pulled me aside before we got into the building. She said she had important information from the night before, because she had adopted my ploy of sitting near a crack in the bedroom door to find out what the grown-ups were talking about.

It seems a certain conversation started because Sister Hodges asked why I couldn't be brought inside along with the other two. Mum started to cry and she heard Dad ask her to buck up because they were in company. Mrs Hodges's voice sounded kind and although Ruthy couldn't hear everything, she heard Dad say he was worried Mum would have another breakdown if she didn't pull herself together. From what Ruthy could make out, Mum had come to Australia to do nursing, but when she arrived and found her uncle was dead and she had no one else she knew here, she went to stay in these tin housing things called Nissen huts, which Ruthy was going to look up in the library. They were something soldiers lived in, she thought. Mum started her nursing studies at the Royal Adelaide, but it was all too much for her, and she had to drop out. She heard Sister Hodges ask what Glenside was like, and Ruthy was pretty sure she was talking about Glenside mental home.

We looked at each other with our mouths open for a minute. I asked Ruthy if she thought this was true, and she said yes, she thought our mum used to be a bit mental when she was young, and maybe this was why she had Jesus days and head days and stuff like that. Ruthy took my hand and we just sat together until the bell rang. I had no idea what to do with this information, but I thought I might talk to Maynard about it. Although then I thought Mum might not want anyone to know her big secret, so I thought I might not.

The whole nuthouse story, as Ruthy and I referred to it in whispers, made me feel very worried about ever having to spend a night in a driveway again. I wasn't sure I wanted to find out more about Mum like this. A couple of weeks later when Mum told us we were going to stay in the car for the evening at Sister Palmer's, Ruthy and I agreed we would be on our best behaviour so no one would have to go inside and learn more grown-up secret things.

In the Palmers' driveway I decided to only think about lovely family car stories. Mum and Dad did strange things with us in the car when we went to the drive-in. We didn't go very often, but every now and again there would be a Disney movie we were allowed to see. Mum would pack dinner for us. Dad was really excellent at parking in exactly the right spot to be able to wind down the window and put the big speaker in it, and then wind it up tight so we could all hear. We always pretended we needed to go to the toilet more than we did, because the toilets were near the big shop that was full of lollies and hot chips, but Mum was never tempted to go in and we would get a smack if we asked more than once.

The strange bit was that when we were queuing up in the car to get into the drive-in, Mum would leave me sitting up in the back but squash Caleb and Ruthy on the floor with a rug over them and tell them to be perfectly still and quiet. When it was our turn, Dad would say, 'Two adults and one under twelve,' and pretend Caleb and Ruthy weren't in the car.

I said, 'Isn't that telling a lie and like stealing?' and Dad said no because we didn't say they weren't there, and the person could have checked for themselves, but I think it wasn't quite right. And given Mum used to constantly look at me and say, 'Would you have done that if Jesus was standing next to you?' I wondered what she'd say if I asked her the exact same question. But I never did of course, because I am often naughty, but I'm not stupid.

CHAPTER 10

All of a sudden it was the Saturday of the church union exams. Caleb was still unwell but said he wanted to do his exam, which made Mum very happy and proud. She called him her little disciple. She had had a few Jesus days in that time. This usually happened when she went to the church's women's group or Bible class and came home feeling more godly and calm. For some reason she went to more of these classes for a couple of weeks around this time, and we all got the benefit.

I asked Ruthy if she thought Mum was going more often because she was sad about Sixpence, but she just snorted and said it was more likely that she was praying for precious Caleb, which wasn't like Ruthy, who usually took Mum's side, even when she's cross. Dad seemed pleased Mum was going frequently, so they didn't argue quite as much. We were relieved when Ruthy could write 'Jesus day' on the top of a journal page, and we tried to keep everything as happy as possible so they would last.

We helped each other to be good. Ruthy was especially helpful because she seemed to naturally be a better child and could catch me or Caleb starting to do the wrong thing and hiss a warning at us, which often made us stop and get out of Mum's way.

I had been trying to do some extra revision, and Ruthy tutored me after we went to bed. In the weeks before the exam, Mum and Dad allowed us an extra hour to study with the light on before we went to sleep. Ruthy was nicer to me than usual, but she said it was because I was nicer than usual and I don't know which one of those was true. I don't think I was nicer. I think I was just sadder.

I thought about Sixpence every day. I visited her grave after school. Mr Driver and Ruthy had helped me build a little house to mark the spot where she was buried. It was about eight inches square, and it had a door and two windows, and Mr Driver made a little postbox to go with it. Mr Driver made it out of bits of timber, and screwed and glued it together for us, and Ruthy helped me paint it. I painted it sky blue with big white dots on it, and Ruthy said she thought it was a bit bright for a tombstone but Mr Driver said he thought it was fine and he was happy to have it in his garden. He pulled up weeds around it and planted some little white seaside daisies he said Mrs Kerfoops across the street let him have for nothing. I don't think her name was Mrs Kerfoops, but for some reason it's what all the neighbours called her. Ruthy said it was because she had a very long, complicated Greek name that no one could say properly.

I thought the grave was lovely. Mr Driver put a little chair next to the bit of garden where we planted her, and every day I would sit for a while and tell her what had happened. Sometimes I saw him looking at me out of his kitchen window, and he would wave, but he didn't ever interrupt me or ask me to go home, and I felt calmer there than anywhere else.

Although no one would ever replace her, I admitted to myself I would love to have another pet because Sixpence couldn't talk back to me or snuggle into my jumper anymore. I missed visiting the animals at the Johnsons, but even I didn't have to be told to stay away from them again. I started to think in my head that if I tried very hard to be good until Christmas, and did better in my union exam than the year before, I might be able to talk to Dad about another guinea pig.

Mum and I seemed to have reached an uneasy truce. She didn't get as cross with me, but she didn't talk to me much either. I must have been scratching my head in the night more than usual because my head was often sore in the morning, but she just took the pillowcases off the bed and put them in the laundry without nagging me or making me wrap my hair in ringlet rags at night.

Ruthy's hair was golden white and curly, but mine was a dark brown colour and dead straight to halfway down my back if left alone. The problem with it being shiny was that the big pieces of sores from my scabs would get stuck in my hair and you could see them sitting on the surface sometimes. Rufus's nasty friend Robert Bridge started to call me Leprosy, and Rufus called me Scabhead. Maynard kindly looked over my hair in the lunch hours and pointed out bits he could see so we could try to pick them out. He wasn't at all fussed about this. He wanted to be a doctor and said this was nothing compared to the blood and guts he would have to get used to. In fact he seemed quite fascinated by it all and even wrapped some of the bigger bits of scabs in his hanky to look at under his microscope at home.

Mum must have been right though about me being a terrible child, because sometimes even though I knew I shouldn't do things I just came right out and did them anyway. The morning of the exam Mum and Dad sat around the kitchen table helping us with our revision questions. Mum made pancakes for breakfast and, even though it was all about getting ready for the exams, it felt like a family holiday thing that we were all working on together. Mum helped Caleb and Ruthy, and Dad helped me. He asked me lots of questions about the Daniel in the Bible in particular. Dad was a bit of a Daniel fan, as far as I could tell, and he was really enjoying himself. He knew a lot of things about him that weren't in my Sunday school notes, and he made him sound a lot more interesting than Sister Joyce, my teacher, ever did. I told him he should be a Sunday school teacher, and he said he was when he was younger, which was fascinating because I didn't know that about him. I told him I'd like to be a Sunday school teacher too and he said that was a fine ambition, but I'd better learn the stories if I wanted to do that, and I thought this was good advice and made a lot of sense.

We parked in Halifax Street and Mum and Dad walked around to the rear hall with us. They left Ruthy and I there and we found our classes at the big trestle tables. Everyone was a bit nervous, and Mr Walters, who was in charge of making sure all the exams were done properly, was strutting around giving out orders. I heard Mum say 'Pompous git' under her breath, which made Ruthy and I giggle very quietly and feel quite pleased with her, because we thought he was too.

Mum and Dad then went through the middle hall to take Caleb upstairs to the baby's Sunday school rooms, where Caleb would do his exam. They told us they would wait for us in the car. Mum had made them sandwiches and a big flask of tea, and they said they would be fine until we were ready to come home, and not to worry about them or rush our answers. A lot of parents waited out the front on union exam day. Most of them got out of their cars and had a sort of social event on the footpath, sharing what they'd brought for lunch and talking nine to the dozen. Anne King, who always finished the exam early because she just wasn't that interested and was allowed to leave the hall, had told me the year before that my mum just stayed in the car by herself, and that some other mums thought she was sad and some thought she was stuck up because she was sort of beautiful and didn't mind showing it. So I lost a few minutes at the start of the exam worrying about whether Mum would join the party outside of the ecclesial hall, or just be miserable by herself. I looked in front of me and could see Ruthy writing away with her pen sliding fast along the page and her tongue stuck out, so I thought I'd better get on with it too.

After the exam, I was feeling pretty optimistic. I had been able to answer all of the questions at least in part, and when I checked some of what I'd written with Ruthy, she thought I might have done quite well too. We were all together in the car driving back home from the exam, and Mum had us all singing 'Lead, Kindly Light' and 'Jesus Wants Me for a Sunbeam'. She had a very lovely voice, and so did my dad, and sometimes they sang a duet at the family nights and everyone admired them because they were both so handsome and beautiful and sang like songbirds together. Mum was a contralto. That means she can sing a bit lower than other women. She sings the boring sort of not tuneful lines, but when you sing that way with the people who do sing the main tune of the songs, it makes it all sound rather wonderful.

I should have just sang songs and kept myself quiet, but I was so happy that I might actually do well in the exam, I heard words coming out of my mouth again before I could stop them.

'Dad, if I get a first-class certificate in my exams instead of a second-class certificate, could I have a guinea pig for Christmas?' I asked.

As soon as I asked this question, I knew I had started something very big and very bad. Mum immediately stopped singing. Caleb and Ruthy froze. Dad said nothing for a minute but I saw his arms go tight around the steering wheel. He stared straight ahead for a few seconds and then I saw him look at me in the rear-view mirror. It was a sad look and made me feel bad. Mum's shoulders were very straight and stiff and didn't move for a long time. Caleb looked at Ruthy who made a very small 'no' with her mouth, and we travelled on that way for what seemed like miles and miles.

'So, Dorcas,' Mum finally said through gritted teeth, 'despite your brother nearly dying of an asthma attack only a few weeks ago, you want to bring an animal into the house that might kill him. That's what you think of him, is it? And you want your dad and me to have no sleep taking turns of sitting in his room with him all night because he can't breathe? And you want us to have more hospital bills? And all so you can have a dirty little rat in the garden? I don't know why I send you to Sunday school. You don't seem to be able to learn anything about caring for other people at all.'

'That's enough, Agnes,' said Dad quietly.

'Oh, that's right.' Mum's voice was getting louder now, with sharp spikes in her words like the teeth on Dad's saw. 'You stand up for her. You always do. I'm never first with you.'

'Don't be ridiculous, and let's talk about this when we get home.'

'That's right. Sweep it all under the rug like you always do. Nothing will change. Nothing ever does. I'm stuck here in this dreadful house with naughty children and no family to support me while you swan off to work with your mates, too scared to tell Henry he exploits you. It's not turning the other cheek, you know. It's just weakness. You're weak. And because you're weak I will never see my family again.' Her voice was filling up the car now like a dangerous gas. It was getting hard to breathe.

'Just stop it, Agnes,' said Dad quietly. 'Just calm down.'

Even I knew it was never a good idea to tell Mum to calm down. It was like pouring petrol on a fire. Up she goes. Up she goes!

'Can't you see you are going to be sacrificed? Henry is sacrificing you at the altar of his own greed. He will kill you and I will be left with the children and no support. Can't you see what's going to happen? Do you even care? You come home later and later, and more and more tired. You have no energy for me or for the children. We never do anything together anymore. He is going to kill you and you don't even care!'

Dad made the car skid to a sudden stop, which made all three of us in the back seat gasp. Ruthy put her hands over her mouth, and Caleb covered his eyes. I couldn't stop looking. This was a worse fight than usual.

'Dad ...' I said, although I didn't know what I was going to say next.

Dad turned and looked at me with a look I hadn't seen on his face before. Then he reached over the back of the seat and hit me across the face. 'Dorcas. For once. Will you shut up. Stop causing trouble. You will never have a guinea pig or a pet. It would make your brother sick. It will make your mother sick. Stop being so selfish. And. Just. Shut. Up!'

Mum was sobbing now. Caleb was sobbing too. Ruthy was crying with no noise coming out of her mouth but with her face all twisted up and her mouth opened and a long line of spittle from her lip to the collar of her blouse. I felt a sort of shock. I put my hand to the place where Dad had hit me and it felt hot and stinging, but not as bad as my heart did, which I thought might burst out of my chest in a huge explosion. My lungs didn't seem to be working properly, and I was having trouble finding my breath.

Dad put on the indicator and pulled back out into the street, and we drove home with just crying noises filling up the car. And then Caleb started to wail.

'Don't be sacrificed, Dad,' he said. 'Don't be sacrificed. I don't want you to be nailed on a cross like Jesus. Mum, tell him not to be sacrificed.'

Ruthy tried to calm him down by patting his shoulder. 'He won't be sacrificed, Caleb,' she said. 'Mum doesn't mean that, do you, Mum? She just means he works too hard for his boss, don't you, Mum? Don't cry, Caleb. She doesn't mean that.'

Dad turned to look at Caleb and said, 'Of course not, Caleb. Of course not. Don't be silly now. Mum didn't mean it, did you, Agnes?'

But Mum would neither affirm nor deny, as they said on cop shows on tellie, and Caleb started to scream and cry hysterically. And then he started to wheeze. And my mother sat like a statue in the front seat next to my dad.

CHAPTER 11

Caleb had asthma all through the night after the fight in the car. I could hear him coughing, and Mum's voice trying to soothe him. She piled up pillows behind him so he could breathe better sitting up, rubbed Vicks VapoRub on his chest and thumped his back gently to try to get all the muck out of his lungs.

I sometimes wished I could invent a pump that we could put down his throat and into his lungs to hoover up all the bad stuff so he could breathe again. I once asked Dad why they didn't invent such a thing. He said he didn't know, but perhaps I would grow up to be an inventor and make one for all the asthmatics in the world, which seemed like a noble thing to do. I put it on my mental list of possible things to do as an adult.

I could tell from the sound of the cough this time that it was going to be quite a bad attack. It was a very loud barky cough, and it went on and on and on. Mum slept in his room but in the early hours of the morning I heard her call to Dad in an urgent voice, and I crept to the door to listen at the crack.

'What is it, Dorcas?' Ruthy asked from behind me. 'What's going on?'

'Nothing, Ruthy. Just Caleb wheezing. Go back to sleep,' I said, and she turned over and resumed her little poppy snoring noises.

I heard a lot of moving around, and I knew Mum must have dressed because I could hear her heels clattering on the kitchen floor. I heard her talking to Dad, and although I couldn't hear what they were saying, I could tell from the sound of their voices they were worried about Caleb. I decided it would be best not to go outside my room, in case Mum pointed out that it was my fault Caleb had had another attack because of the car incident the day before. I was feeling worried about him because I had good radar for when he was a bit sick and when he was very sick, and I could tell he was quite unwell this time.

Then I heard the back door bang shut and the car pull out of the drive. I ran to the lounge room window and watched Mum and Dad and Caleb drive away. Mum was sitting in the back seat with Caleb. I couldn't see him but I knew she would have him propped up with a pillow on her shoulder. I went into the kitchen and there was a note on the table from Dad that said we should make breakfast and stay in the house until he rang us from the hospital. At the end it said: *DORCAS. Please don't cause any trouble today. Just do as we ask and stay in the house and don't make a mess.*

Ruthy was still asleep, so I made some toast and marmalade, took it into the lounge room and switched on the TV. I felt a thrill as I turned on the tellie. It was Sunday morning and I had no idea what would be on the tube because we were not allowed to watch on Sundays.

This made me think of Aunty Maisie, who said we only had the tellie because Mum was too lenient and worldly. I asked her how come she had a television then, and she got very cross and said it was for Grandpa because he was a boxing fan, and had to have some small comforts at his age, but I know for a fact she watched tellie too because I heard her discussing a show called *Bellbird* with her best friend, Sister Thatchman.

When Ruthy got out of bed and I told her that Mum and Dad had taken Caleb to hospital, she followed me into the lounge and said, 'Um, Dorcas. You'll get into trouble for putting the tellie on.'

'Not if you keep your big pooswiddle mouth shut I won't,' I said to her in my best threatening voice.

She stood in the doorway and looked at me for a minute, and then grinned and said, 'What they don't know won't hurt them,' and ran and jumped on to the sofa, which we are never allowed to do. We made more toast together and sat and watched a sports show. We weren't really paying attention, but it was fun and we threw pillows at each other and played tag and then found a show with hymns on it and sang silly words to them and had rather a good time.

Then the phone rang and gave us a fright for a minute, until we remembered that meant Mum and Dad weren't coming home yet, and we weren't in trouble. Ruthy rushed to answer it. Dad said Caleb was still very sick and they would be a few more hours. He said we were NOT to leave the house for any reason or make a mess, but we could have as much toast as we wanted if we were hungry. Ruthy answered with her good girl voice to reassure him.

When we got off the phone, we played chasey right round the house, bounced up and down on Mum and Dad's bed, and made necklaces out of fruit loops and Mum's gardening string. Then I opened Mum's wardrobe and we put on some of her shoes and blouses and looked at ourselves in the long mirror by her window. I decided to try some lipstick on.

This made Ruthy scared for a minute, but then she tried some on too. When we finished, we rubbed it off with toilet paper that we flushed to make sure there was no evidence and checked there was none left on each other. I noticed a tiny bit of orange lipstick on Mum's good white blouse, but I didn't show Ruthy and decided to carefully hang it up and hope Mum thought she did it herself.

Then Ruthy said we'd better clean up or there'd be trouble, but I didn't feel like it and we had an argument and I walked out the back door and slammed it to make the point that it would be up to her. This was a bit mean, but Ruthy was good at tidying up and would get all the praise anyway. I walked to the olive grove and climbed my tree with a piece of toast, which was a bit difficult because although my hand wasn't swollen any more, it was still a bit weak and sore if I didn't use it carefully.

It was a beautiful Adelaide October day. The sky was very blue and very bright and made me squint when I looked up at it. Lots of fresh new weeds were growing up around the olive trees that had new leaves on them. Soursobs were waving up at me from big ponds of yellow. I had trouble stopping myself from eating soursobs, even though they gave me a stomach ache. Mrs Kerfoops's cat Aristotle was stalking invisible mice. There was a mother magpie with babies that swooped on us lately, but she was in a happy mood today and left me quite alone. I had picked a pile of small stones and put them in my pocket to throw at things from up the tree, just in case.

Teddy Edwards turned up and climbed my tree without asking, but the sun made me warm and a bit floppy, and I didn't complain or order him down. He asked how come I was out on a Sunday morning and not getting ready for church. I told him about Caleb being sick again and in the Royal Children's Hospital with Mum and Dad, and he said he was sorry and he hoped he got well soon.

Sadly for Teddy, he is what my dad calls 'badly put together'. His very short, thick legs were bowed, so we teased him that we could see between his knees on a regular basis. He had a barrel chest and thick square hands with nails that were always black. His grandma cut his hair, and it stuck out in all directions. He had a double chin and very small grey eyes that sat warily beneath a large bone across his eyebrows that looked like a ridge. Ruthy said it made him look like a Neanderthal, which means ancient stone age man or something like that. He smelled of unwashed clothes and sour milk.

Most kids wouldn't go into his place because it looked abandoned and a bit scary. There were two old cars in the front yard that clearly didn't work because they were rusty and had plants growing out of them, and plastic bags of rubbish on the seats. There wasn't a garden really, just a track where the weeds were flattened by Teddy's boots. The paint was peeling everywhere and there were nests in the drainpipes and even some small trees growing out of them. Inside was very dark and smelled of dust and old food and wee and garlic, which lots of New Australians liked to eat, but which is very stinky and tastes funny. There were old pieces of furniture everywhere, and piles and piles of books and papers. Teddy said his gran didn't like to throw things out. I'd been there a couple of times and I thought it was good on the inside even if a bit rough on the outside.

He said what was good about living with his gran was that he never had to make his bed or change his sheets. She didn't go into his room so he had plenty of privacy to do his own projects. And what the other kids didn't know, because they would never visit him and he would never tell them, was that he made the most beautiful model planes you have ever seen. They hung from his ceiling on little hooks he put up himself with his gran's old ladder. He spent hours and hours on them. His desk, if you could give the old trestle table that grand title, was covered in tiny pieces of models, small tins of paints and pots of brushes. Everywhere else in his house was filthy except this desk, which was organised into categories and very clean. He said you couldn't afford to get dust in your work or it ruined the final product. I suggested he take some of his planes to school to show people how talented he was, but he just shrugged and said they would only claim someone else had made them.

He wanted to be a pilot in the Air Force when he grew up, unless I agreed to marry him, in which case he planned to work for Ansett Airlines so he could be home with me and the children most of the time. When he told me this, I reminded him of my Knights of the Round Table choice, but he just shrugged again and looked at me sideways and said he would wait. Sometimes when Mum says no one will have me when I grow up, I think of telling her about Teddy, but I have a feeling it won't help my cause.

Teddy suggested that, given Mum and Dad weren't going to church, I could go back to his place. He said his grandma had made lasagna, which is an Italian dish I had once in a restaurant and really loved. Teddy's grandma is half Italian and half Polish, so the food he described always sounded rather delicious, although having walked past the kitchen I am not sure my mum would approve of how dirty it was. Still, lasagna was a temptation, and I was sick of toast. I wasn't entirely sure that the lasagna thing was true. I knew

Teddy remembered everything I said to him and stored it away to work out how to please me, but it was a beautiful day and I didn't think Mum and Dad would be home for ages. For a minute I worried about Ruthy being alone in the house, but I knew she could always go to see Mr Driver if she was worried, so I dropped out of the tree and challenged him to a race to his place.

I won the race, although I had a feeling he let me, but still, it was a win and I made quite a point about it. When we got to his broken front gate, I hesitated for a minute. Was it really a good idea to be here when Caleb was sick in hospital? But whatever I was doing wasn't going to make a difference to Caleb's lungs, so I turned to Teddy and indicated I'd follow him in.

As soon as I walked into the house, I could smell delicious cooking. Teddy took me in to see his grandma in the kitchen.

'Hello, Mrs Edwards,' I said.

She turned and smiled at me, put her big stirring spoon down and gave me a huge hug.

'Are you going to have lunch with us today, Dorcas?' she asked. 'Well that is wonderful. Teddy get another dish down for me, and both of you take a seat. It's a little bit early but who cares about the rules, eh?'

Mrs Edwards gave me a large white bowl full of the hot, cheesy, meaty dish, and it was heavenly. At first I didn't think I could eat it all, particularly as I had already eaten so much toast, but I just couldn't stop shovelling it in. As we ate, Mrs Edwards chatted away about lots of things, and I realised she wasn't as old as I'd thought. I guess I think most people called Grandma are ancient. In our church once you're a grandma you get fat, wear flowery dresses, let your hair go all grey and wiry, and wear black orthopaedic shoes.

Mrs Edwards had piles of very messy hair stuck up with lots of kirby grips, with bits escaping all over the place, but which looked quite fetching when you thought about it. Her skin was an olive colour and she had dark bags under her eyes, but her teeth were good and she had a big mouth with a warm smile. Her nails had chipped red polish on them, and even though Mum always said this was a sign of no self-respect, it sort of looked right on her. She had a jumper over a skirt that didn't match but made her look a bit like a cheerful gypsy. I finished all my lasagna and she asked if I would like more, but I said no thank you I was full to the bosoms, which made her laugh. She made us both a strong, strong cup of black coffee that was too bitter for me, but I did feel a bit grown-up trying it. Teddy was clearly delighted I had enjoyed lunch. I asked if I could help to do the dishes but Mrs Edwards just shooed us out of the kitchen and told us to have some fun.

I asked Teddy how old his grandma was and he said forty-something, which was old, but not actually that much older than my mum, which I thought deserved some thinking about later. For the first time ever, I asked why he lived with his grandma, and he told me that his mum had him when she was very young and wasn't married and didn't cope very well. She went to Torrens House with him when he was born and left him there with the nurses. She ran away with his father to Sydney, and they didn't know where she was now. I put my hand on his forearm and said I was very sorry because this sounded like one of the saddest things ever, but he did a Teddy shrug and said it was okay because his grandma was the best really and loved him, and as long as you have someone to love you the world wasn't too bad.

He said that's why he would wait for me to marry him, because that way when his grandma died, he would have the next person to love. That made me feel a bit like a convenience, but given it wasn't going to happen anyway, I didn't worry. He would probably find a girl fighter pilot in the air force and that would make him happy. I hoped so anyway. I decided he really was quite a nice boy and I would consider him a friend.

We played in his room for a while, and he let me paint a tiny red tip on one of his planes, which was pretty special. I'm not sure I did it as well as he would, so it was also kind. After a while, his grandma knocked on his door and asked if we would like a piece of warm cake and cream, and we both yelled out yes and ran into the kitchen after her.

It was truly delicious cake and again I was amazed I could fit it in. While we were eating, Mrs Edwards was chatting away again and asking lots of questions.

'How come you not at church today, bella?' she asked. Italiany people call girls Bella, just like my Scottish mum calls people 'hen' but doesn't really think they are chickens.

'Mum left in the car with Caleb early this morning and so we didn't have to go,' I said.

'Oh no. I'm so sorry,' she said. 'We all knew she wouldn't stay but we were hopeful.'

I just looked at her, a bit confused. 'Oh no, Mrs Edwards. She always takes Caleb,' I said.

'No! She has left you before? I did not know that. I just heard from Alice that she was planning to go soon. I'm sorry, Dorcas. It must be very sad for you and for your dad.'

'Well ...' I said. 'Not really. Dad is sort of used to it too, although she usually goes when he is at work, and he doesn't usually drive her.'

'He drove her away today? Well, I don't know what to think about that,' said Mrs Edwards, surprised.

We both stopped talking for a minute.

'Mrs Edwards, Mum and Dad took Caleb to the hospital because of his asthma. That's why I'm not at church. Why wouldn't Dad drive them if he was home from work?'

'Oh. Oh. I see,' said Mrs Edwards. 'I misunderstand you, bella. Don't pay no attention to me. That's good they go together. That's good. I hope that little boy is fine. I will pray for him. I know your family doesn't like the Catholic, but our prayers are just as good as yours, I'm sure of it. Now, eat more cake and go and play.'

But I thought it might be time to go home in case Mum and Dad beat me to it, so I thanked her. Teddy said he would walk me home but I told him not to because I had to think about what Mrs Edwards had just said.

I didn't know Mum's hair client Alice Johns knew Mrs Edwards, and a whole world of women in the area talking to each other had just opened up. And what had Alice been telling Mrs Edwards, and maybe telling other mothers too? I know I made Mum cross, but she would never go away. My heart started to jump up and down in my chest and I felt scared and worried.

CHAPTER 12

I knew I was in trouble as soon as I neared the house and saw the car in the drive.

I stopped dead in my tracks for a minute and considered my options. All kinds of pictures raced through my brain like little pieces of film, but none of them offered a solution. I thought about visiting Mr Driver and then pretending he had been ill and I had been helping him, but I didn't want to implicate him in my dilemma. I thought about saying we had used up all the bread and I had gone to the shop to get a new loaf, but then realised I didn't have one as evidence. I briefly considered the idea that I wanted to understand more about the Catholics, and that this was a good day to go and look at their church because usually I couldn't because we were at our church, and I said some of the words out loud to try them out and knew they wouldn't make the grade.

I thought about pretending what I had done was preventative. It was Sunday and we shouldn't fight on Sunday and Ruthy was baiting me and I thought it was better to leave than to have an argument, because that would have been disrespectful to Jesus. It was thin – very thin – but it was all I had. And I knew from all our family games of Snap and Canasta that you have to play the cards in your hand.

I walked up the back steps quietly and peered through the screen door into the kitchen. There was no one in that room, so I quietly opened the door and let myself in. I crept into our bedroom, where Ruthy was sitting crying on her bed hugging Milly Molly Mandy. She was doing that irritating kind of crying that was more like a continuous moan. Her mouth was all out of shape and she looked ugly. I thought of telling her that, but luckily stopped myself.

'Mum! She's here!' screamed Ruthy, despite my hushing noises and flapping arms trying to communicate the need for stealth.

'Dorcas. What on earth do you think you were up to?' asked Dad at the bedroom door, in a much angrier voice than he usually used. 'Didn't I tell you to stay in the house until we got home? Was that so much to ask when your brother was so sick?' he hollered.

'Is he all right, Dad?' I asked, suddenly frightened. There was something going on here that was bigger than my unauthorised absence.

'No, he's not all right but he will be fine, no thanks to you. Now explain yourself.' By this stage, Mum was standing next to him with her arms crossed and her chin stuck out and thunder on her features.

'I … I … Ruthy was annoying me so I thought it was better to go for a walk than to have a big fight on the Lord's day … and …'

'Don't try that nonsense on me. I'm not in the mood, Dorcas. And don't blame your sister. She's already told us about bouncing on the beds and watching TV and the lipstick on your mother's blouse. I am so disappointed in you both. And all this when Caleb was sick in hospital and had to have another adrenaline injection. I just don't know what to say to you.'

My head snapped to look in amazement at Ruthy, even though I would have told it not to because it was definitely going to make things worse.

'And don't look at your sister like that. We came in and found the tellie on. At least she told us the truth when we asked what had happened. Imagine a grown-up girl like you leaving her in the house all on her own, and with all the mess to clean up. Really, Dorcas, this is the living end. The living end,' said Dad.

He hadn't struck me yet. Dad preferred not to hit us. But when Mum was really upset she handed him the wooden spoon and insisted he give us a good smack across the back of the legs. When he walked out of the room, I presumed I was about to get the spoon, and stayed stock-still on the bed in fearful anticipation. Instead, I heard the back door slam and the car pull out of the drive.

Mum was still standing with her arms folded, and her lips squished into a thin line pointing downwards at each end.

'I hope you're happy,' she said.

'Where's Dad gone?' I was almost too scared to ask. I felt decidedly less safe without him in the house.

'He's gone to work of course,' said Mum. 'On top of everything else he's gone to work. On a Sunday. For Henry. Henry calls and he sacrifices everything because Henry sacrifices him.'

'Mum,' Caleb called out weakly. 'I don't want Dad to be sacrificed.' And then he had a coughing fit that at least drove Mum to his side and stayed what I was sure would be my execution.

'Why did you tell her?' I hissed to Ruthy when she'd gone.

'You left me everything to do, and that wasn't fair. When they walked in I was trying to get the lipstick off the shirt because I saw what you did, Dorcas. And you can't blame me for telling them because you are the oldest and you started it all and you should be a role model.'

She started bawling her head off until Mum came to the door and said, 'Dorcas, leave that girl alone. Haven't you created enough trouble for one day?'

'Is Caleb okay?' I asked Ruthy when Mum had gone.

'He's sicker than usual, I think. He's all white and shallow breathing and noisy wheezing. They wanted to keep him in the hospital but Mum says hospitals are full of germs, and nurses are too busy to look after children and so she asked to take him home. She's really upset, Dorcas. Like, I mean, really upset. Dorcas, she ate two biscuits!' Ruthy then returned to more of the ugly, moaning crying.

'What?' I said in amazement.

Could this day be any more worrying and confusing? My mother was always doing what she called watching her waistline, which Caleb thought was very funny because he said it meant she would have to go everywhere with her head pointed down or she wouldn't be able to watch it. It was pretty much unheard of for Mum to eat anything sweet, or actually anything much at all. This was a very bad sign.

And now Dad had gone to work on a Sunday. I couldn't ever remember that happening before because Mr Bednarski knew we were Christadelphians and always said he respected Dad's beliefs. And that he'd rather have a good Christian family man working for him than a heathen, even if Christadelphians were a funny kind of Christian if you asked him anything about it. But Mr Bednarski was a Jew, and that meant he didn't work on Saturday but he did work on a Sunday.

I was scared that Dad had gone to work after what Mrs Edwards had said about Mum leaving, but then I realised I was confused because Dad had left, not Mum, and it was to go to work, not to go to Scotland, and so I calmed down a bit. Ruthy's moaning was really getting on my nerves now, and I considered threatening to push her into the wee patch if she didn't stop, or even telling her what Mrs Edwards had said, but knew I wouldn't do that because it would frighten her to death and she might tell Mum and then Mum would know I had lasagna when I left Ruthy by herself and so all round this would not be a good idea.

Sometimes when I had to work things out, or I wanted to make myself small and invisible because I was in trouble,

I crawled into our wardrobe and sat in the dark. This seemed like a good wardrobe day, and I took off my shoes, pushed things around to make a kind of nest, climbed in and closed the door behind me. Thinking in the quiet can help when the world gets a bit too big or busy. I screwed my eyes shut and made a low humming noise, so I wouldn't notice doors closing and people's voices and Ruthy coming in and out of the bedroom. I tried thinking about the palace I'd live in when I became a knight. I would choose only pink and blue and white flowers – no orange ones. And I'd move Sixpence's grave to the garden and put a special arbour over it. I don't think an arbour counts as an idol, so it shouldn't cause trouble with the Arranging Brethren. And because I am a very selfish child, just as my mother says, I started to think that if Caleb could just stop getting sick, I might one day have a guinea pig.

CHAPTER 13

Things were pretty frosty in our house for the next couple of weeks.

Usually within a few days of a fight, Mum and Dad made up and it would be okay again for a while, but Mum wouldn't thaw this time, and Dad seemed to have given up. We heard them speaking in clipped, urgent voices in their room at night, and that felt strangely better than when there were no words coming from their room at all. Dad didn't say goodbye to Mum in the mornings as far as I could tell, and sometimes he forgot to say goodbye to us too. I took to standing by his car door when I'd had my breakfast so I could at least see him before he left, and although he always looked sad, he would at least mess up my hair and smile at me before telling me to go inside before my mother started to look for me.

Mum didn't go to church for two whole weeks. In fact, she didn't go anywhere much for two whole weeks and was rarely out of her nightdress. She said Caleb was too sick for her to leave the house. Dad said Caleb would be fine wrapped up warmly in the middle hall.

Mum said, 'There you go – you don't really care about us. You just want to make sure you get to your precious meetings with all your friends and that monster of a sister-in-law.'

Dad said, 'That monster of a sister-in-law was like a mother to me.'

Mum said, 'Well aren't you lucky you have her around given my mother is thousands of miles across the sea and I'll probably never see her again.'

Dad said, 'I'm not sure I could deal with two of you anyway.'

Mum said, and this worried me the most, 'Well I can fix it so you don't have to deal with either of us if you like.'

Mum started to eat food. As I've already made clear, this was not usual for her at all. She made four pieces of toast for her breakfast with lots of butter and jam, when she usually only had one slice with nothing on it. She started to put sugar and milk in her tea and had a biscuit with each cuppa, which was unheard of. She made more puddings than usual, which of course was a good thing as far as I was concerned, but then she ate a lot of them too. When she made rice pudding, which was my absolute favourite, she put big dollops of cream on the top of hers and kept her eyes on Dad's eyes as she did it. He watched, but he didn't say a word, which I thought was quite wise of him.

Caleb couldn't keep his mouth shut as usual though and said, 'Mum, I thought you were watching your waistline?'

Mum said, 'Well, it doesn't really matter anymore, does it?'

'Why doesn't it matter, Mum?' Caleb asked.

Dad said, 'Just eat your pudding, Caleb.'

Caleb didn't go back to school for two weeks. He lost a lot of weight I wouldn't have thought he had to lose and was always tired and breathless. His little grey trousers hung on him like an old man's pants, and Mum had to make two new notches in his belt. When that didn't work either, she tied a bit of rope through the loops and yanked them up to his bosoms so they wouldn't drag on the ground. Most of the time he stayed in his pyjamas, so it didn't matter too much.

I seemed to make Caleb nervous. Ruthy said he told her that I made Mum cross too much and it scared him. He also continued to be worried about Dad being sacrificed.

He regularly woke up from nightmares, calling out for someone to take Dad off the cross. He told Ruthy he could see Dad nailed up on bits of old tree in a graveyard, and Dad kept talking to him and saying it would be okay but blood was coming out of him in all sorts of places and he knew he would be taken up to Our Heavenly Father.

Ruthy reminded him we didn't believe you went to heaven when you died, you just got buried and got all mouldy in the ground until the bugs ate you, and that only Jesus had ascended to the right hand of God. This made Caleb much worse and he had to go on his breathing machine for quite a while. Mum asked him what had upset him, but he just looked at us through the clear plastic mask and didn't say anything, which Ruthy and I agreed was lucky.

Dad worked later than usual most nights and didn't come home for tellie and chocolate nights two Fridays in a row, which was very sad-making. He also wouldn't let me go to the Sunday night meetings with him, which I think was the worst thing of all for me, because I couldn't talk to him or mind his books or put paper markers in his hymn book or breathe in his nice smell. I think he was worried I would ask him questions or say things about what was happening and he didn't want to have to answer me. When I did try to talk to him at home, he would make up a reason I had to go and do something else, or he had to do something else, and Ruthy said it was because I had a reputation for asking awkward questions.

I wrote him a note that said:

Dear Dad,

If you take me to the Sunday night meeting with you, I promise not to speak or ask a question from the time we get into the car until the time we get home. I will sit very still in the meeting and listen to every word. I will not turn around to look at the teenagers. I won't whisper about people's hats. I won't kick the chair in front of me. I won't hang around Brother Davies in case he gives me a mint before the meeting starts.

I love you.

Your oldest daughter,

Dorcas

I showed it to Ruthy, but she said I should just wait to see what happened and surely everything would go back to normal soon. What she didn't know, or course, was what Mrs Edwards had told me about Mum wanting to leave us, so I thought I'd just keep that to myself and take her advice. Ruthy was, after all, much better at keeping the peace than me.

Ruthy and I spent a good amount of our time in the tree house when we returned from school, because Mum was definitely tied up in a long string of head or cross days. It wasn't really fair of me, but I blamed Caleb for a lot of the troubles we were having. It seemed to me very convenient that as soon as things were tricky for him, he could get sick and then get all the attention and the tiny bit of love that Mum seemed to have left in her. She pampered him and made him his favourite dinners to encourage him to eat. She slept in a chair in his room for the first part of every night, and I think would have stayed in there with him if there had been enough room. She read a story to him before she turned the light off but wouldn't let Ruthy and I come in to listen. She would grab him and hug him at the strangest moments and get quite teary as she did it.

I asked Ruthy at one point if she thought Caleb was going to die, and was that the reason Mum kept hugging him, but Ruthy said she thought Mum had so little happiness in her at the moment she had to spend it on just one person because there wasn't enough to go around. We talked about why she was especially unhappy, and Ruthy brought paper out to the tree house for us to make our lists. We agreed we should write what we thought was the honest truth.

Her list said: *Mum is worried about Caleb's asthma and all Dorcas talks about is having a guinea pig which Mum believes will make him sicker. Mum is upset Dad is working more hours for Mr Bednarski but isn't making enough money to bring Grandma for a visit from Scotland.*

My list said: *Dad has to work more because it's too sad to be home and this is making Mum even crosser. Mum misses Grandma, who I think might be an especially good kind of mother because Mum misses her so much, and if she was here, perhaps Mum would be less cross. Mum's heart has shrivelled up into a little unripe olive. Caleb is sick and Mum thinks I make him that way by causing trouble and fights. Mum doesn't want me to have a pet to love and pretends Caleb will be allergic so she doesn't mind he gets sick because it makes her story better. Mum only loves me because God says she has to because I am her kid, but she's not going to church much now and that means God can't remind her to love me so it's getting harder.*

Ruthy put her arm around me when she read my list. I noticed that she didn't disagree. We didn't move the beads on the string because Caleb wasn't with us, but we agreed if he had been, we would probably have moved mine pretty much to the end of the rope.

In the past, I had been able to go over to see Mrs Johnson when I wasn't sure about things, and she would sit and listen very quietly and patiently. She didn't always know the answer, but she would pat my hand and smile at me and that made me feel that I wasn't silly for having my thoughts. She told me life was an obstacle race, and I had to get fit enough to jump over each hurdle as I met it. I asked how to get fit to do that, and she said I had to have good friends to talk to, and that probably what I learned in church would be very helpful too. She didn't believe in God, but she said any powerful belief could feed your heart and help you jump rather than falter. She said it was like physical food; we might all eat different things, such as we might all believe different things, but it all added up to nutrition for the body just as belief fed the soul.

This sounded a bit like Dad's words about snakes and ladders, so it made me feel even more that my dad was very wise. And I certainly agreed with the idea that friends could help you because Anne King at Sunday school, and Maynard at school, and even Venita when she wasn't fussing about clothes or what she looked like or her mother's private parts, could somehow give me bits of energy to keep going. I said to myself it was like being plugged into a power socket and charged up. I thought this was a good analogy, and raced to tell Ruthy about it, who was impressed and wrote it down in her notebook. So it was terrible not being able to talk to Mrs Johnson about what was happening. I thought about breaking my promise and going to see her, but things were already so bad I decided it was just too risky.

I sat in Mr Driver's garden next to Sixpence quite a bit, and sometimes wished and wished he would come and sit next to me and ask me what was going on, but he would just wave from his kitchen window, and I didn't know what I could say to go and start a conversation with him.

One day though, when I was feeling very low, I started to cry on the little seat by Sixpence's house. Mr Driver didn't talk to me, but he came out of the house, picked me up, took me into the kitchen and sat in his chair with me on his knee. He put my head on his shoulder and patted me and said, 'There, there, you'll get another pet.' Although I wasn't really crying for Sixpence right then, that was about the most wonderful thing that had happened to me for a long time. I wished it would go on forever. Mr Driver smelled of wood and Palmolive soap and machine oil. His wrists were old and stringy and had lots of black dots and scars on them, but his arms were strong and he held me tight, and I wondered if God had sent me to Mr Driver because my Aunty Maisie says God never tests us beyond our endurance and I think I was nearly endured right out.

I seemed to get into trouble even more than usual at school, and I don't really know why because I was trying very hard. Every morning I would wake up and say to myself, 'Today you have to be perfect at everything'. And I would start out quite cheerful with that thought in mind, but in no time flat, as Mr Driver used to say, I'd queer my pitch. My bright, shiny intentions to be like a saint weren't strong enough to make me behave like a good child.

I whispered in class so much I was sent to the headmistress three times in one week, and they sent a letter home to Mum, which of course I didn't give her, and which Maynard signed for me instead. Rufus kept calling me Scabhead so I went into his classroom in the lunch break and took all his pencils to the electric sharpener on his teacher's desk and sharpened them until they were just little stubs his fat fingers wouldn't be able to manage. Unfortunately I didn't do a good job of cleaning up all the curly wooden shavings, and some of them got in my hair and all over my clothes, so Maynard had to sign another note that was meant for Mum.

In weekly assembly I was at the top of a marching line and was meant to take all the babies behind me to the left towards the flag, but I decided to take them to the right, which meant the whole pattern of marching got messed up and there were children everywhere. When the teachers started to shout, I couldn't help laughing and that meant another long sit outside the headmistress's rooms to be told off.

On another day, when we were chanting the words for the flag – 'I love my county. I salute her flag. I honour her queen. I promise to obey her laws.' – I changed all the hand signals that are meant to go with the words, and some other children got confused and copied me. The neat pattern the teachers liked was all wrecked again and Mr Foster grabbed me by the plait and dragged me out the front and told me off in front of everyone.

Ruthy went all quiet and spent more time than usual in our room cross-legged on the bed writing in her journals. She was quickly filling the latest one up. She was what she called 'in the throes of an enthusiasm'. She had several throes in the past. One had been to try to classify all the faces in the world into twenty types. She would watch someone and make notes of their features and decide which category to put them in. She had a page for each of the types and would add their name and a description of them to explain her choice. She said she was developing a typology. Every now and again when we were at the shops for Mum or at the meeting, she would point to someone and say, 'That's type thirteen – pointy,' or 'That's type seventeen – fleshy.'

Another time she developed an enthusiasm for reading all the books in the library about Eskimo. She spent hours and hours poring over big stacks of school library books looking for any reference to them. When her enthusiasm wore off, she would look up surprised, as though she hadn't noticed the world had kept spinning and that she had been away for a long time.

Since the day in the car after the union exams, Ruthy had developed a new enthusiasm about expanding her vocabulary. She chose three words every day and wrote them out, along with their definition, over and over again to help her remember them. She set herself the task of using them in a sentence that day too. As a result, at teatime we heard: 'I think you should learn some new words Dorcas because of the impecunious nature of your vocab'; 'Dad, can you think of an antonym for headstrong?'; and my favourite, 'Mr Driver bears the loss of Mrs Driver with longanimity.' I didn't tease her about this, partly because at the moment any teasing between us seemed to end in an argument between Mum and Dad, and also because I was quite proud of her.

Instead of keeping her journal in the tin in our tree house with the rest of her collection of filled-up books, she kept the current one under her pillow and sometimes woke up in the night and wrote things in it using a torch. She wrote two letters to our brother Daniel, but wouldn't show me what she wrote. I hoped it wasn't bad things about me, because when I was very sad, I imagined Daniel coming home and telling me he wanted to spend all his free time with me because he loved me the best. And then he would go to school and beat up Rufus, and then punch Mr Johnson on the nose and speak sternly to Mum to remind her she was a Sister in Christ and should be happier more often.

Mr Driver gave each of us a torch on our birthday that year, but Mum had taken mine away because in art class I had decided to see what it would look like if I painted blue polka dots on my white school shirt and the stains didn't come out. During the days since the exams, because I was so sad, and picking the sores in my head more than usual, if we both woke up in the night sometimes Ruthy would come into my bed with the torch and we would put it on under the covers so Mum and Dad wouldn't see the light, and we would put our arms around each other and tell each other stories until one of us fell asleep.

Ruthy told very good stories. They were about children who did amazing things and won awards and travelled to exciting places and were on tellie a lot. She described what they wore and gave details about their friends and families. My favourite stories were the ones about a girl called

Anastasia Armistad, who was very brave and invented cures for cancers and strokes and problems with your bowels. We agreed the cures for bowel problems were her greatest inventions because who would not want to be able to go to the toilet without someone helping you? Maynard told me that his grandpa had to wear a big nappy in his nursing home and sometimes it fell off a bit and stuff would ooze out and as a result Maynard didn't really like to hug him and tried to sit a fair way away from him. His mother wouldn't let him hold his nose, which is what he wanted to do, because she said it was disrespectful, but Maynard said his grandpa was disrespectful stinking everyone out to high heaven.

I asked Ruthy if I was as brave as Anastasia Armistad, but she said you weren't really brave if you did risky things without even thinking about it, and I considered that for quite a while and decided it was probably true. She said I was more impetuous, impulsive and injudicious than brave, which made me guess she was studying words starting with the letter I.

I made up stories about kings and queens and knights. All the best knights were girls in my stories. Ruthy said this was quite unrealistic, but I pointed out they were my stories so that's the way it would be. All the girl knights wore armour but had a special hinge so they could sit down for the toilet, because that was a problem that I had pondered for some time. When we'd made armour out of cardboard boxes Dad brought home from his work, it was quite an ordeal to unstick, unhook, un-staple and un-tape oneself when nature called. Caleb sometimes didn't bother and wet himself, which made the cardboard go quite soggy, but he didn't care.

My favourite story of my own was about a castle where there was only a queen and princesses and all the knights were girls. It was called Caramel, which is a bit like Camelot, but not quite. When other countries couldn't kill their dragons or their enemies, they would send someone to Caramel and all the knights would have a meeting in a very lovely garden where rabbits and guinea pigs and dogs and cats ran all over the place, and they would decide whether to go to help or not. The price, if the knights of Caramel agreed to help, was that the country needing help had to give them one little girl baby as a reward, because the Caramel knights didn't like all that sexing stuff Venita told me about at school, and it was better just to be given a baby than have to have it come out of your insides as you screamed blue murder for hours, which, according to Venita, was exactly how it happened.

In my story I was elected the head knight. Every girl knight had decorated armour, and mine had blue and green polka dots on top of the solid silver metal bits. I had a sweet little baby of my own called Arabella and a puppy called

Plops, and a guinea pig called Thruppence, and the four of us lived in a small castle of our own and loved each other very much. Ruthy didn't like the name Plops, but I had to remind her it was my story and therefore my choice.

In the third week after Caleb went to hospital, he went back to school. I hoped that would mean things would go back to normal, and Mum would get up and get dressed in the mornings, but she didn't. When we got home from school each day, the house was cold and dark and quiet, and she was still in bed asleep. We crept in and put our bags away, and then agreed we should go to the tree house so we didn't wake her up.

Caleb's lungs seemed a bit better. He didn't need to go on the nebuliser, and as long as he had his Ventolin spray in his pocket, he seemed to manage pretty well. But although his breathing was better, he was fidgety and shaky and anxious. He jumped from one topic to another, sometimes halfway through a sentence. He hopped up and down and squirmed and sort of darted about the place. The asthma medication could make him a bit like that anyway but he kept worrying about Dad being sacrificed and wanting to talk about it over and over again. Ruthy and I tried to reassure him that it wasn't going to happen. It wasn't what Mum meant. She just meant that Dad was going to keep working too hard for

Mr Bednarski, but Caleb wasn't convinced. He said he knew from the Bible that before they put Jesus on the cross, all the people around him started fighting with each other and being weird and that was exactly what was happening at home.

I got a bit sick of hearing about it and asked him how he knew it would be on the cross anyway. People had been sacrificed in lots of different ways in the past. Ruthy told me to stop but I went on about people who were tied to four posts and then stretched to death, and people who were put on altars and cut up into little pieces or thrown into fiery volcanos, and about Joan of Arc who was tied to a post with firewood under her and set alight.

Caleb gasped when I mentioned Joan of Arc and said that in his dream Dad was definitely stuck on a tree, so maybe he was going to be burned at the stake instead of hung on the cross. He ran round and round us on the floor of the tree house, which was very irritating, because there wasn't really room to do that, and said he wouldn't sit still until we told him about Joan of Arc.

Ruthy said okay, okay, if he sat down, we'd tell him what we knew, and that calmed him down a bit and he dropped next to us, crossed his legs and put his elbows on his knees to listen. Ruthy said she was pretty sure Joan was a French person, and it was something to do with religion, but she wasn't sure what. Caleb asked if we were sure it was Joan, and not John, because Dad's middle name was John, but we both said no it was a story about a girl. I knew a little bit about it because when I borrowed some books on knights from the state children's library on North Terrace, there was a picture of her dressed as a sort of knight, so I read that section. I told Caleb I thought she was a Catholic saint because of being burnt, and he decided he'd ask his best school friend, Lincoln Waterford, because Lincoln was Catholic and would probably know the story.

Mum and Dad didn't like us to have Catholic friends. They said that Catholics made up their own bibles that weren't really properly the word of God but written to suit themselves. They had priests who were men who wore long dresses and lots of jewellery and did the job fulltime, whereas in our church the baptised people voted for all the positions in the church, and you had to do your ordinary job as well as your church job on the weekends and you didn't get paid anything for it. Mum and Dad said the Catholics worshipped idols, which I knew for sure God said you shouldn't do, and they had lots of crosses and statues of saints and things they would bow and scrape to, and this was very wrong. Dad said they also just gave jobs to other Catholics, which wasn't really fair, and that's why he was grateful Mr Bednarski didn't only give jobs to other Jews.

I asked once if we could go and look at the Catholic heathens, but Mum and Dad both said they wouldn't set foot in one of those churches. They said the men in dresses who ran the show walked around swinging balls full of smoke and that would give Caleb asthma and we wouldn't like the smell. They said we wouldn't understand the services, which were in Latin and deliberately impossible to understand so the men in dresses could keep all the secrets and the money and the power.

Mum said they made you stand up and go to a big step at the front and kneel down on the cold floor and they put a circle of white plastic stuff on your tongue, and then made you all drink out of one big wine thing and the priest wiped the dribble off your chin afterwards. We liked the way the Serving Brothers at our church passed the dishes of fresh white bread and little glasses of wine down the rows so we could help ourselves. Caleb said yuck about wiping the dribble off your chin and then made a really long string of spit and leaned over until it was almost touching the ground and Mum smacked his leg, but only gently.

Mum said Catholics had to go into a little room with a screen and tell the priest all their sins and then he would say amen and away you'd go with not a worry in the world. This seemed like getting off pretty lightly to me, and Mum said yes, it was ridiculous because only God could hear your real thoughts and read your heart and it was up to each of us to develop our own relationship with him and to work hard for his forgiveness.

She also said, 'Besides, Dorcas, you would have to just live in one of those confessional boxes you'd have so much to say.' We all laughed and Caleb said he'd bring me a mattress and pillow if that happened.

Dad said Catholics left all the hard work to the priests, and that Catholics hardly knew what the Bible said or went to youth class or midweek Bible class or Saturday night special classes or Bible conferences or Sunday school or Sunday night meetings.

Dad said most of the government was run by Catholics who put their spin on everything, which he didn't think was right. I asked why the Christadelphians didn't try to take over the government, but Dad said Jesus in the Book of Matthew said, 'Render unto Caesar the things that are Caesar's and unto God the things that are God's', and that this meant we could not interfere in the running of the world because everything was God's will, and we might accidentally do something that wasn't in His plans.

This is why Christadelphians don't vote. They might accidentally vote for the wrong man and then they would be getting in the way of God's will, and he might get pretty shirty about it. And you have to admit, if God gets shirty, he really gets a huff up. He drowns people, sends plagues, turns them to salt, kills their families and makes them walk miles and miles in the desert from one country to another without any real houses at the end of the walk.

Mum seemed very worried that if we had Catholic friends at school, they might tempt us over to their club somehow, and at the first sniff that a friend might go to the Catholic Church, she told us we shouldn't play with them at school or go to their houses afterwards. As a result, the three of us had made a pact not to tell Mum or Dad about the Catholic kids at school, because we thought most of them were pretty nice, and it seemed a shame to stop talking to them. Not once did any of them ask us to say things in Latin or say bad things about Jesus or try to stop us going to Sunday school, so we thought it was a good secret thing to do.

Maynard wasn't Catholic. His family was Church of England. He said his father called it the 'one true religion', but his oldest brother said it only existed because a horny old king wanted to get rid of his old wife and marry some young girl and made up the whole church so he could change things to suit himself, and then he got sick of her anyway and had her head cut off. I knew at least most of this was true, because I won a book on the Tudors as a Sunday school consolation prize, and there was a picture of Anne Boleyn in it, and one of Henry the Eighth who had the biggest calves I've ever seen. So I couldn't see why this church was better than ours, because I'm pretty sure no Christadelphians had killed anyone and divorce wasn't allowed so no Arranging Brother had ever changed the rules so he could marry another Sister as far as I knew.

After the union exams, nothing was much better at home. We couldn't remember a fight between Mum and Dad lasting this long. In the past there had been noisier ones, where Mum would scream she was leaving and walk out the door, and Dad would let her go for half an hour and if she didn't come back, he would get in the car and look for her and bring her back. Usually by the next morning they were a bit careful, as though there were actual bruises on their hearts but that were clearly starting to heal, and we were careful and didn't make the situation worse, which usually meant if I didn't make the situation worse by the next teatime we could all breathe a sigh of relief.

We were coming up to a record for the coldness in our house, and it didn't look like it was going to end anytime soon.

CHAPTER 14

Caleb consulted his best friend Lincoln Waterford about Saint Joan of Arc.

Lincoln was as large and noisy as Caleb was small and quiet. Caleb loved him and considered him the last word on most things, and started a lot of his sentences with 'Lincoln Waterford said ...' Lincoln was a tall child who had the look of a person who had been put together out of bits left over from other people. He had long, straight, shapely legs with enormous knobbly knees and thick ankles. He had a flat tummy and broad shoulders, but also a large round bottom that didn't seem to belong to the rest of him. He had thin, elegant arms and wrists that supported enormous, square hands. He had a charming smile, flashing beautiful teeth, because his mum made him wear a wire mouth plate at night to keep them straight, but he also had three huge warty things on his chin. I allowed him to be in one of my plays once because he was quite theatrical, looked older than he was and could quickly imagine things. But he needed to be the centre of attention, which could be tiring, and he had a habit of changing my scripts to words he liked better.

Lincoln insisted that Caleb and a little girl called Janet get his milk bottle in the recess times and fetch his lunch from his locker and bring it to him in the schoolyard. Lincoln also expected Caleb and Janet to take turns finishing his homework. We told Caleb to stop, but he and Janet both seemed to like working for Lincoln. When Caleb heard the headmistress telling Lincoln he was a born leader, it reinforced his view of his nine-year-old hero.

Lincoln was unable to shed much light on Saint Joan because he said there were thousands and thousands of saints and there was no way he could keep up. He said his father's favourite was Saint Brigid. She was a Catholic celebrity because she changed her dirty old bathwater into beer. She also changed bathwater from a whole pile of leprosy people into beer too, but why you would want to drink either beat me. Surely there would be bits of skin and scabs and even fingers and things in the leprosy beer? When we asked

Lincoln about this, he said his dad just said, 'Beer is beer, and all the better if it's holy.'

Ruthy said the Catholic saints weren't really able to do miracles, or they would be in the Bible. This resulted in an interesting conversation about the difference between magic and miracles. We concluded that anything magic that was about God or Jesus was a miracle, and everything else was just plain magic or a trick. As a result, the bathwater thing was either a hoax, like you saw at the circus sometimes, or it was magic.

Caleb developed a total fascination with Catholic saints. He said our church was very boring because no one could do anything special at all, except for Brother Steve Wilbur who had a puppet in a box called Brian he could bring out and make talk, even though we all knew it was really Brother Steve throwing his voice. Some of Caleb's favourite saints included Saint Joseph of Cupertino, who could fly and used to sit in trees and tell people the view was nice; Father Paul of Moll, who could make birds come to sing to him and when they did their feathers changed colour; and Saint John Bosco who could make a dog called Grigio turn up out of nowhere to protect him when he was in danger.

Lincoln also offered to ask his mum about Saint Joan. Caleb asked him to do so as soon as possible because the matter was urgent.

Caleb nagged Ruthy to find out about Saint Joan too, and Ruthy agreed to have something for him by the weekend if he would just shut up and leave it alone for a few days. He agreed but didn't keep his promise and asked her at least twice a night if she was reading anything important about the burnt soldier. If he asked too loudly, we shushed him quiet. It wouldn't do for Mum to find out we were reading about a Catholic when she was already so down.

Now that Caleb was feeling a bit better, I convinced them to play a game of which I was particularly fond. We would put the record player on the kitchen table and open the window so we could hear the music in the garden. I would put on one of the few records we had, 'Colonel Bogey March' from the film *The Bridge on the River Kwai*, and make the others line up and march behind me. I sent Ruthy to go down the street to see who else was at home and might be convinced to join my troupe, and before long we had seven children in our line-up. That gave me the chance to drill them rather than march myself, and I stood on the sidelines and yelled orders and criticism of their marching style, until I made Rose Partington from number 17 cry and she and her brother went home. Ruthy said I had to learn to be less bossy if I wanted kids to play with us, but I said that it was my job to get them all up to speed or we wouldn't win marching competitions, and Ruthy said there weren't any competitions to win, which means she missed the point.

Ruthy presented her research to my little brother. She had worked on it all week, asking the school librarian, Mrs Sandicock, to help her find books and references, and then sat at the little table in our room after tea to work on her report. She got up just as the light was creeping in under the little torn corner of the blind in our room on Saturday morning to copy out her notes on to her favourite lined pad that she used for homework. We took it into Caleb's bedroom together and shook him awake. Ruthy handed it over. He was very excited in a nervous kind of way and sat straight up in bed to read it. Ruthy got in with him so she could see her writing and help him with any words that were hard for him. In the end, he handed it back and just asked her to read it out loud. I crawled in next to them and put my arms around Caleb so we could listen together, as though it was a story time with Mum or Dad, even though Ruthy and I hadn't had one of those for quite a long time. Ruthy read her report in her best ABC newsreader voice.

'Joan of Arc was a French girl who was born in 1412. She was called the Maid of Orleans. You don't say Orleans the way we would say it, because it has a little dooverlacky over the letter 'e' and the French people know to make that sound a bit different, but it doesn't matter really. And Maid of Orleans didn't mean she did people's cleaning but I am not sure why she was called that.

'Her dad's name was Jacques d'Arc, which Mrs Sandicock says you would say like "Jark da ark", which sounds quite funny, but they probably didn't think so. When she was only one year older than Daniel is now, that is eighteen years old, she led the French army into a battle that they won. There had been a prophecy that a girl like her would lead an army. I searched Dad's Bible concordance and she is not mentioned so this was a made-up prophesy and not a proper one from God.

'She claimed that when she was thirteen, she started to hear voices in the garden that told her what to do. She believed they were from God, but as we know, Maynard's grandpa hears voices all the time and they are definitely in his head and not from God, who would not bother to ask the nurses to remove the frogs from his jelly. The voices said the English were bad people and she had to save France from them. This seems strange to us because Grandpa Wilson is from England

and he is not a bad person, but this happened a long time ago so perhaps they were then. Her voices told her she would be struck in the chest by an arrow. That's exactly what happened, so people believed her voices in the garden were from God. The French king was very happy with her and made up a coat of arms for her that he drew himself. It had a sword holding a crown with a picture of a flower on each side.

'She got captured after a battle and someone sold her to the English for a lot of gold. They took her to an English court that was run by Catholic priests who put her on a bed and tied her down. They told her she had to say she didn't really hear the voices, but she wouldn't do it. After a time she gave up because torture is very terrible, but they still burned her to death anyway. Her last words were "Jesus, Jesus, Jesus".'

Both Ruthy and I were hoping this homework would be the end of Caleb's obsession, but instead he let out a rip-roaring scream and we cuddled him hard to try to make him quiet before Mum got out of bed.

'Caleb! Shhhhhh! Mum's still in bed. And we have to be good or she'll have a worse than usual head day,' said Ruthy.

'What's that noise about?' we heard Dad call out from the bedroom. 'What's going on? You all right, Caleb? Need your nebuliser?'

'He's fine, Dad. He just saw a spider,' I called out. Ruthy had her hand over Caleb's mouth trying to calm him down.

'What's wrong, Caleb?' she said. 'This is what you wanted, isn't it? I finished it this morning for you. What's wrong?'

'This proves that Dad is going to be sacrificed,' he said, white with panic.

'Don't be ridiculous,' I said, tired of the game now. 'Dad. Is. Not. Going. To. Be. Sacrificed.' I thumped the bed next to him with each word.

'Yes, he is, Dorcas. Yes, he is. Because yesterday you drew a picture of a crown and sword, like the army coat from the king, and Ruthy drew some flowers.' His little bottom lip was trembling and his eyes were as wide as a full moon.

'But Caleb, I am *always* drawing swords and armour and crowns, and Ruthy is *always* drawing flowers,' I said, exasperated. Really, boys could drive me nuts. I made a mental note to be sure no boy knights came to live at Caramel.

'But when I saw Dad tied up to the tree in my dream, he kept saying not to worry, and then he said, "Jesus, Jesus, Jesus",' insisted Caleb.

'Caleb, that was just a dream,' said Ruthy, patting his back now because he had started to hiccup between words.

'But Joan Dark had dreams too, and they came true and they sacrificed her.' His face was crumpling up in the way it did when he was about to lose it, so we were both patting him and stroking him, and I was holding his Ventolin ready to help him use it if he started to panic and wheeze.

'Want me to come and get the spider?' called out Dad.

'No!' Ruthy and I both called out at once.

'Dorcas got it and squashed it with her shoe and it's quite dead,' called out Ruthy.

'You'd better not have squashed a spider on my clean sheets,' called out Mum.

At least we could call out one true thing when we sang back, 'No.'

CHAPTER 15

The next day was a Friday, and it should have been an excellent day because Dad said he was taking the morning off work and that we were going on an outing. We thought this might help Caleb to let go of this sacrifice theory because Ruthy and I were plumb out of ideas about how to help him get past it. Ruthy and Caleb were very excited because I think they saw this as the end of what Ruthy called 'the Cold War' between Mum and Dad, but I had a feeling in my guts that said it wasn't going to be so easy to get Mum back to a good place. As it turned out, it was a terrible day. It was even worse than the day I found Sixpence dead in the box, and that's saying a lot because I didn't think any day could ever be that bad again.

We got ready to go. Dad said we were going to Cleland conservation park to see the animals, and that sounded like the best idea ever. We got dressed and put things in the back of the station wagon we thought we might need, like Ruthy's notebook and Caleb's Ventolin and Milly Molly Mandy and a yellow truck and three jars with holes punched in the lid Mr Driver had made for me in case we found interesting insects, and Ruthy's torch and a pair of scissors in case we needed to cut something interesting.

I ran into Mr Driver's place to tell him about the outing, but he seemed rather sad and just mussed up my hair and told me to try to have the best day I could have. Something in my insides did a little somersault when he said this, but I pushed that thought away, ran down to Sixpence's grave to tell her where we were going, and raced back to the car. Mum and Dad weren't ready, but I was full of light, air and energy and ran down to the end of the street and back just for something to do while I waited. I was out of breath and a bit sweaty when I got back, and my parents still weren't in the car so I ran back to Sixpence to tell her what kind of animals I hoped I would see.

The first sign that it was going to be a bad day was that Dad told us to get in the car and then he got in too and started the motor. Caleb started laughing and said Dad was a duffer because he had forgotten Mum, but Dad said Mum wasn't coming with us to Cleland, which made us all go very quiet and perfectly still in the back seat. Caleb asked how come Mum wasn't coming, and Dad said she had a busy day and needed some time to sort things out for herself. He seemed cross more than sad about it, but he said it in a voice that invited no comment.

Ruthy and Caleb looked at me, but I didn't look back, because the thing inside me that went a bit haywire when things were bad was rushing around my innards and I was feeling quite panicky.

We drove to the park in silence. It was quite a long way, so there was quite a lot of silence. Dad didn't look in the rear-view mirror to check on us, which he usually did. Caleb curled up in a little ball and Ruthy hung on tight to Milly Molly Mandy and buried her head in the rag doll's woollen hair. When we reached the park, we all got out of the car quietly, and just sort of stood around it for a minute. Usually we would have already run to the gate and be screaming for Dad to hurry up.

Inside the park, Dad walked to a shelter shed and put our lunch basket on a bench. He sat down and took out his newspaper and told us to go and have a good time. Caleb asked if he was going to come with us, but he said, 'Not right now, off you go and play.' This didn't feel right, but after a few minutes we raced off to explore, and for a little while we forgot that Mum wasn't with us and Dad didn't look happy.

Normally we would have disappeared for hours but after a while we met up at a water fountain and decided we should go back to see Dad and to ask him to look at the kangaroos with us. When we ran back to the table, he was just sitting and looking at nothing. His paper was folded flat. Caleb pulled at his shirt and asked him to come to feed the animals with us, but he said he wasn't really in the mood. He took some stale bread out of the picnic basket and told us to go and feed things with it.

We went to a little lake and threw the bread to some birds that were hanging around. They seemed to enjoy it enormously, and I thought it was good that someone was having a good day. Caleb plonked himself down on the ground by the water and started to cry. Ruthy sat next to him and put her arm around his shoulders and I noticed she didn't tell him there was nothing to worry about, because we all knew there was, even though we didn't understand what it was exactly.

'Dorcas, you think it's just that Mum is having a head day?' asked Ruthy.

I shook my head no.

'Well, what do you think it is then?' she asked.

Part of me wanted to tell her what Mrs Edwards had told me about Mum leaving, but my mouth couldn't make those words come out of it because they were too scary and sad. We sat there together for quite a long time, not saying anything, Caleb whimpering quietly. I wanted to cry a bit, but my throat was all tight and sort of strangled.

We saw Dad's shadow before we saw him. It was tall and thin and his head of dark bouncy curls made a nice curly shape on top. He came and sat down next to Caleb. The four of us were a sad, little row. Dad stretched his arm out so it went around all three of us. His hand was on my shoulder. It felt heavy.

After a while, he said, 'I have something to tell you, and I need you to be very brave.'

We waited. I don't think I was breathing.

'Your mum has left for Scotland today. She needs to visit your grandma. You know she has been missing her mum very much, and although I wanted Grandma to come to visit us, she is not very well and can't travel, so Mum is going to see her.'

'But can we go with her?' asked Caleb.

'No, we have to stay here and keep going to work and school and the meetings. That's what she would want us to do. And she will come back and tell you stories and bring you presents, and she will probably be wearing a kilt like everyone does in Scotland and she will be very happy because she's seen her family again.'

'Will she be able to play the bagpipes?' asked Caleb.

'Possibly. Who knows,' said Dad.

'Why didn't she come with us today, Dad?' I asked.

'She is leaving this morning and she thought it would be a bit sad for us to see her get on the plane so Mr Driver is going to take her to the Adelaide Airport. She wanted you to be having a lovely time somewhere when she got on the plane so she could remember you all happy and excited,' said Dad.

'But she won't remember us all happy and excited because she didn't even get out of bed to see us and she didn't say goodbye,' I said. Ruthy started to bawl now.

'She didn't say goodbye to you when you were awake, but last night when you were asleep she sat next to each one of you and stroked your hair and told you she loved you very much and that it would break her heart not to see you every single morning and every single night,' said Dad.

'Did ... did she mean that? Even for me?' I asked.

'She did mean that, and she meant it just as much for you as for Ruthy and Caleb. She loves you very much, Dorcas.

Sometimes her sadness just gets in the way of her showing it,' said Dad.

'Will she be home by next Friday for tellie and chocolate?' asked Caleb.

'No,' said Dad.

'Will she be home to wash my school shirts for next week?' asked Caleb.

'No,' said Dad.

'Will she be home for the Sunday school prize night?' asked Ruthy.

'No, Ruthy. But she's finished your frocks and they are waiting for you in her wardrobe. They are very beautiful yellow dresses with white dots on them, so you will be very happy, Dorcas.'

'But, Dad,' said Ruthy, 'prize night is still weeks away. How long will Mum be gone for?'

'She will have Christmas with her family,' said Dad, 'so she will be away for quite a long time.'

'Noooo,' howled Caleb. 'I want my mum. I want my mum.'

Dad wrapped himself around Caleb and rocked him to and fro.

'Come on, Caleb,' said Dad. 'Don't be a baby now. Big boys don't cry. Don't you want your mum to be happy that she can see her family?'

'No,' said Caleb. 'I want her to be happy here with us.'

'Not going to happen,' I heard myself say, and Dad snapped his head to look at me but didn't say anything.

'But why didn't Mum say goodbye to us?' said Ruthy, who had tears rolling down her cheeks now. 'Doesn't she love us anymore?'

'I told you, she did say goodbye, and of course she loves us,' said Dad. But that was all he said.

'But who will make our lunches and look after us when you are at work?' asked Ruthy.

And that was the question that shot a big bullet of fear right through my gut. I could feel the blood rushing to my face. My hands got all sticky and sweaty. I held my breath again, waiting for what I was dreading to know.

'Well. It's going to be fine really. Caleb is going to stay with Aunty Maisie and Grandpa. Because they live so close, he will be able to finish the school year at Rostrevor.' He addressed Caleb, 'Aunty Maisie will walk you to school every day and pick you up. And you will be able to see Grandpa every day and that will be lovely.

'Ruthy, you are going to stay with Brother and Sister Hodgeson, who really love you and can't wait to see you. I've spoken to your teachers and they are going to give you a big packet of work to do at the Hodgesons. They said you are very clever and it won't put you behind.

'And Dorcas, you are going to stay with the Roystons. You've known them all your life, and Maudie and Helen and Peter will be your friends. You are going to go to school with Maudie until the end of the year, and your teachers say you can sit their exams instead of the ones at your school and it won't be a problem,' said Dad.

We were all three crying now. Caleb was making noises that sounded like *'woa, woa, woa'*. Ruthy was doing her very distressed cry where she stops breathing and her face is all screwed up and her mouth is an ugly big hole with dribble coming out of it. I had tears streaming from my eyes but made no sound. There wasn't a sound that could match the awfulness of it all. I was pretty sure my eyes would leak forever.

A couple walking past us slowed down as they heard us crying and turned to look as they went past. The woman made a little 'oh what a shame, poor poppets' face, but I couldn't hear what they were saying. A little boy raced past us then noticed we were something interesting, came to a halt, stood stock-still just a little way behind me, staring and listening. Then he ran off calling to his mother, 'There's people crying, Mum. There's people crying over here.'

Dad didn't say anything else. He just sat with us and stared out at the water. In a way, I thought that was okay because he was being honest about the terribleness. But I also wanted him to say things to make it all right. This silent Dad was part of the huge bubble of misery that was getting bigger and bigger in my chest.

After a few minutes that felt like days, Dad said, 'Come on, you three. Let's go and get an ice-cream.'

Ruthy said, 'I don't want one, Dad.' But he stood up and gently pulled her to her feet, and Caleb and I followed. We all walked silently to the shop. Dad said we could have any ice-cream we wanted. Caleb was still hiccupping, and my eyes were still raining on my cheeks. Ruthy had her little pouty face going on. The woman in the shop had purple hair. I thought, *Mum would never agree to dye someone's hair that colour.* I wondered if Mum would take Orlay's Audrey Auburn hair colour with her to Scotland. What if they don't have Audrey Auburn there? What if she comes home with different-coloured hair? Would she go black? Or blond? Would she look the same?

'They can get overtired on outings, can't they?' said the purple-headed serving lady. I noticed her roots were very grey for a good half an inch around the line of her face. I also noticed she was wearing an orange jumper. Mum would have said, 'What are you thinking wearing purple with orange?'

Dad just nodded and handed her some money.

'I make mine have a lie-down before I take them out,' she said. 'About your ones' ages I'd say.' She leaned into the freezer and pulled out our ice-creams. 'Oh, they don't like it, of course. But I say, no lie-down, no treat. I'd try that, a lie-down before you leave. We see a lot of tired crying and tantrums here. I always recommend the lie-down.'

Dad just nodded again.

* * *

When we pulled into the driveway Caleb said, 'Dad, will Mum be inside?' and Dad said, 'No, Caleb. Your mum has gone to Scotland.' We all walked to the back door because it wasn't a running kind of event. There was no one in the kitchen. The house was quiet and empty. It didn't feel right that everything looked the same, when nothing was really the same. Dad told us to put our things away. We went into our bedrooms, and then we all started to cry again, because Mum had packed a suitcase for each of us and put it on our beds.

'But, Dad,' howled Ruthy, 'we don't have to go right now, do we? Can't we stay with you, Dad? We will be really good and we can do the cooking and cleaning and Dorcas can look after us until you get home from work and we can get Mr Driver if there are snakes or spiders or robbers.' She was pleading.

'Or pirates,' added Caleb, a bit hopefully for a minute.

'It's too long a time for you to look after yourselves,' said Dad. 'We need to go now so you have time to settle down a bit before the week starts. I'll see you every Sunday and sometimes I'll come and have tea with you during the week.' He picked up Caleb's suitcase and took it through the house. I thought, *They sent Daniel away and he hasn't been back since. They don't see him on Sundays and they don't have tea with him during the week sometimes.*

I suddenly realised I wouldn't be able to see Sixpence every day and raced through the house, and past the car to Mr Driver's, even though I could hear Dad calling me to come back.

I sat on the little stool next to her. I was crying as I explained things, so the words came out a bit stuttery. I felt as though a big hand had reached into my heart and was squeezing it hard. At first I thought it might have been God's hand, but then thought he probably wouldn't squeeze a child's heart, so maybe it was a witch. But then I thought it might have been Jesus because he did say,

'Suffer the little children,' and suffer was a good word for me right now.

I said, 'I love you very much and I will never forget you but Mum has gone to Scotland and I have to stay at the Roystons' until after Christmas. Mr Driver will take very good care of you. It will get lovely and warm soon so you can rest in the spring and I will see you in the summer and water the garden around you so you stay nice and cool. Love, Dorcas.'

Ruthy used to ask me why I spoke to Sixpence as though I had written a letter to her, but Mr Driver said letters were powerful things and that was okay. He said that in the war sometimes letters were the only things that kept a man alive, and you could keep them and read them over and over to keep your heart from stopping from loneliness. Ruthy said sure but Sixpence wasn't at war and I wasn't actually posting a letter to her and Mr Driver said, 'There's more than one way to send a letter,' and neither of us knew what that really meant but I felt Mr Driver had said something that was on my side so I said, 'So there,' to Ruthy, who shut up.

Dad dropped me at the Roystons' first. I asked if I could be last so I could sit in the front seat with him for a while, but he said no, it made sense to do it in this order because of where everyone lived. I thought Caleb should go first because Aunty Maisie lived quite close to us but

Dad said he was having dinner at Maisie's when he took Caleb there, and that made Jesus squeeze my heart again because I thought that might mean he loved us in the order he dropped us off, from least loved to most loved, and it made me think of the beads on our string in the tree house.

That made me gasp and I said, 'Dad, we have to go back and get the beads in the tree house. We can't leave them behind.'

But Dad said, 'Just make a list of anything you need once you're settled in and I can bring it into Sunday school for you. But only things you really need. I can't imagine why you need some beads from the tree house. What are they, anyway? A necklace?'

None of us answered, because we didn't want to explain the way the family was represented on the string to Dad. But as we drove on our way to Henley Beach, where I would be staying, which is quite a long way from home, I thought about those beads and where they should be on the string now. Should we take the Mum bead off altogether for a while? Or should we just make a much bigger space between the Mum and Dad beads? Was the string long enough at all now? And if we took the Mum bead off, should we take mine off too, because I had a feeling Mum would say I was the main reason she had to go to Scotland.

And there it was, my big fear. Was I the reason Mum couldn't wait any longer for Grandma to come to visit us? Was I the reason she had to fly across the world to be with her mum? Was she going to say, 'Honestly, that child is the living end,' as soon as she walked into Grandma's house? I didn't know my grandma, and only got a flowery card from her for my birthday every year that said *Happy birthday from your gran* in spidery writing. But I had always hoped she thought well of me. I had the idea in my head that I was quite like her and so she would like me, and perhaps I would even be a favourite. For Mum to talk to her first and give her a bad impression of me was not ideal.

Caleb whispered loudly to Ruthy, 'I can go and get the beads after school.' But Dad heard him and said, 'No, Caleb. No one is to go home without my permission.'

But Caleb looked at Ruthy and mouthed the words, 'I will. I will get them.'

And then I thought of Daniel. 'Dad, does Daniel know where we will all be now? Does he know about Mum? Will he know where to send Ruthy letters? Can we ring each other and talk sometimes?'

Dad said, 'Enough questions now, Dorcas. Just settle down with the Roystons, and we'll sort everything else out after that. Just hush for a while now.'

I looked at Ruthy who mouthed, 'I'll tell Daniel. Don't worry.' I wondered where Daniel's bead would be now. And then I thought again about my mum, who was flying right across the world all by herself. I worried about who she might have to sit next to. What if it was a man who made bad nose noises like Brother Jupitus did when he sat behind her at the Memorial Meeting on Sundays? She hated men who made sniffy or whistling noises through their nose. Or what if there was a chatty woman next to her? Mum didn't like chatty women. She called them all show and no go. And she might have hours and hours of someone blethering on. I wondered if she'd tell them off, like she'd tell me off. And what if when Mum needed to go to the toilet on the plane, there was a big queue of people? Venita said her mum nearly wee'd herself when they went on a big trip because there's only one toilet and so many people.

And what if Mum was crying all the way to Scotland because she was already missing us so much? Crying and crying and messing up her make-up and running out of tissues. And then I had the worst thought of all.

What if Mum wasn't missing us at all?

CHAPTER 16

I did not enjoy my time at the Roystons' and I'm pretty sure they didn't enjoy having me there either.

The Royston family was made up of Brother Royston, who I called Uncle Paul; Sister Royston, who I called Aunty Jean; Peter, who was seventeen and used to be in the same Sunday school class as my brother Daniel; Helen, who was thirteen and in the first year of Grange High School; and Maudie, who was twelve and in the final year of Grange Primary.

They lived in a cream brick house in what was called a seaside suburb, but their house was near a very boring, busy main road and you couldn't even walk to the ocean, so I think they must have been very disappointed if that's why they bought it. It had no front yard to speak of, just dry grass that Peter had to mow when it was growing, but it was already so hot when I went to stay that it was just short yellow sticks of weeds and straw. The backyard had a big shed in it but it wasn't that interesting and mainly just had their car and a few tools in it.

There was also a very old caravan that had no wheels and smelled of cat's wee when you went into it, which Aunty Jean told me not to do. I went into the shed to have a good look around one day, and Aunty Jean yelled at me to get out before she took the stick to the back of my legs, so I didn't chance a rummage around again. The back garden also had no flowers or shrubs or lawn or furniture except for a broken wooden table with two benches either side. Sister Royston said those who loved God and spent their time at the meeting all weekend had no time for fripperies like gardens. She said garden beds were a sign of materialism and vanity. When I said, 'Didn't God make the flowers and tell us to consider the lilies of the field?', she said He did, and I could go and look for lilies in fields any time I liked and consider them there.

This was one of probably a thousand things I said in the weeks I stayed with them that I wished I hadn't.

Aunty Jean was scary. She was enormously tall and very fat, but not that floppy kind of fat. She seemed so firm that

I often wanted to poke her to see if she was as hard as she looked. I saw some strange underwear on the line one day that made me suspect she bound herself up with elastic all-in-ones to pretend she had a shape. Someone should have told her it wasn't working, and she should just let go and breathe. Although, perhaps if she did, she would unfold into a huge wobbly jelly.

Aunty Jean's favourite expression was grumpy. She was a great friend of my Aunty Maisie, and it seemed to me that if you liked Aunty Maisie, you had to end up looking a bit like her to stay in her club. This, I was sure, was a club to which I never wished to belong.

Aunty Jean had three chins, and the main one under her mouth had lots of thick grey and white bristles on it, and some hairs that were so long they curled up. She had the most enormous blackheads I've ever seen. Caleb called them The Pocks of Poo. I had to try not to keep looking at them because they were sort of fascinating. She looked very old but Mum said that she was only a few years older than her and she only looked that way because she was one of those matrons who refused to dye her hair and immediately moved to flat shoes and shapeless flowery dresses when she turned forty. Mum said that's what happened to most women over forty in our church meeting, and there was no need for it because there wasn't a commandment that said 'Thou shalt look like an old bag of potatoes when you leave your thirties'.

Before the union exams, I had made Aunty Jean cross one Sunday by calling out across the church's middle hall, 'Aunty Jean, your teeth look very beautiful and shiny today.' She stomped over to me and grabbed me by the elbow and shook me so hard my teeth sort of chattered independently in my mouth.

She said, 'You dreadful child. You know fine well they are new and false. What a mean thing to say out loud.' I honestly hadn't realised they were false, and just kept saying, 'Sorry, sorry,' but she stayed cross with me. So I was a bit surprised they had agreed to take me in. I had asked Dad on the way to the Roystons' if I couldn't go and stay with my best friend Anne King, but Dad said the Kings were going on a big trip as soon as school finished and so it wouldn't work out. I said I didn't think that was right because Anne would have told me but Dad said it was going to be a surprise for her and I shouldn't tell her. Dad should have known not telling Anne was going to be a big challenge right there.

If Peter Royston had shown any interest in knights, I might have considered marrying him. Although I didn't like boys that much, I sometimes got a bit goofy around him and said mad things I didn't intend. Once I had made a paper fortune-teller, one of those things where you fold up the paper into triangles and make them go in and out with your fingers. Anne called them chatterboxes. When I had asked it who I would marry, it had said Peter. I told Anne this, but she pointed out I had written all the names in it, and had written his name five times, so there was a good chance it was going to give me the name I wanted. But I was pretty sure there was some magic going on there and refused to accept her doubt.

Peter didn't pay a lot of attention to me but we had to eat dinner together every night, so I got to see him then. I combed my hair before I went to the table, which I didn't do at home, but when Helen asked me what I was doing I said my mum always required us to straighten our clothes and comb our hair before 'being summoned to dine'. This wasn't true. I was usually screamed at to get to the table, threatened if I didn't hurry up, criticised for looking like a rag and bone man's assistant and smacked for being so grubby. But Mum would have liked us to smarten up for tea, so it was sort of right, and Helen and Maudie were very impressed.

I found myself telling stories over dinner about all sorts of amazing things, but Peter kept snorting and saying, 'That's just not true. You are a little liar.' Uncle Paul would just make pushing down motions with his hand and say, 'Bring it down, Peter, bring it down.' Aunty Jean cuffed him on the head and said not to be rude to guests, but then said, 'Dorcas, you shouldn't tell fibs.' The problem was when I was telling the story I believed it was true.

For example, I was absolutely positive that not long before my visit a whole family was found living in the belly of a whale. When the whale swallowed pirate ships and such like, all the bits floated in and the family was a bit like a clan from the book about the Borrowers by Miss Mary Norton. The Borrowers were tiny people who turned everyday things into useful objects, and they would have turned all the flotsam and jetsam into household items to make their stay in the whale cosier. Peter said that was an out-and-out lie, and I insisted he was wrong and it was in a newspaper, or else how would I know the term flotsam and jetsam, but he said Ruthy would have taught me those words because everyone knew she was the brains in our family. If he kept this up, I thought, he was going to have a hard time of it when he proposed to me.

Mum always said Helen turned dowdy at eight. I sort of knew what she meant. She was as skinny as Aunty Jean was round, and short like Uncle Paul. She wore knitted grey tights all year round that were baggy around her ankles. Her grey glasses had thick, coke-bottle bottoms in them, which gave her a slightly scary owl quality when she looked at you, because they made her eyes too big for her face. Her sturdy black shoes had a strap across them and she wore very bulky jumpers in winter and large crocheted tops she made for herself in summer. Mum used to say that Helen must have hunted through the rubbish tips to find the wool she used to make her tops, because it was always of the ugliest possible shade and other people must have thrown it out. She didn't seem to be comfortable with herself and was always hitching her tops down as though to cover bits she wasn't that keen on.

She was quite a nice girl, but rather too godly for me. She never seemed to do anything wrong and was always polite and kind, and read her Bible every day and crocheted rugs for poor people in Africa. I asked her once why poor people in Africa would need those rugs, given it was very hot, but she said the Christadelphian missionaries asked for them and they would know best.

Maudie was okay. I neither liked nor disliked her because she was a sort of blancmange. She was pale and thin with mousey brown curly hair that seemed to be falling out, a bit like a man going bald. You could see her bright pink scalp between the curls. She wore clothes that were far too big for her; usually long box-pleated skirts that were higher up at the back than the front, and little jumpers with things like cats and fairies stitched on to them. The best word for her was beige, I thought. She was an all-round beige person.

I sensed all the girls in the Royston family saw me as a bit ungodly, and somehow dangerous. I stayed on the top bunk in the two-bunk room Maudie and Helen shared. There was only room for a tiny desk under the window between the bunk beds, and the girls had a roster to share it to do homework and Bible study. They offered to change the roster to give me a space, but I wasn't one for homework and decided if I couldn't go to my own school, I wouldn't bother too much anyway.

By far the nicest person in the family was Uncle Paul. He was a tiny, very thin man who walked with a crooked back, bent over quite a long way. Brian Dirk and Bruce Munsford at the meeting were often rude about him. They did Quasimodo impersonations behind his back and walked around saying they couldn't remember his name, but his face rang a bell.

I'm pretty sure Uncle Paul knew about this but he never complained or punished them. I would have stuck a knife in their bike tyres at least. He was very clever, and although he worked as a clerk somewhere and didn't make much money, everyone at church said he was a genius and if he had been a worldly person, which he wasn't, he would have been a great professor or scientist or something equally important.

But the story was he devoted his brain to the study of Revelations and had written two books about it that were printed by the church and even sold in the big book cupboard in the entrance hall of our meeting. I thought he would only read Bible things, but he read all kinds of interesting books. He told me he was very fond of insects and showed me a collection of books on his shelves about them. Many had fascinating drawings or photos blown up so you could see all their bits and pieces, and he told me stories about them I could have listened to for the longest time. I told him one day I wished he had been one of my teachers at school because he made everything sound so interesting. He kindly said he wished he had been one of my teachers, because he would have been lucky to have an excellent learner in his class. No one had ever called me that before, so I was pretty chuffed and rolled those words around and around in my head for a long time later, particularly when things were a bit dark.

Lots of little bad things and five very big bad things happened during my stay with the Roystons.

The first very bad thing was that I hated, hated, hated Maudie's school. Because it was nearly the end of the year, everyone had already made friends, and there were no friend spaces available anywhere. I missed Venita and Maynard and hoped someone would explain to them why I had suddenly disappeared. I wondered who they would be friends with now, and whether they wouldn't need me anymore when I went back next year. I thought about writing a letter to Maynard, but I realised I didn't know his address. I asked if I could look in the Roystons' telephone directory to find it but they said they didn't keep one – all the numbers they needed were in the list of church members that were copied and distributed at the beginning of each year.

My temporary teacher seemed okay but didn't try very hard to help me fit in, and largely left me alone. She seemed perpetually exhausted. Sometimes she set us work and rested her forehead on the desk at the front of the room. One day she didn't even look up when the bell sounded; she just lifted her right hand and waved us all away. Her name was Gloria Gizzard, and I wondered to what extent an ugly name had contributed to a tired life.

I spent the breaks by myself, although for the first couple of days Maudie and her friend Susan came to find me. But I could tell Susan wasn't that keen about being friends with me and by the end of the first week they gave up. Maudie walked to school with me, but I walked home by myself.

I spent a fair amount of time in the library. The librarian was nice, although not as good as Mrs Sandicock at Rostrevor Primary. They had three books on knights I hadn't seen before, so that was a bit of a highlight. I asked if I could see a telephone book, but she said they didn't keep them in the library and I wasn't allowed to go into the staffroom. One lunchtime I decided to go and look in a phone booth I had seen on the way to school. I took a pencil and a piece of paper so I could write down addresses. I would look up Maynard's address, the Hodgesons' address and Aunty Maisie's address so I could at least write people letters and let them know where they could reach me.

I didn't know you weren't allowed to leave the school yard without permission, although I should have realised that when I was the only one to walk out of the front gates. I must have taken a lot longer to walk to the box and find all the names than I realised because when I returned to school, everyone was back in class. There were three prefects walking around the grounds, pretending, as I found out later, to be looking for me, but really they were just having an extended lunchtime and giggling together.

One saw me and pointed and they all ran towards me calling out my name, which was a bit unnerving. They marched me to the head's office. I kept twisting and pulling myself away from them, but they were treating me like an escaped prisoner they'd found, and each of them was hanging on to a handful of my shirt or skirt. I must have started yelling at them and pushing back, because the note that went home to Aunty Jean said I had been violent and abusive, having run away from school. None of this was true of course, but no one believed me. I wasn't planning on giving Aunty Jean the note, but they were smarter at Grange Primary than at Rostrevor and sent a copy of it home with Maudie.

The headmistress asked me a pile of questions that made it clear she had already made up her mind about what had happened and asked me to turn out my pockets. She took my note with the addresses and phone numbers away. She had tried to ring Aunty Jean, but luckily I knew she had gone to ladies' Bible class that day, so I thought I would be safe. I didn't know then about the duplicate note with Maudie.

The very worst thing about this was that Aunty Jean rang my dad and put me on the phone to him. I tried to explain I was just looking for addresses and phone numbers because we had left before I could get them, but this seemed to make Dad cross.

'So this is all my fault, Dorcas, is it? Because I wouldn't let you go to your own school after your mum left, you had to misbehave?'

'No! Dad! I'm not saying it's your fault. I'm just saying this is why I had to leave school to go to a phone box to get all the details. I wanted to write some letters.'

'Dorcas, you don't even write to your brother Daniel, so why did you have to write to everyone else when you'll see them soon enough?'

'But I don't know when I'll see Maynard and I don't get pocket money here because Aunty Jean said you didn't leave any for me and they can't subsidise me so I can't ring. But Uncle Paul says he will give me stamps, and I want to make sure Maynard is still my friend next year.'

Nothing changed his mind about my motives or my guilt. Yet another grown-up had made a decision without knowing the facts. I knew my brother Daniel secretly wanted to be a lawyer, even though our church frowned on this and no one so far had become one. I decided I'd urge him on so he could take on cases like mine and sue for justice. Although hearing my dad's voice was comforting, the fact he was so cross with me was not.

Luckily for me, Uncle Paul was listening to all of this from his little study room, and after the call he summoned me. There was almost no room for me to be in the space with him. It was more a cupboard than a study really, and I think it might have been made from half of the laundry.

It had shelves that went from the floor to the ceiling all the way around, with a very small window on one side with his desk pushed up beneath the shelves. There were so many books crammed on the shelves they all sagged in the middle.

He asked me to tell him right from the beginning what had happened. And before I started he said, 'Now, my dear Dorcas. You and I know you are a splendid teller of tales, a quality I much admire because I myself am a man of infinitesimal imagination. However, on this occasion, I would be most grateful if you would look hard at the words you are saying, and check that they match up perfectly with the events of the day. Is that a reasonable request?'

'Right-o, Uncle Paul,' I said. This meant I spoke quite slowly and screwed my eyes up a bit in the telling to make sure I did the matching thing he was seeking. I explained everything to him, including my fear that Maynard wouldn't remember me, and that I needed to check that Ruthy and Caleb and Mr Driver were okay, although I knew Mr Driver's details, so that wasn't a problem. I explained that I didn't write to Daniel because Ruthy did that for all of us, and he didn't write back much anyway.

Uncle Paul listened very carefully. He looked at me the whole way through the story, a bit like the way Mrs Johnson and Mr Driver used to do. When I was finished, he said to leave it to him and he would make sure I had all the addresses and numbers I needed. He took me into the kitchen where, in the corner, was a little telephone table with a green Telecom phone on it. We didn't have a phone that sat on a table anymore. Mum had asked Dad for an apricot-coloured one that hung on the wall. But I knew the Roystons wouldn't want the latest phone, probably just on principle, but maybe because they were poorer than us.

He told me to sit down and get ready for some talking. He looked up the Christadelphian phone book, and he rang Aunty Maisie and asked her to put Caleb on the phone. I couldn't believe my luck. Aunty Jean came into the kitchen and asked what was going on, and he just turned and gave her a look and she stormed out again. I have a feeling he didn't use that look all that often, but when he did, Aunty Jean knew he meant it. There's a bit in the Bible that says the man is the head of the family and wives have to obey their husbands. I didn't really like this quote, but at that point in time I could see some benefits. After I'd spoken to Caleb, who was still very worried about the sacrifice thing, for a few minutes I hung up and wondered what I should do next. Uncle Paul came out of his little room and looked up another number. He rang the Hodgesons and asked them to put Ruthy on the phone.

Ruthy seemed to be having quite a nice time with them but was very homesick and cried for a while on the phone, which made me want to cry too, but I was worried if I did, Aunty Jean would say I couldn't ring and upset her, so I sniffed all the snot up. After that call, Uncle Paul said he didn't have the number for Daniel or for Maynard, but he would look them up at work and bring the numbers home the following night. I ran to him and gave him a hug, which wasn't hard, because he wasn't much bigger than me all bent over, and he patted me on the back and said I was welcome. He also told me to come to see him any time I was worried about something and we would problem-solve together, rather than me making up a solution by myself. This was such a reassuring idea that I hugged him again. I'm not sure how much he got hugged, because he really seemed to appreciate it. He kept forgetting to get the other two numbers and addresses, but I was sure eventually he would remember because he was a kind person. I didn't nag him because I thought if Aunty Jean heard me, she would interfere. At least I had two numbers now and I had heard Caleb and Ruthy's voices, which was better than only seeing them on Sundays.

The second very bad thing that happened was at Sunday school prize night. I got to see Dad on Sunday mornings at the Memorial Meeting, when all three of us sat next to him in a row. We were always so glad to see him that we didn't play up and he told us he was very proud of us. If there was a communal lunch, he had lunch with us and then said goodbye as we got ready to go into Sunday school at 3 pm. He picked Caleb up from Sunday school at four and had dinner with Aunty Maisie, and that made Caleb very lucky because he got to see Dad for most of the day. I used to run out of the hall as soon as my class finished and wait on the pavement so I could see him before he took Caleb away. I tried to be brave and cheerful so I wouldn't upset him. But I could feel my heart breaking and breaking and breaking when his car drove off, and sometimes I had to go into the girls' toilets and cry a bit before I let the Roystons find me to go home.

I wanted to go into the Sunday night meeting so I could nurse his Bible and hymn book and sit with him, but Aunty Jean said I would be too tired for school on Monday and made me stay at home with Maudie and Helen. This caused me to be sad and bad-tempered and meant I often tried to pick a fight with them. They would just look at me in surprise and refuse to have an argument back. I suspect this is because they were more godly than me by quite a long way. I did wonder sometimes though if godly and boring went hand in hand. I didn't want to be boring, so did that mean I would never be accepted into the Kingdom of God when Jesus came back and we all came up out of the dust of the earth to be judged?

The terrible bit was every Sunday I asked Dad if he could bring in our prize night dresses, and every Sunday he forgot. Eventually he put our dresses in the back of the station wagon, and somehow spilled oil all over mine. Ruthy's was fine, and she got to wear it, and it was really lovely. Aunty Jean said I had to wear my usual Sunday school dress, even though even her girls had a new frock for prize night. I possibly had a bit of a tantrum about it, and she put me in the bedroom and told the other two to stay out of there until I learned to be less vain and more grateful.

It wasn't really about having a new dress that upset me the most. It was that Mum had made that dress for me, and made it with polka dots on it, and hadn't made it orange, and she hadn't said goodbye to me but had finished my dress. I continued to be upset and sullen all day before the prize night, until Aunty Jean decided I couldn't go at all for being so bad, and could stay home with Peter in my room. This threw me into a panic – not because I wouldn't go on the stage in a new dress, but because I wouldn't see my dad at all, and he would hear I had been badly behaved and would be very upset with me. I begged. I pleaded. I cried. I made promises. I couldn't call on Uncle Paul for help because he had gone into Halifax Street early to hear the testimony of a boy called Iain Walters who wanted to be baptised. I didn't get to go to prize night, and my Dad was so disappointed in my behaviour I thought he might not pick me up and take me home when Mum came back from Scotland. That night, I thought it was possible to die of sadness, but later I learned that it could get even worse.

The third very bad thing that happened was something Peter told me about Daniel. I was hanging around the door of his room one day after school, and he had told to go away and play with the other babies, which made me cross. For some reason I thought responding with 'You're the baby' was a smart reply. I picked up a pen that had fallen out of his school bag near his door and threw it at him. He said he knew I was in love with him but he'd rather marry his mother's old mop, even after she'd used it to wash the toilet floor, than an idiot like me. I felt the need to comment on the large number of zits covering his face, and I believe I called him Chokito features. I had apparently poked the bear too hard with this comment, and he came back at me in a fury. He rose from his chair, came over to the door and stood over me so his face was only an inch from mine. His breath was very stinky, and right there and then I decided the wedding was off. I didn't flinch because that would show girls were weaker than boys.

'You're going to go just the way of your brother, aren't you? You're all the same in your family. Too sure of yourselves by half. So sure everyone will adore you. Think you are all so good-looking and clever. Well, Daniel-boy wasn't so clever when they found him with Esther Dangerfield with their pants down behind the kitchens at the interstate youth camp, was he?' he sneered.

This was news to me. I felt the shock that came with instinctively knowing I had been told a truth. I knew Daniel had done something he shouldn't have, and although we kids had tried to guess what it was, we didn't really know. We had made lists to try to work it out, and these had included the following possible reasons: he stole money from the collection plates when he helped Dad tally the takings on Sunday morning; he kept saying he was going to be a lawyer, even though Christadelphians said you shouldn't be because you might help a judge make a decision that was against God's will; and he'd refused to go to Aunty Maisie's for Christmas lunch because she made us eat her manky prawn cocktail.

We had agreed that we just couldn't see Daniel stealing, and that the other two items didn't seem bad enough to cause Mum and Dad to send him away. As Ruthy said, it was an enigma, which apparently is a thing wrapped in a thing that's a mystery, or some such.

'Well, at least Esther Dangerfield was the prettiest girl at the camp, and she liked my brother the best and I bet she didn't like you,' I said, not guessing until much later that this was an arrow straight to his heart.

'Yeah. Well look where that got him,' shouted Peter, who pushed me into the corridor and slammed the door. He barely spoke to me for the rest of my stay, and could hardly bear to look at me ever again.

The fourth very bad thing was the caravan. Every day the teacher made a long list of revision homework we should do for the exams. Although my school had told Dad the curriculum would be largely the same, I didn't recognise much of the work we were revising in the classroom, and the homework may have been written in Zulu for all I could understand it. And I just couldn't find the energy to do schoolwork when I got home. I would take my library books and sit on the top bunk and look through them until teatime, but homework just seemed a waste of time when I was so far behind.

Unfortunately, while my new temporary teacher barely had the energy to lift her head from the desk, she found the get up and go to write a note to Aunty Jean, again delivered through Maudie, to complain that I had not done a skerrick of homework since arriving at the school. Maudie had tried to be loyal and warned me she'd been given the letter, but I felt angry that I was even at her stupid school and just shrugged away the chance to fix the problem.

Aunty Jean was furious. I decided I would have to rely on the kindness of Uncle Paul to get me through this mess and waited in the driveway for his car to pull up from work. But Maudie came out to say her mum wanted to see me, and when I said I was waiting for her dad, she said there would be no point because he had gone to Keith for work and wouldn't be home until Sunday morning.

What can she do to me that she hasn't already done? I thought, as I walked in behind Maudie, feeling quite defiant. But once again I learned that grown-ups can surprise you and even nasty, bad-tempered women with no imaginations like Aunty Jean can make up new ways to make you sad. She grabbed me by the elbow and dragged me into the back garden. She threw open the door of the cat-wee-smelling old caravan, pushed me in and closed the door. Through the broken window I could just see her mean eyes and a sprinkling of the Pocks of Poo.

'You can stay there until I see some homework out of you. Maudie will bring your school bag out. You won't come in until I call you for dinner, and you'd better have some work to show me when I do.'

She trudged back inside, flattening any green shoot or little insect that foolishly tried to thrive in her pathway. I imagined being as small as a beetle, wondering why this giant had come to kill and crush her way through a tiny world. I hoped there were no Borrowers living anywhere near the Roystons, because contact with one of those enormous fleshy feet could mean the end of a whole family. I could imagine Mr Clock shaking his little fist at the enormous battleship of a human bean that was my Aunt Jean.

For the next few weeks, I was sent to the stinky, skanky, dirty, cobwebby prison that was the caravan. I hated it and was often a bit scared of it. I sat at the formica table and did as little as I could to suggest some progress. But when they called me for dinner, I put on an acting face for them. I would whistle as I walked to the back door, smile at Aunty Jean and hand over my work, which thankfully, after a night or two, she didn't even look at, and say how much I loved the caravan and could I sleep out there and have my dinner there because it was so much fun.

This irritated Aunty Jean no end, but it didn't fool Maudie, who kindly snuck out some cleaning rags and warm soapy water in jars for me to try to make at least a few spots clean enough to bear. Helen donated a poor African person's crocheted rug for me to sit on, and wrote out the answers to some of my homework questions so I could copy them into my exercise book to maintain just enough peace for the last few weeks of school. I was managing it all pretty well, I thought, until one night after tea, when we were studying the Bible together, Aunty Jean made a point of reading 1 Timothy 2:9: 'Likewise also that women should adorn themselves in respectable apparel, with modesty and self-control, not with braided hair and gold or pearls or costly attire.'

Stupid Poo-head Peter, as I now referred to him in my head, sniggered, and he and his mother looked at each other in a knowing way.

'My mum might wear fancy dresses and high heels, but our house is always clean, and she would be ashamed of the filthy caravan in your garden and I can't wait to tell my Aunty Maisie about it because she's a neat freak and will be very, very interested,' I said, and I ran out of the room, down the back steps and into my prison, even though it was now quite dark and therefore extra scary.

It was Uncle Paul who coaxed me out and walked me to my room so I wouldn't have to bear the wrath of the Bearded Boodlesnot, as I now referred to Aunty Jean in my head. Helen and Maudie were quite kind and suggested I just lay low for a few days, but that night I wasn't sure I could take it much longer and planned to run away to Anne King's house and explain I could just live in the empty house when they went on holidays.

The next morning, I knew my escape plans were hopeless, but Uncle Paul came into our bedroom with my school things out of the caravan and told me I wouldn't be going down there again. This signalled an uneasy truce between me, the Bearded Boodlesnot and Poo-head Peter. It would seem my Aunty Maisie was good for something after all.

But the fifth very bad thing was very bad and definitely the worst. One night, we girls were all sitting on our beds talking. They were asking me what I thought about boys, and I noticed I had quite a few views to share with them about all sorts of things. Maudie and Helen were so quiet and meek they made a good audience, and I found I would talk and talk and talk and they would happily sit and listen. Maudie asked if I had ever kissed a boy, and I said no but that I did have someone ready to marry me whenever I said yes. They asked me about Teddy Edwards and it may be true that I coloured in a few things about him. I might have suggested that he was sixteen, and that his dad was very wealthy and drove a Rolls Royce. I might have advised them that he had his own plane and flew us to Melbourne for picnics sometimes. I could have described his house as having fifteen rooms with a butler. I might have described a crown he had made for our wedding with diamonds and pearls in it.

After we had discussed whether I should marry him or not, I asked them which part of themselves they would cover up if they were in the bath and the house caught on fire and they had to rush out to save their lives and they only had a small handtowel. Maudie said she would cover her chest up and Helen said she would cover her front bottom. I discussed the value of the back bottom cover-up for some time, but we agreed that front bottoms or bosoms would be the way to go because you could always sit down or back up to a wall to cover the back side. I hadn't realised the door had opened a tiny bit and Aunty Jean was listening.

She rushed into the room, dragged me down from the top bunk, and smacked me hard on the backside. She said I was a vain and rebellious child, and she would not have me dragging her girls into sin and from the path of Light. She said it wasn't surprising given the antics of my mother, with her fashionable dresses and orange hair and high heels and lipstick, and she wouldn't be surprised if what they said was true, and that Mum and Dad were divorcing and Mum was never coming home again because she could not live The Way anymore. She waved a little key at me and I realised it was the key that could lock their Telecom green phone.

'You will make no more calls from this house. You can see your brother and sister on Sundays. I will not reward this kind of behaviour.' She triumphantly put the key down the front of her dress, and goodness knows she may as well have put it in the Cracks of Doom from *The Lord of the Rings* as between those two enormous melons.

But it wasn't the key to the phone that upset me. It was what she said about Mum never coming home. Because these nasty words matched up with the words I heard in my nightmares at night. Jesus seemed to have decided to use Aunty Jean as the prophet of misery. Those words were out in the air now, and I couldn't pretend otherwise.

CHAPTER 17

The Hodgesons were very kind to Ruthy. Sister Hodgeson asked her to call them Aunty Ada and Uncle Ken, but she was so used to hearing them called Brother and Sister Hodgeson by Mum and Dad she just couldn't do it.

Sister Hodgeson sat down with her on the first night with them and made a list of all of Ruthy's favourite foods, the games she liked to play and the books she preferred to read. She was allowed to watch television with them for the whole evening if she wished and stayed up half an hour later each night than we were allowed at home. She was allocated a seat of her own in the television room, and a rug and pillow on it to snuggle up if she wanted to. Next to it was a small side table just for her, that always had a drink and treat on it.

When she went to bed, they both came into her room with a chair and took turns reading a story to her.

They bought her new clothes, new books and five new exercise books. For the first three weeks after Mum left, she turned up at Sunday school with a new outfit on each time. This freaked Caleb out, who said they must think she belonged to them now, but Ruthy told him not to be stupid. It was just that they had never had a kid of their own and they were enjoying playing happy families.

Mum had put Ruthy's biscuit tin with all of her notebooks in the case she packed for her. That was wise of Mum, because it might have been the last straw for Ruthy if she hadn't been able to keep writing in them, and she liked to take old ones out and review what had happened in the past, but we all had to have a good think about the fact Mum seemed to know the secret location for all of our precious things.

Brother Hodgeson made a special wooden pencil box and carved Ruthy's name on the side of it. Sister Hodgeson filled it up with all sorts of pens. I was particularly jealous of the set of pencils they gave her, with the most wonderful range of rainbow colours. They took her on outings after school and on Saturdays. She went to see *Chitty Chitty Bang Bang* at the movies, during which she was allowed to eat popcorn and a choc-top ice-cream. Sister Hodgeson hugged her quite a bit.

Ruthy said at first this was fine. She was the centre of attention and nothing she said or did made either of them cross – not that Ruthy caused grief at home anyway as a rule. But after a while she found it a bit smothering. She felt like a little doll they wanted to play with. She was paraded in front of their friends like a wind-up toy. She grew tired of been chucked under the chin and asked to sit on the knees of all their old friends. She particularly disliked it when they took her to visit Sister Hodgeson's father in the rest home. His legs were very bony and she kept slipping off them when they put her on his knee. He liked to pick his nose, and sometimes did it the whole way through a visit. He flicked little bits of goobies all over the room, and Ruthy constantly panicked that one would flick on to her and she would scream or faint. He liked to force her mouth open so he could look at her teeth. Sometimes he put his fingers in her mouth and counted them over and over. This made the Hodgesons laugh, but not Ruthy. She told me she was sorely tempted to clamp her teeth shut on his yellow, gnarly fingers, but thought she'd better not. They were so fragile she imagined they would snap off in her mouth and she might accidentally swallow one of them. This might lead to her being taken by ambulance – or police car, given biting off old people's fingers was probably an offence – to the Royal Adelaide Hospital to have them surgically removed from her stomach so they could be sown back on. We agreed this would not be worth the pleasure of biting him.

Her second least-favourite person to visit was a mutual friend of the Hodgesons' and Aunty Maisie called Sister Everude. Well, you can already guess the jokes about that name, but the sad thing was they weren't really jokes because she was rude. She would look at you for a minute and then pass judgement.

'Dorcas Wilson. Your hair is too long. It's dangerous. It will get caught up in machinery and scalp you. Then you'll be a little bald girl. How would you like that?' Or 'Dorcas Wilson. Don't slouch like that. Pull those shoulders back. You don't do justice to what God's given you, girl, and that's disrespectful to the Lord. If you were my girl, I'd strap a back straightener to your waist.'

As well as saying rude things, Sister Everude made chicory essence coffee, which is just about the most disgusting thing in the world you can drink. When Ruthy visited her with the Hodgesons, she insisted Ruthy have a mug full of the nasty stuff. Mr Hodgeson realised she hated it and took her cup to the sink and tipped it out when Sister Everude wasn't looking. He would turn and wink to show they were part of a conspiracy.

Someone Ruthy didn't mind visiting was a very old lady in the rest home. Her name was Sister Ida Rose, and the Hodgesons visited her because she was on their list for a welfare visit. Ruthy said they would take her into the room, sing out hello to Ida Rose, and then leave Ruthy alone with her while they joined other welfare visitors in the tearoom for a good old natter. Apparently there was more tea drinking, cake eating and gossiping between the welfare visitors than actually sitting with the people on their lists.

Ida Rose was a tiny little woman propped up in bed with lots of pillows. She had silvery hair and beautiful soft pink skin. She smelled of talcum powder and roses. Although she was fairly blind, her hearing was top notch, so Ruthy could have conversations with her. She asked Ruthy all sorts of questions about who she was and what she liked to do. Ruthy said they were good questions, not the silly sort most grown-ups asked you like 'Do you like school?' and 'What do you want to be when you grow up?' Ida Rose asked questions such as 'What do you think of the fact that women can't hold office in our meeting?' or 'Have you had much to do with computers and what do you think of them?' She only spoke about herself if Ruthy asked her a question, but when asked, she would tell the truth and wouldn't do a child's version of the answer.

Ruthy asked her what it was like to be very old, and was she scared of dying. Ida Rose told Ruthy you sort of sink into being old without really noticing, and because it happens gradually you get used to it. She said the best thing about it was not having much to worry about except whether they'd put too much salt in the soup. The worst thing about it was that bits of you stopped working properly, you had to let strangers wash you and wipe your bottom, and you forgot bits of who you were sometimes. She said all we really had in life was the story of who we were that lived in our minds, and for some old people, even those stories slipped away. It was like watching your favourite movie with some scenes removed.

She wasn't afraid of dying. She knew a lot about it because she had been a nurse in a palliative care hospital when she was a working person. She said bits of your brain start to die so you don't really know what's going on anyway. She told Ruthy the last sense you lose is your hearing, and so you should always talk to a dying person because that may be the last link they have to this world. Likewise, you should be careful what you talk about in their room when they are on their way out, because you think they can't hear, but they might be able to, and some people's last moments were awful because stupid staff or family members would say mean things about them that might be their last sounds on earth. She also told Ruthy she wasn't worried about dying because many times during her life she'd wished she was dead. She suffered badly from depression, which was considered a weakness or a lack of faith in our church, and she had often wished she could just go to sleep and never wake up.

'Living's not for everyone, Ruthy. Living's not for everyone. And loneliness is everything it's cracked up to be,' she said. Ruthy told me she filled up many pages in her notebook with Ida Rose stories and wisdom. I was pretty sure I'd like Ida Rose too. I made a list of questions I would like to ask her and passed them on to Ruthy in the hope she might try some out on the dear old lady.

1. *Isn't it unfair that only Christadelphians will have a chance to live eternal life? And given there's not many of us, how was God thinking we'd get around to saving everyone anyway?*

2. *Why does God think you should stay with your husband or wife for your whole life? What if your husband gets a weeping ulcer like King Henry VIII and it stinks constantly? What if he grows mean? What if you love animals and he won't let you ever have any?*

3. Why are some sins considered worse than others? If Jesus was without sin, but then he did a little sin, he would no longer be sinless, regardless of the size of it, so how does the order of sins work, and why isn't there a list in the Bible of different ones with different penalties by them? I find it very hard to believe that Jesus didn't at least take the last egg sandwich at the Sunday school lunch even if someone else would have liked it.

4. Why can't girls do things in our church? What was God thinking when he put all that stuff in about women being quiet and covering their heads and obeying blokes? Is God a bit biased to boys, and if so, why is that?

5. What do you think would have happened if God had been a girl?

6. Can you please tell Ruthy quite a bit more about when you suffered from depression. What exactly does it look like? Could it possibly be the same as head days and cross days? Did you yell at people you loved when you had depression? Is it children's behaviour that causes it? When you wanted to die when you had it, did you ever consider getting on a plane instead? Can children cure depression in people if they behave extremely well and refuse to have pets? If you don't have depression now, what was the magic thing that made it go away?

I thought I'd just start with my first six questions and see what happened from there.

All three of us agreed that living with other people was a bit weird, because every family and every house seemed to have its own strangeness about it. Ruthy said the Hodgesons were pretty clean generally, but not as fussy as Mum, and that Mr Hodgeson missed the toilet bowl quite a lot and left bits of beard in the sink when he shaved. Ruthy had taken to tearing off bits of toilet paper and covering the seat and the floor where her feet would touch the ground before she sat down. This had resulted in her completely blocking the toilet one night so nothing would flush, and Brother Hodgeson had to kneel down with a big rubber plunger to unblock it. He didn't get cross though, which was quite relieving, and Ruthy was secretly glad he had to kneel on his own urine dribbles to fix it, because this seemed a bit like justice.

We kids would meet in the ladies' toilets at the meeting on Sundays to swap stories, and sometimes Ruthy cried, which made me cry, and we both wished we could just go home and it would be like it used to be.

Aunty Maisie caught us crying one Sunday, and issued an ultimatum that we were not to speak to each other during the week because I upset the little ones. This meant we had to save everything up for small pieces of time on Sundays and had to find hidey places to meet where we wouldn't be overheard. The best place was behind the store shed in the carpark, and all three of us would run there when we got a chance to see if one of the others was free.

Ruthy's other big problem, besides the bathroom situation, was her writing. It was lovely at first to be given books and pens, but the Hodgesons nagged her to read her notebooks to them. This was definitely not allowed. We had a big rule that no one ever opened Ruthy's notebooks, and even I didn't disobey, although to be honest that was largely because I just wasn't that interested. She started to worry that they snuck in and read them when she was asleep or playing outside. This became a constant worry for her.

She decided to set a test to see if she was right. The first thing she did was to find a hiding place for her notebooks. This wasn't an easy thing to do in a house you don't know, because it was hard to work out what the Hodgesons might use regularly.

She wasn't going to school, so she couldn't ask a friend to look after them for her. In the end, I asked Anne King if she would care for Ruthy's books, and she said of course she would. Ruthy and I agreed she was trustworthy. We met behind the store shed one Sunday for the handover, and Anne offered to cut her wrist a bit if Ruthy wanted to do the same to make a blood oath, but Ruthy said that was okay, she trusted her. I find a bit of blood quite interesting, but it makes Ruthy queasy.

Ruthy kept one book as her real notebook, and one that would be her test one. She found a loose panel in her wardrobe she could put the real one in and left the test one under her pillow. At first in the pretend one she wrote just ordinary accounts of what was happening. This was to set the scene of the crime and to give us time to work out our strategy for the trap.

We invited Anne King to join us behind the store shed between the Memorial Meeting and Sunday school to work out what Ruthy should write as bait. Each of us agreed to think hard about it all week and to come up with at least three good ideas. Here are the ideas we pooled.

Caleb's list:

- *Brother Hodgeson smells like poo*
- *Brother Hodgeson breaks wind all the time*
- *Brother Hodgeson is a big burper*

We said thank you very much to Caleb, because he had tried very hard, but we didn't think any of these would get the reaction we were seeking. Caleb said he didn't mind. But he was pretty sure his points would be right anyway because Brother Hodgeson had the look of a burper.

Anne's list:

- *Sister Hodgeson's cooking is making Ruthy ill*
- *There are hundreds of cockroaches living under the bathroom carpet*
- *Ruthy would like to watch* Bandstand *with Mr Brian Henderson*

We agreed that the *Bandstand* idea should be on the short list, because they seemed so eager to please Ruthy. They didn't watch it, and if they suddenly turned it on or asked if she'd like to see it, we knew we'd be on to something.

Ruthy's list:

- *Aunty Maisie says Sister Hodgeson is vain and a terrible cook*
- *Aunty Maisie says she wants to pick Ruthy up from the Hodgesons' and keep her at Aunty Maisie's place because the Hodgesons are spoiling her*
- *Aunty Maisie is going to make Ruthy leave behind all the clothes and presents the Hodgesons have given her when it's time to go home*

We congratulated Ruthy for this set. It was clever to use Aunty Maisie, who was like a Christadelphian army general, to lure the Hodgesons into a trap. The trouble was, even if they were brave enough to mention any of these ideas to Aunty Maisie, it might all be kept from us, so we might not know what effect we had had.

I waited patiently until we'd worked through all the other lists because, as Dad used to say, you're not a leader if there's no one following you. In the past, when the others had refused to participate in my plays, or to do marching drills to the records in the backyard, Dad had said my problem was that I just ran very fast in front of people rather than taking them with me. He said I had to work more on my psychology. I had to walk back to where people were, take them by the hand and lead them to the new place, listening to them first to work out what story would work for them, instead of just imposing my view.

So I decided I would hear everyone else's ideas first, respectfully discuss them, and then drop mine, which would be the winning one, right at the end. That way everyone would have had a turn, even though it would be a bit of a waste of time. I only had the one thing on my list, but I knew it was a beauty.

My list:

- *Write that you are planning to run away*

Because Caleb was a runner, and everyone knew about it, I thought they'd believe this one easily. And there is no way the Hodgesons would want anyone else to know Ruthy had scarpered while they were caring for her.

There was a unanimous chorus of yes from the trio of fellow conspirators, and we spent the rest of our meeting discussing exactly what Ruthy should write. Caleb insisted we give the mission a code name. The three of us didn't think this was a good idea but went along with it given we had clearly rejected all his bodily functions suggestions for Brother Hodgeson. We called it operation Fly Away. We also gave in to using a code suggested by Caleb. 'The pigeons are pooing' would mean there was a problem, and 'the cat's had kittens' would mean it was going well.

Caleb's advice would turn out to be useful.

* * *

During Sunday school, instead of writing notes about what the teacher was saying as Ruthy usually liked to do, she drafted her letter so we could hear it before we disbanded for the week. We all ran to the usual spot as soon as the last prayer was over, even though we would get into trouble for holding up the adults who wanted to take us straight home.

Here is what Ruthy planned to write.

I am so lonesome for Dorcas and Caleb and Mr Driver next door. I am forbidden to ring them during the week and it is breaking my heart. None of us have been allowed to ring Mr Driver, and I am very worried about him because he is an old, old man with a wooden leg from the war, and might have fallen in his shed and hit his head. I have nightmares about him calling for help with no one able to hear him. In my dreams I hear him wail: 'Ruthy! Ruthy! Come to my aid, my angel!' I have undertaken the research about how to get back to check on him. If I take the number 19 bus into Grenfell Street in the city, and walk along until I see the sign for the number 23 that will take me to St Bernards Road, I think I can find my way home from there. I plan to leave next Friday morning after Brother Hodgeson leaves for bowls. I will slip out the back door when Sister Hodgeson isn't looking. I can't bear the worry any longer.

I thought the bit about 'come to my aid, my angel' was bunging it on a bit thick, but otherwise this was a work of art. For the first time in ages, it was almost fun to go our separate ways, operation Fly Away in train.

We were all desperate for a report. Anne King rang me on Wednesday night, and I was allowed to take the call because she was a King girl. I told her I hadn't heard anything, of course, and she should ring Ruthy.

She rang back an hour later to say that Ruthy couldn't say much because she was being overheard, but she sounded very happy and said 'the cat has had kittens'. We tried to work out a way to tell Caleb, but even Anne King was scared to ring because Aunty Maisie would answer. She came up with the brilliant idea that she could ring and ask Aunty Maisie if she would like a kitten because they had a spare one from a new litter. We knew Aunty Maisie hated cats, but with a bit of luck Caleb would hear about the call and know that things were going to plan.

We all met behind the shed as soon as possible the following Sunday, and Ruthy was ecstatic. She said the first thing that happened was that Sister Hodgeson asked her what she'd meant when she said the cat had kittens. This confirmed her theory that they were always listening to her on the phone. She said Anne King's cat had given birth and they were all very excited about the dear little babies.

The next thing that happened was that all the money she had saved disappeared from her purse. She guessed this was so she didn't have the bus fare on Friday morning. The third thing that happened was that the Hodgesons asked if there was anyone she hadn't heard from for a time she would like them to call, and Ruthy said she would make a list for them. Finally, Mr Hodgeson stayed home from bowls on Friday morning, and when Ruthy decided to try opening the back door to see what happened, she found it locked for the very first time.

At first we were jubilant. We had proved that the scheming Hodgesons were untrustworthy, just as we expected. But after the excitement wore off, Anne King asked what would happen next.

Ruthy said one thing that would happen is she would have to be careful what she wrote even in her hidden book and would keep looking for new hiding places for it. But she admitted that the cost of being right was that her guardians now never let her out of their sight and were even more smothering than ever. We decided she had better write something about wondering why she had been so silly as to think she would run away when the Hodgesons were the best people ever, and hope this would create some ease. She agreed and later told us that after she'd done this there was a noticeable sense of relief about the house, but that they remained watchful.

The only other tricky thing about our campaign was that Aunty Maisie stomped up to Sister King the following Sunday asking what all this nonsense was about kittens. Anne's mum asked Anne afterwards why she had rung Aunty Maisie and offered her a non-existent cat. Anne said none of the kids at Sunday school liked Aunty Maisie, and knew she was allergic to cats, and she did it as a dare. Anne's mum said, 'Well. I'm not sure that's a nice thing to do, Anne, and I'd rather you didn't do it again,' but Anne said her mum gave her father a look that said, 'Isn't that a hoot?' and that night when Anne listened at their door she heard them laughing about it. They said it was a brilliant idea and perhaps they'd sneak a couple of big cats into Aunty Maisie's old Holden and let them piss all over it because nothing, absolutely nothing, gets that smell out of a car.

The best thing about Ruthy staying with the Hodgesons though, as far as I was concerned, was the message Ida Rose sent back to me. Ruthie had written it down carefully in her notebook, so she could relate the old woman's thinking as accurately as possible. Ida had dictated a letter for me, which I thought showed she was a very serious and respectful person. Ruthy said Ida was very patient, saying a few words slowly in little bundles so Ruthy could get them all down.

Dear Dorcas,

Thank you for sending me an excellent set of questions. I hope you don't mind, but I don't always have a lot of breath, so I thought I'd spend it all on the answer to question number six. I suffered from depression most of my life. I use the word 'suffered' because it's a good word to describe how you feel. Life seems desperate and hard and some days you can't find any light in it. You feel very heavy inside and you don't always have energy left over to deal with life's problems or the people around you. I have a feeling from what your sister has told me that your question relates to your mother. If it does, it's not your fault if she is depressed. It's something that happens in the chemicals in your body, and it's not due to naughty children or failing to pray.

Do you know much about the Dorcas of the Bible? She was a good person who helped other people. But did you know she was so good that when she died and they told Peter the Apostle about it, he came to see her body and brought her back to life?

Although it's not your fault if your mum is very sad, remember Dorcas's good works, and see if you can help your mother by helping others. Even if the value you bring is for other people and not your mother, she will appreciate it when she comes home and you are all together again, and it will make her proud and happier.

But did you know that Dorcas means gazelle? I think this might be appropriate for you, Dorcas. Gazelles are very adaptable, even if they are living in a desert. They can run very fast, and always keep their heads held high. They make different sounds to signal annoyance and danger. They do this to help keep others safe. So stay adaptable at the Roystons, even if it feels like a desert, keep your brother and sister safe as you have always done, and most of all, keep your head high like the gazelle you are.

Your friend in Jesus,

Ida Rose

CHAPTER 18

Mum didn't contact us.

She didn't ring us and she didn't really write to us, even though Ruthy sent her a letter every week at the same time she posted one to Daniel. In the first three weeks we were apart, we all received one postcard each. It was exactly the same card and said exactly the same thing on the back.

Dear children, I am having a wonderful adventure and hope you are too. I love you very much and will see you soon. Grandma and all your Scottish relatives send their love.

As Ruthy said, would it have hurt to have at least put our own names on the cards? What I hadn't said to Ruthy is that the writing didn't exactly look like Mum's writing, and I wondered if she'd even written them.

Dad said Mum didn't call us because Grandma couldn't afford Mum to make four different calls every week, and that he would tell us every Sunday how she was going. The trouble was I didn't believe the reports he gave us. He claimed she rang him on Saturday nights, and he said things like 'she's finding the weather very cold', or 'she's enjoying spending time with all her cousins and sisters', or 'Grandma is so glad to see her', but I could have just as easily made up those sentences. He also didn't sound convincing when he told us. There was no bounce in his voice, he didn't look us in the eye, and he wouldn't elaborate. I worried and worried and worried about what it all meant, but when I tried to talk to Dad about it, he just said everything was fine and we should be happy Mum was having a great time with her family. He wouldn't be drawn into conversation about when she might return either. 'After Christmas' seemed like an eternity to all of us.

Sitting next to him on Sunday mornings, I felt him grow sadder and sadder. He didn't sing with the same energy. Usually he would lift up his face as though he was singing to the top of the enormous pipe organ in our main hall, and really belt out the hymns in his lovely tenor voice. When he sang the harmony, it was as though he was racing around us, weaving in and out of our song, sometimes making us go all quiet and thoughtful, and sometimes raising us up to feel the joy he felt when he offered God a hymn. He really did sound as though he was praising God when he sang, and although I wasn't sure how I felt about this God fellow sometimes, Dad's certainty made me feel comforted and hopeful, peaceful and confident. Every Sunday I would feel I could be a better child, a better friend, a better daughter, and for at least an hour or two, I was able to be the perfect child I so badly wanted to be despite the devil in me.

But now he kept his face on the page as though he had never seen the words before, as though they were a surprise and he had to follow them one by one. These days he sang the main tune quietly along with everyone else, and never offered the harmony, even though I knew he knew the funny notes by heart, the ones that sounded so discordant if sung alone. Now I couldn't always even pick out his voice. Since Mum left, it sounded as though he'd lost his puff, his ability to take others with him to a holy place, and it felt as though perhaps he didn't believe any more. Hymns sounded sad rather than reverential and joyful to me now.

He had grown thinner. Never a fleshy person in the first place, he started to look like the photos you see of people who walked out of the concentration camps after the war. Well, perhaps that is an exaggeration – perhaps Peter was right when he called me Dorcas-prone-to-exaggeration-Wilson – but his skinniness was noticeable. He had put more holes in his Sunday belt and his pants had a gathered look about them. His cuffs hung over his shoes, and I noticed he must have stepped back on them a few times because they looked a bit grubby and raggedy. His suit jacket used to fit him just right, but now it had lots of room between his buttons and his tummy. And his white shirt gaped around his neck, even with a tie knotted around it. He wore the same blue tie every week, even though it had a gravy stain on it. He didn't smell of Old Spice. He smelled of unaired suit and the air-conditioner stuff Mum sprayed in the car.

He hadn't been to the barber since Mum had left and the curls in his black hair were unruly and had lost their shine. The tiny bits of grey he used to have just at the temples had spread like an infection down his sideburns and into the big curls at either side of his part. Dad grew a beard very fast, and although he shaved every morning, by the time he got home from work, you could see the dark shadow where the beard was desperately trying to force its way onto his face. Some nights, before Mum had left for Scotland, he would chase us and rub his bristly chin on our faces until we worked ourselves up to something that was a cross between hysterical laughing and screaming in fear. One Sunday I was pretty sure he hadn't shaved at all.

Caleb still liked to shine Dad's shoes, and on Sundays would insist Dad took them off when he visited Aunty Maisie for tea, so he could take them to the laundry for a good going-over. Caleb said it was obvious Dad wasn't cleaning them himself, and that worried all of us, because Dad and Mum had always been sticklers for clean shoes.

When Caleb told Ruthy and I about the shoes we both gasped, and Ruthy covered her mouth with her hands in shock. I reminded them of what Mum called one of her 'maxims': 'There's no excuse for being any less than clean, polite and well shod'. But then I felt sad because I heard myself say, 'Mum used to say,' rather than using the present or the future tense. I wondered what my future tense would be.

But the worst sign of all was the hanky. Dad always had a clean, ironed hanky in his pocket. It had to have no stains on it at all for Sunday use, and he liked to match the stripe on his hanky with the colour of his tie. And it wasn't that Mum wasn't around to do it for him, because this was something Dad did himself. After Mum had done the ironing in the lounge room, she would sit with a cup of tea and Dad would press his hankies and iron them into exactly the size and shape he liked for his pockets.

I had asked Dad if I could borrow his hanky one Sunday when my nose threatened to drip all over my Bible, and he stuck his hand in his right coat pocket and out came ... nothing. I wiped my nose on the hem of my dress, not because my sleeve wasn't available, but because I didn't want him to see my lip tremble and a tear squeeze out of my eyes.

Realising he didn't have a hanky felt like a huge shock. It felt as though someone had hit me hard in the stomach. Who did he have to love him and take care of him now? We hardly saw him, and he was so alone all those nights after work. Who was feeding him and washing his clothes and asking about his day? People often told me I looked like my mum except for the red hair. I wondered if this was why, when Dad turned to me sometimes, his face seemed so sad, and he quickly looked away. I wondered that morning, not for the first time, what would happen to us all if Mum took too much longer to come home.

CHAPTER 19

Ruthy was coping by writing and writing and I was picking great sores in my head and Caleb was beside himself.

He said he kept wetting the bed and that made Aunty Maisie cross, and she had taken to insisting he wear a big nappy at night like the ones she put on Grandpa. This made him cry and cry. He said she didn't say mean things to him or smack him, but she was like a strict sergeant major and just roared out rules and commands to be obeyed, and he was always frightened. She made him eat porridge for breakfast, which he hated, and once he chucked it up on her new breakfast banquette, which she'd had reupholstered with orange and avocado flowers on it. This made her very angry. She gave him a rag and told him to clean it up and then made another bowl of porridge and put it in front of him when he had stopped puking.

She slicked down his cowlicks with too much sugar in the water, and he said he looked as though he had horns when he went to school. He rushed to the long drinking troughs at school and stuck his head under a tap most mornings to try to fix them, but that meant water sloshed all over him and down the front of his clothes. Bruce Wauch and Barry Plover called out, 'Wilson's a wetter! Wilson's a wetter!', and his friend Lincoln punched Barry at recess time and told him to lay off or he'd piss on his sports shoes when he wasn't looking. So Caleb stopped trying to tame the mess with water and decided to try to trim the sugar-starched horns himself with crimping scissors from the art classroom. This was, to say the least, an unsuccessful strategy, and Aunty Maisie had a fit when he went home with jagged hair and bald patches at his forehead and crown. She marched him to a local barber who shaved almost all of his beautiful snow-white wavy hair off, and he wet the bed again that night despite the nappy. Aunty Maisie said he was an evil boy who did it deliberately, despite him promising and promising that wasn't true.

He was at least able to go to our usual school, which was a blessing for him compared to Ruthy and I, because at least he had his friends and some things seemed familiar. At Sunday school, I would hand him a note for Maynard, and he would sneak an answer back to me the next week. He had to be very careful Aunty Maisie didn't see it in case she decided to take it hostage. Maynard's notes were reassuring and newsy, and some weeks it was the only thing I had to hang on to from one weekend to the next. Caleb said his teacher asked him if he was okay, and he said yes, but he wished he had said, 'No, I am living with an evil witch and someone needs to rescue me.' But he knew that would just make Dad cross.

At least on Sundays he spent more time with Dad than we did, which I was jealous about, but which seemed fair given he was just a little boy. Sometimes Dad took him for drives in the car or to pick up things for Aunty Maisie from the few shops that opened on Sundays. They brought Grandpa out of his sunroom bedroom when Dad visited, and Caleb rather liked sitting next to Grandpa, who didn't say much but whom Caleb felt sent out kindly sorts of feelings into the room. Caleb liked Grandpa's white moustache and big hands and the fact that he always wore a tartan waistcoat, suit trousers and black shoes and socks even when it was very hot. He cleaned Grandpa's shoes for him every day, and if Grandpa wasn't well enough for him to take them in to see him, he left them on a rag by the door for Aunty Maisie to take in when she dressed him. He admired Grandpa's gold Waltham pocket watch he was given as a retirement present, and which he was never without. Caleb thought he might sleep with it on but he snuck into Grandpa's room one night and found it on his night stand. Most Sundays Grandpa let him open it up and put it to his ear.

He was still obsessed with the idea that Dad was going to be sacrificed, and every Sunday asked Ruthy if she had done more research on how we could prevent it from happening. He was sure that we had been farmed out to different families because Mum wasn't coming back and Dad was going to be hung on a tree branch with nails like Jesus. He said he couldn't cope with living with Aunty Maisie forever and we had to do something to stop Dad from being crucified.

One of his theories was that Mr Bednarski had sent Mum away so she couldn't stop him from sacrificing Dad on account of Mr Bednarski being a Jew and that was who had done Jesus in. And because Mr Bednarski also had a building business, Caleb was sure this meant he would have the materials needed to nail Dad up in a cemetery when the time came. It was all he wanted to talk about when we caught up, and it didn't matter what we said to him, he was quite convinced he had it right.

He would become so upset when Dad was due to leave after dinner on Sunday night that Dad would promise to come to see him after the evening meeting to say goodnight and sit with him until he went to sleep. I only know this because Aunty Maisie told Sister Everude who told Sister Jack who told Anne King's mum who told Anne who told me.

Caleb wrote a letter to Daniel and asked Ruthy to post it for him. It was already sealed when he handed it to her, so Ruthy didn't like to open it. I was quite happy to do so, but she told me it wasn't our business and what could it say anyway? Suddenly there were more letters from Daniel than ever before, and all of them were handed over by Dad to Ruthy on Sundays. Ruthy said some of them didn't make sense to her. It was as though Daniel thought he had explained things to us when he hadn't and was referring to situations he'd never written about before. She handed them on to me, and I studied them carefully. After reading a few I had a suspicion that at first I didn't want to consider, but did seem pretty obvious to me. I thought Daniel had written to us a lot more than we knew, and something had happened to some of his letters. And I had a horrible feeling I knew what it was.

It prompted me to write to him myself. I sent him all three of our addresses just to be sure he knew where to find each of us, and I wrote the following:

Dear Daniel,

First, we miss you like mad. I hope you are impressed that I started with 'first' and not 'firstly'. As you can see, Ruthy is rubbing off on me.

I have read the last three letters Ruthy passed on to me. I'm not sure if you know this, but we usually only get a letter from you every six weeks or so. I now think you've been writing to us much more often than that. I wouldn't like to say what happened to them, but the good news is at the moment Dad is handing them straight over to us, so you can be pretty sure we will see them all at least for the time being.

I don't want to worry you because I am sure you have enough to worry about as it is, but I don't know what's going on. We don't know when Mum will be back, and it is very hard on Ruthy, and Caleb in particular. If you have any news, can you send it to me, or ring me on the number I put on the back of the envelope? If you know anything hard, can you tell me first so we can work out how to tell the little ones?

Dad is getting very skinny and he doesn't sing the tenor bit in the hymns anymore, and he doesn't have a hanky in his pocket, even a snotty one. I am sorry I haven't written to you before but you know what I'm like and I know Ruthy does it for all of us. Please ring me if you can. We are sad, but we are okay so don't worry.

Love Dorcas

PS And we really miss you and I wish you were home.

PPS I don't care what Peter Royston says, whatever happened you were right.

PPPS I was considering marrying Peter Royston if a knight didn't show up, but I would rather live in Peter's old footy boot with his socks after a long game in summer than live with him now, so don't worry about him being your brother-in-law.

One night after dinner the phone rang and Aunty Jean answered it. Her voice sounded weird straight away. She said, 'She isn't here right now but I can take a message,' and I thought that was strange for a minute because all the 'shes' in the house were definitely home. I wondered if it was a boy for one of the girls but thought that unlikely. I had a feeling it was Daniel, but I couldn't be sure, and there was no point making a fuss about it. I went to Uncle Paul's room to ask if I could ring Daniel, but he said it would be best to ask Aunty Jean first, so I gave that up as a bad joke.

I had posted the letter to Daniel on a Monday, and the following Monday he wrote back.

Dear Dorcas,

I tried to call you but Aunty Jean said you were out. I hope you were doing something fun.

I have written to Ruthy almost every week, so it is strange you haven't had many letters from me. I'm glad Dad is passing them all on to you.

I don't know any more than you do really. I have tried to talk to Dad about it but he just says Mum is on a holiday and will be home soon. I'm sure that's right. I rang Ruthy last week and she cried on the phone but she said the Hodgesons are very kind to her and she doesn't mind too much. I'm not sure that's true. I rang Caleb and he seems sure Dad is going to be crucified. Where on earth did that come from? I felt a bit worried about him, but I'm sure Aunty Maisie will make sure he is okay.

Try to comfort the little ones as much as you can. I am going to ring Mr Driver to see if he has any news we don't have. I miss you, Dorcas, and thank you for looking after the babies and for writing to me.

Love you always.

Your big brother,

Daniel

Well, I must have read that letter about twenty times the first night I got it. It made me sad, happy, sad, happy, sad and then happy. But most of all, it made me feel relieved that my big brother knew how we felt and was going to try to get more information. I could have kicked myself for not thinking of Mr Driver. I bet he knew stuff we didn't. For the first time in weeks, that night I didn't pick the sores in my head and I didn't have nightmares.

The next Sunday behind the store shed at church we all met up and swapped any news we had. Caleb looked a bit shocking with his head almost shaved. I could tell when Dad first saw him on Sunday morning he wasn't at all pleased, but there wasn't much he could do about it. Caleb said he was teased at school about it and the nasty boys called him Caleb the Bald Eagle. I thought it might have been worse, but anything called out in a nasty way sounds upsetting, even if it's 'Beautiful! Beautiful!'. It's often not about the words, I reckon.

Caleb was even more certain now this was all part of a lead-up to Dad being sacrificed. He said Lincoln told him at school that they shaved the heads of sympathisers in the war, and he didn't know exactly what that meant, but he had a lot of sympathy for Dad, so he could see this was a bad sign.

I wish now I had listened to Caleb more carefully, or asked him more questions about what he was thinking, or found a way to reassure him. I wish I had told Dad about how upset he was getting. But I didn't.

CHAPTER 20

I've heard grown-ups say, 'Be careful what you wish for'. I know what that means now.

It had seemed so unfair that Dad had dinner at Aunty Maisie's every Sunday, which meant that Caleb got to see him for so much extra time. And a couple of times he went to tea at the Hodgesons'. But he never came to Henley Beach. So when I heard Aunty Jean answer the phone as I walked past it, and was pretty sure I heard Dad's voice, I hoped this meant it was my turn to have him come over to tea. I was afraid to ask outright, and Aunty Jean just gave me a glowering look until I had walked away. I huddled near the door, but I couldn't hear anything. I was so keen to see him that I actually did some Sunday school homework to show Aunty Jean to get into her good books.

I took it to her at the time I was expected to present for inspection, and was pleased to see that Uncle Paul was already home, which surprised me because he was often late from work, but I'd never known him to be early. I thought perhaps Dad was coming for tea that very night and Uncle Paul had come home especially early to have time with him too. I wouldn't mind sharing Dad with Uncle Paul. Well, actually I would, but another thing grown-ups say is 'Beggars can't be choosers'.

When I walked into the kitchen, Aunty Jean and Uncle Paul were sitting close to each other at the dining table, leaning in and whispering. For a moment I had a horrible feeling Dad was coming over because I'd done something wrong again. I stood at the kitchen door for a moment, allowing the movie of the last couple of weeks to roll over in my head, but I couldn't put my finger on anything I should worry about.

Since Ida Rose's letter, I really had been trying to do nice things for people like Dorcas in the Bible. I had done Maudie's turn of drying the dishes three times without being asked. I had taken the hoover out and vacuumed the lounge and our bedroom. I'd shined up the kitchen sink with Vim the way I'd seen Aunty Jean do it, and I'd tidied up all the newspapers in the laundry into a neat pile and tied them up with string ready for the rag and bone man.

Aunty Jean realised I was standing watching them, and tapped Uncle Paul on the shoulder. He turned around and looked at me. At that very moment, I heard a car pull up in the driveway, and I just knew it was my Dad.

'Who is it?' I cried out. 'Who is it? Is it Ruthy? Is it Caleb? Is it Mr Driver? Is it Mum? Has something happened to Mum?'

They just stared at me, and there was no colour in Uncle Paul's white face.

I ran to the front flywire door, and wrestled with the snib that kept it closed. It seemed to me that it was deliberately getting in my way so I couldn't get to Dad, who seemed to be just sitting in the car.

Finally I got through the door and ran across the dead grass. I was in my socks, and a bindi stuck into my foot, but I just hopped the last few yards to the car door. I pulled at the door, but Dad still had the little black rubber stopper down, and it wouldn't open. I leaned down to look at him through the glass, and I felt I saw the end of the world on his darling face.

* * *

Ruthy gave me an account of what happened, explained to her by Dad after a visit from the police.

She took a lot of notes after he spoke to her so she could tell me as much as possible, seeing as I wasn't allowed to go home straight away. We went over and over the story together. For a while I just couldn't get enough of it, and needed to talk about every sentence, every thought, every idea, so I could get a feeling for what Caleb had been through. After she told me, I found some paper and made notes of questions I thought she might be able to answer, or at least discuss together. As a result, the story I ran over and over in my head is now quite detailed. On several occasions Ruthy went to Lincoln Waterford's house to ask him what she called supplementary questions. He was very sad and very happy to talk about it and to try to help. He hadn't been to school since, and his parents were making him talk to a priest every day for a while to help him get over what happened.

When Ruthy first turned up at the Waterfords' door, she said Mrs Waterford wouldn't let her inside. She pushed her back on to the porch and asked what she wanted with Lincoln. Ruthy said she thinks she is quite a good mother and was probably worried we would blame her for what happened, but Ruthy told her straight away we didn't, and that we were very glad Caleb had a terrific friend like

Lincoln who really tried to help, and that something would have happened anyway because Caleb was trying hard to rescue Dad. Mrs Waterford stepped towards Ruthy, grabbed her in the tightest hug in the world, and cried and cried. They let her in to see Lincoln, who also seemed wary for a few minutes, and who then also cried and cried and said how sorry he was. He was eager to talk and Ruthy took lots of notes so she could share the story with me.

So from what we can piece together, Caleb had consulted Lincoln Waterford daily about how to stop Dad from being sacrificed. Lincoln had asked his mum, his dad, an old priest and a couple of nuns whether there was anything that could have been done to stop Jesus from being nailed to the cross, but apparently they had said no, he had to sacrifice himself to save the world. This didn't seem fair to me, because I'm not convinced he was really given a choice, even though at our church they said he was. I think this is a bit like saying Daniel had a choice at seventeen about whether he had to be sent to New South Wales, or whether he could be a lawyer when he left school, but when you are brought up to hear the same thing year after year, and told to obey your parents, in my opinion it's pretty hard to pick something you know everyone will be upset about, so I think Jesus, just like Daniel, didn't really have an option.

Lincoln tried to cheer Caleb up by pointing out that our dad wasn't, as far as he could tell, the Son of God or part of the Holy Trinity, whatever that was, and therefore he couldn't be expected to die for everybody. Caleb sent him back to the Catholic experts with this question, which I thought was a good one: 'He may not be *the* Son of God, but could he be *another* Son of God?' Apparently the answer was something along the lines of 'don't be ridiculous', so the boys crossed that off the list of concerns. As a result, in Lincoln's opinion, if they could find a suitable alternative sacrifice, Dad should be okay.

Caleb was much cheered by this advice, but had no clues as to what the alternative sacrifice might be. Caleb remembered that someone or other had sacrificed a sheep, but they felt this would be too cruel and they weren't sure where they'd get one. Lincoln thought Sampson had cut off his hair as a sacrifice, but Caleb said no, some girl cut if off when he was asleep. What they did agree on was there seemed to be a lot of stuff about burnt offerings, so they were settled on fire as part of the deal.

Once again, Caleb's hero and mentor, Lincoln Waterford, stepped into the breach as Ruthy put it. She said this was what very brave people did when something hard had to be done that took courage, so I am happy to agree to this term.

Having given it a lot of thought, Caleb and Lincoln decided that if they could steal a cross from a church and burn it like Joan of Arc, this should do the trick.

Caleb liked the idea of burning a cross because he felt it sorted out the nailed-to-a-cross business, along with the burning of Joan of Arc business, and apparently said, like his favourite character Virgil in *Thunderbirds*, 'Thunderbirds are go!'

The next problem was how to find the right cross. Lincoln Waterford suggested one from our church would work best because it seemed it was our god that was causing the trouble. This confused Caleb, who had been told there was only one God, but Lincoln Waterford said he was sure his god and Caleb's were not the same, and that ours was probably a more junior version. He felt it was likely that our god was like the captain of the Sturt Football Club in South Australia, whereas his god was like the captain of Carlton in the Victorian Football League, which was more important.

Lincoln was shocked when Caleb explained we didn't have any crosses in our church because it was considered worshipping idols. He asked what other sacred objects we had that might serve the purpose, but all Caleb could think of was the little glasses in the wooden trays that held the wine, or the little tin dishes that held the bread. When

Lincoln found out everyone could handle these, and in fact Caleb sometimes had to do a turn drying them in the middle hall after the Memorial Meeting, he was sure they wouldn't fit the bill.

They discussed further the possibility of junior and senior gods, and compared it to whether all the Thunderbirds were equal. They finally decided that our god was probably more like the Brains character because we had to do church exams, whereas Lincoln's was probably more like Jeff Tracy who was an ex-astronaut and founder of the Thunderbirds, and definitely the boss. They agreed that a cross from a more senior god was required.

Lincoln Waterford said they might be in luck, because things had changed at his church that just might sort out the problem. Apparently something called Vatican II happened, which was a really big deal in Italy somewhere. I gather it was a bit like our annual Christadelphian Conference that was held in a different city every year. When it was in Adelaide, we had to hire a whole high school for it. But theirs involved men in white and red robes and hats, whereas we just wore our Sunday best, and I gather there was quite a lot more fuss made about theirs.

The boss of their church, who I take it is the Pope, decided they should make a few changes. The priests in the long white frocks would stop praying to a big cross on the wall with their back to the audience, and would turn around and look at them across a big table with a smallish cross on it. This was ideal for Caleb, who told Lincoln Waterford that perhaps it was in God's plan to save Dad after all, and that's why God did a toy version of the idol they could steal. All they had to do was to snatch one of the new smaller crosses and burn it somewhere.

According to Lincoln Waterford, this wouldn't be too much of a problem because he was in an upcoming Christmas play, and he had a practice straight after school in the church on Thursday night. If Caleb asked permission to go to his house to play after school, they could both turn up to practice and Caleb could check out the cross to see if he thought it would do a bang-up job. They would find a way to snaffle the cross and hide it somewhere overnight. Apparently this wouldn't be too hard, because the practice was in their Sunday school room, not the main bit of the church hall, so it wouldn't be noticed straight away. They could both sneak out of home very early the next morning, meet to burn the booty, and be back in time for school with Dad rendered quite safe.

Lincoln was a bit leery about stealing the cross, and they had a discussion about whether God might strike them dead, or send them boils and leprosy, or take their bikes away as a punishment. But Caleb pointed out that the more senior god probably wouldn't bother about what a kid from a more junior god got up to. He asked Lincoln if Lincoln thought the coach of Carlton would know or care what the coach of Sturt was up to, and they both agreed this would be unlikely, and Lincoln felt more relaxed.

Their scheme ran to plan and they got the cross. They had a lot of discussion about where to burn it. Caleb was sure the tree house was the right place, because Dad had made it, no one would expect them to be there, and because of the beads on the string hanging on the tree. He explained the family string theory to Lincoln, who was quite impressed, and said he'd like to see the beads. He asked if a bead could be added for him, given he was helping to rescue Dad, and Caleb said he'd be happy to discuss this with the three of us when the sacrifice problem was solved.

So the boys agreed to burn the cross in our tree house, and they hid in a tree in the olive grove until Dad pulled out early the next morning to go to work. They had also pinched a lot of candles from the Catholic Church, because Lincoln said there were candles all over the place, and it would help make the sacrifice properly serious. They put all the stolen loot, along with two boxes of matches – Lincoln said they didn't have to steal those because he and Caleb had always agreed a boy should have a box in his pocket for unexpected adventures – on a little branch we regularly used as a narrow table, and discussed the best way to do it.

The main problem was that the cross was metal, and they weren't sure it would burn properly, but Caleb said he'd seen pictures of Joan of Arc where they tied her to a pole and put lots of kindling around her so that she would go up properly, so they built a nest on the floor of the tree house and sat the cross in the centre. Apparently, given it was so hot and dry by then, the pyre went up in no time flat with just a couple of matches.

Of course it quickly spread along the tree branches and the floor caught alight in no time. Lincoln raced down the steps calling for Caleb to follow, but Caleb kept saying he needed to see the cross start to burn, and Lincoln left him to it. Lincoln told Ruthy this was the thing that gave him the worst nightmares. Perhaps if he'd gone back and pulled Caleb out, he could have avoided what happened next. Ruthy told him she doubted it. She said Caleb was a sweet, skinny, sickly boy but he had a big streak of stubbornness and bravery in him, and nothing would have changed his mind. I think this was quite kind of Ruthy, and I wouldn't have thought to say this.

Within minutes our timber picket back fence was ablaze, and Lincoln heard the neighbours start to shout. He ran as fast as he could to the olive grove and climbed a tree, waiting for Caleb to join him. He saw Mr Driver and a tall boy run out of Mr Driver's house to the backyard, and other neighbours come out onto the street, screaming. Mr Driver spotted Lincoln and sent the tall boy to ask him what was going on. Lincoln was crying and said 'Caleb' and pointed to the backyard. The tall boy raced down the drive of our house to the backyard, calling out to Mr Driver that Caleb was in the garden. Lincoln didn't see what happened in the garden but he saw the fire brigade arrive, and then ran home.

The fire destroyed the olive tree, the tree house, the back fence, parts of four neighbouring fences, Mr Driver's greenhouse, Dad's shed and the big shed belonging to the Spinelli family who lived behind us. Luckily a few neighbours were able to manage it until the fire truck arrived, and the firemen put it out before it burned houses to the ground.

The tall boy Lincoln had seen was my brother Daniel. We didn't know it, but he had hitchhiked home and arrived late the night before. He had arranged to stay with Mr Driver until he could ring Dad to tell him he was home and to ask if they could talk. Mr Driver and Daniel were pretty much responsible for saving all the neighbours' houses, but they couldn't save Caleb.

Daniel ran into the fire and pulled him out, which was very brave, and resulted in burns on his arms and legs that meant he had to go in an ambulance to the hospital, but Caleb was already dead when he carried him out to the street screaming for help. Caleb wasn't all burned up, but he had breathed in too much smoke, fallen as he tried to escape, and gone to sleep forever.

Ruthy told me they found the cross intact in the fire mess. She had gone to look for the string with our beads on it, but it had been burned up. She said there was a poetic justice in that, which I don't understand, but I liked the sound of the word poetic given everything was so sad.

CHAPTER 21

The day after Mum came home was hot, well over ninety degrees, and the road in front of the house shimmered so you weren't always sure where the edges were.

I looked out of the lounge room windows and noticed all the plants were starting to lie over sideways in the heat. They just didn't have the heart to fight the blazing, relentless sun, and I didn't blame them. Mr Driver had been up watering at 6 am, but that wasn't going to make a difference. Today was the day flowers were going to die on him. I did all this noticing not from our lounge room window, but from Mr Driver's.

The day before, the day Mum had actually returned from Scotland at last, Mr Driver had taken his car to the Adelaide Airport to collect Mum from the plane with us, because we

needed two vehicles to fit everyone and all Mum's bags. Dad
had rung Mum to come home, but she had gone on a trip
with a cousin somewhere far away and they weren't able to
contact her. They said they might not see her for weeks and
weeks. We buried Caleb six weeks before she touched down
in Adelaide. Dad asked Ruthy and I to stay with the families
we were living with until Mum came home because he had
lots of things to sort out about Caleb and trying to find
Mum to bring her home. And I think he asked us to stay
where we were because he was so sad and because I should
have told him about the sacrifice thing, and I didn't.

Aunty Jean got crosser and crosser with me because I
picked my head so much in the night, and she would only
let me sleep on one old pillow that was stained yellow from
snot and ear wax and dribble, and which was covered in an
old towel she had pinned around it.

Ruthy and I were allowed to go to the main service when
we buried Caleb, but we had to go home to the Roystons
and the Hodgesons straight after because they didn't think
it was suitable for children to go to the graveside. I think
they were very wrong about that, and I had two kinds of
nightmares for the longest time afterwards.

The first nightmare was like a play where I was a Catholic
priest who was organising the service, but I couldn't get

everyone to behave and line up by the graveside. I wanted them all to march around the grave to 'Colonel Bogey' from *Bridge on the River Kwai*, but they just wouldn't do it properly, even though I waved a big ball of incense at them and threatened I could send them all to Hell. And then we were all standing by the open grave but the dirt kept dropping into the hole and filling up and I had to get down into the grave with a spade to try to get it out. When we finally buried Caleb, Ruthy and I cried and cried and cried, and then Ruthy would say, 'Dorcas, you forgot to put him in the box – we have to do it all again,' and the play would start from the beginning.

The second dream was worse. I think Caleb must have handed it on to me somehow. I was in a graveyard next to the shop from which we bought the fresh bread on Sundays. When I came out of the shop with the bread, I did the wrong thing and started to eat it because it was so soft and fragrant. I noticed Dad on a cross in a small graveyard next to the shop, and ran to him to try to get him down. He said he couldn't get down because I had the bread of life in my hands and I'd picked a big hole in it, and because of that he'd have to die to save Caleb now. He said I'd never believed Caleb's lungs were really bad, and if I hadn't wanted a guinea pig so badly, none of this would have happened. He started to cry big drops of blood, and they splashed on the loaf of bread. He said, 'Take, eat, this is my body. Take, drink. This is my blood,' in his lovely tenor voice, and I walked back to the car with the bloody bread, but there was no one there. I just sat in the back by myself for a long time feeling like a giant stone was sitting in my heart until I woke up crying and scratching my scalp.

I did not know you could feel so bad. I thought Sixpence dying was the worst thing that could happen to me, but I was wrong. Losing Caleb meant I thought about Sixpence all the time again, every day. But at least I had been able to make her a bed and give her a kiss and say goodbye. At least she was in Mr Driver's garden and I would be able to visit her every day when I got home. I didn't know where Caleb was. I didn't have a picture in my head about it. I kept trying to imagine what that place would look like. Would he have a nice tree overhead to keep him cool? Who was asleep next to him? Was it a nice person who would look after him at the resurrection until I could find him? I was pretty sure I was too naughty to be judged and given eternal life when Jesus came back, but if Jesus was at all kind, he would at least drag me out of the mud to check that Caleb had a friend and wasn't too scared before he consigned me to everlasting death.

During the day I would sometimes think Caleb would turn up somewhere, laughing at us for being silly, and I would be able to run and hug him or perhaps give him tickle-death for giving us all such a scare. That would make me so happy for just a minute and then the happiness would burst like a big blister and all the hope would run out like blister water down my foot.

Normally any reason to go the airport was exciting, but it was Caleb in particular who would beg and beg and beg to go to see the planes, so the day we went to get Mum just felt heavy and sad. The Roystons picked up Ruthy and took us both to the airport, and handed us over to Dad. Mr Driver was there. Daniel had travelled in his car with him. There were crowds of people waiting to see people they loved come down the stairs from the front and back of the plane, and across the tarmac, which shimmered in the sun as though there was magic in the air.

Mr Driver stayed a step away from us, to give us family privacy. I took his hand to bring him with us, but he just shook his head no very sadly and gently pushed me forward. We waited and waited. She seemed to be almost the last person to come through the chute. Ruthy and I saw her first and screamed, 'Mum, Mum.' Most people looked so happy to see friends and family when they came out of the tunnel from the plane, but Mum didn't rush to where we stood. She just walked over carefully and elegantly on her high-heeled shoes, looking as though she'd just come fresh from the beauty parlour. She seemed taller and thinner and was wearing a dress I'd never seen before. It was baby blue with an empire line and no sleeves. Her sandals were the same shade of blue, and her bag was white leather with a shiny silver clasp and blue piping. Her hair was a different colour red than usual, and she had changed her eyeliner and mascara. She looked like our mum, but she also didn't look like her.

She walked over to us at a usual kind of walking speed, handed Dad her flight bag and let him give her a peck on the cheek. She dropped to her knees to give Ruthy a cuddle, and then stood up to hug Daniel. Mum wouldn't look at me and ignored me when I tugged at her arm to say hello. I was pretty sure my heart was going to break into pieces and come out of my mouth. I felt sick and confused and embarrassed and left out and ashamed all at the same time. I felt like running and running and running, but at the same time, I could hardly move. Dad pulled me to him and put his arm around my neck, and pushed my face into his shirt, which smelled like ironing aid and sweat and a bit of aftershave I didn't recognise. So part of Mum didn't seem the same, and part of Dad didn't smell the same, and this felt wrong rather than interesting. I was very glad though that he didn't let go until we were walking to the cars. I tried to stop the tears but they just kept falling and falling and I didn't make a noise but I gave up the struggle and let them splash wherever they wanted.

Mr Driver walked a few feet behind us, and when I looked back at him to check he was okay and wouldn't get lost in the crowds, he had the saddest look on his face. When we stepped out of the airport into the scorching sunlight, he asked if I would go in his car to keep him company on the way home. I wanted to be with my family, but Daniel said he'd come with us too, and that I could sit in the front. I didn't argue. This wasn't an arguing day. And, in fact, I didn't seem to have any words available at that point in time. I felt a bit dizzy and as though I was somehow watching myself from a few feet away. It was like watching the old Super 8 movies Dad used to make of birthdays and Christmas. You knew they were real, and you knew you were in them, but somehow they seemed made up.

When we got home, I started to follow Daniel into the house, but he stopped me and he and Mr Driver gave each other a grown-up sort of look. He asked me to go with him for a minute into Mr Driver's house and the three of us walked down the side drive to Mr Driver's back door, and into the kitchen. Daniel took me over to Mr Driver's chair and pulled me to sit on his knee. He hugged me and kissed my hair and stroked my cheek and when I looked up at him, his tears plonked on my face, and I wiped them away with my sleeve. I put my head on his chest and I felt him take a very deep breath.

'Dorcas. You know this is a sad time for everyone, and especially for Mum because she … didn't see Caleb before … before … well … and she's a bit mixed-up and unhappy at the moment. And so she … we … she … thinks it would be a good idea if you stayed here with Mr Driver, just for a few days, until she gets over all her travelling tiredness.'

'But I want to be home in my own room with Ruthy and my things and the wee patch and Mum and Dad and you,' I said. 'I really, really badly want that, Daniel. I've been away for so long. Is it because … because it's my fault … about Caleb?' I asked in a whisper. This was the question I knew had been hanging around in my head ever since the fire. It was like a blowfly in my brain. I could sort of hear it, and it came and went, and it was upsetting, but it would fly away from my thinking when I tried to catch it or swat it. It was definitely a blowfly not a butterfly, and I would quite like to catch it and squash it.

'It's not your fault!' said Mr Driver. 'None of this is your fault. You are a wonderful, wonderful girl and anyone who knows you knows that for sure. It's not your fault your mum is very upset. But I would consider it a great favour to me if you would take my spare room, Dorcas, and just keep me company for a few days. Daniel and Ruthy and your dad are welcome in this house whenever they want to be, and in no time we'll have you back in your room.'

I felt like a block of lead. My legs felt too heavy to carry me. My head felt too heavy for my neck to hold it up. My eyes were leaking, and Jesus was squeezing my heart again. Daniel let me hang on to him for ages, and Mr Driver made him a cup of coffee that he drank by sort of leaning it on the top of my head, which I didn't mind at all. I could hear him slurping and I could hear it going into his insides. I could smell peanut paste and spearmint toothpaste and the funky smell boys had sometimes. I didn't want to move, but eventually we heard Dad calling over the fence, and Daniel hugged me extra tight and nudged me to get up. He stood and looked at Mr Driver, who said, 'It will be all right, son. She'll be fine here. You know she's always been my special girl. I won't let anything happen to her, and when your mum is ready, you'll all find a way forward.'

They shook hands, which reminded me that my brother was a grown-up man now, but then Daniel stepped towards Mr Driver and hugged him briefly before turning and walking out the door. It wasn't just Mum and Dad that looked and smelled different. Daniel had grown taller and more handsome. His shoulders were broader and his bottom was littler. Dad's lovely big brown eyes had copied themselves onto his face, as had Mum's high cheekbones and thin, neat nose. I found myself staring at him very hard, as though I thought he'd leave me again, and I wanted to remember every bit of him I could.

When he left, I just stood at the back door. I didn't know what to do. After an hour that was about a minute, Mr Driver took my hand and led me outside. We walked down to Sixpence's house, and he put another chair next to mine, and said why didn't I tell Sixpence about today. He was pretty sure she would want to know, even all the sad bits. But I couldn't find my words. After a while he led me back inside, and he didn't leave me until he tucked me into bed. He sat next to me, and I could tell he was trying to find kind things to say. I heard his back door open and sat up in bed straight up like a rocket ship. I hoped against hope it was my mum or my dad, but it was Daniel. He had brought over my *Don Quixote* book, which I had forgotten to take back to the school library before I went to the Roystons'. He changed places with Mr Driver and started to read.

I listened to the story I had come to know well. Like me, Don Quixote loved knights and chivalry, and decided he should be a knight-errant in search of adventures. He makes his tired old horse Rocinante take him to an inn he thinks in his mixed-up brain is a castle, and decides to rescue Dulcinea, who is a neighbour who doesn't even like him much and doesn't feel the least need to be rescued. It's a good story, but it's a sad one too, because Don Quixote made everything up and wasn't right in the head and couldn't see the world the way it really was. And I lay there thinking that this was my problem too. I wanted what I wanted and I didn't notice what the real world looked like. In the real world, Caleb had bad lungs and that was more important than me needing a pet. In the real world, Mum was sick and I was naughty and didn't help her enough. In the real world, I was meant to notice my little brother was upset and let a grown-up know properly, but I was too busy with my own dreams that had dried up my brain like Mr Quixote.

After a while Daniel's words drifted away, and I must have gone to sleep for a short time. I woke up to the sound of the two men talking. They had left the door open a crack,

I guess in case I woke up and was a bit scared, and I crawled out of bed and sat at the door to listen.

'She told me not to come here. She told us all not to come to see her,' I heard Daniel say, and then he made a kind of choking noise. 'I told her the time for her to be telling me what to do was over, and that if she didn't want me back in New South Wales, she'd better think twice before she used me to punish Dorcas, or she'd go from two sons to no sons.'

'Good for you, lad. Good for you. I hope it won't take long to sort itself out.'

'How can she be like this?' I heard Daniel ask. 'I just don't understand.'

'I think you do understand, son. Maybe you don't agree, but you do understand. Look what she put you through. After all, it was your mother, not your father, who insisted you leave after … after the incident. I think she's just got so little fuel in her tank that she can't face it when things don't line up properly. She has to tidy them up and trim them straight and try to change their colour, just like she does with all the ladies' hair.'

'She didn't write to me or contact me for the nine months I was away,' said Daniel.

'Not even a note?' I could tell from his voice Mr Driver was very surprised.

'No. Thank goodness for my weekly call from Dad, and all the letters from Ruthy.'

Mr Driver leaned over and I think he patted Daniel on the hand. 'I don't think anything in the world could stop that child writing.'

'I told Mum and Dad last night I'm going to law school next year.' There was a silence.

'I thought your church frowned on going to law school, not that I ever understood why,' said Mr Driver.

'They think it sets you up to make decisions that might be against God's will, or some such rubbish. But I'm going to go. And if they try to fight it, I'll stop going to church. I've had enough of all this Christian goodness. Look where it gets us all.'

'Well, for what it's worth, I've always thought you'd make a very good lawyer. If they don't let you stay with them, son, you can have my spare room here if you'd like it. I'll swap you for some maintenance around the place and free legal advice about how to stop Mrs Kerfoops's cat from urinating all over my veggies.'

They both laughed. It made me smile for a minute. I heard a chair scrape, and Daniel say, 'I'll just look in on her before I go'.

'You do that, son, and don't worry about her. I'll take good care of her. She's my mate.'

I jumped into bed and pretended I was asleep as he quietly opened the door to look in on me. I wasn't ready to talk about what I'd just heard. I put my head under the blankets and thought about Mum not handing over Daniel's letters, and Mum and Dad forbidding Daniel to be a lawyer, and most of all, Mum being the one who made Daniel go away, and some of me was frightened, but a tiny, pinky-toe-sized piece of me thought, *Well I'm not the only one she's pushed away. I'm not the only one she's pushed away. I'm not the only one ...*

CHAPTER 22

A few days' stay with Mr Driver stretched into a few weeks.

Mr Bednarski gave Daniel a job until he could start his university course the following year. Daniel said Dad was quite fine about him becoming a lawyer, and I could tell this made him feel very relieved. He didn't say anything about Mum, and I didn't ask. Dad and Daniel left for work together every morning and went straight in to see Mum as soon as they got home. They took it in turns to slip over to Mr Driver's to see me when they could. Every time I heard Dad or Daniel come through the back door, I hoped they were coming to take me home. But they asked me to stay put for a while longer because Mum was quite unwell and not getting over Caleb's death yet.

The Christadelphians held a special Sunday school meeting for everyone to remember Caleb. They'd waited for Mum to come home to hold the ceremony, but she was too upset to attend, so they went ahead without her. So many people wanted to come that they took over the rear hall because the Sunday school rooms upstairs weren't big enough. Dad attended the Memorial Meeting in the morning and drove back to collect us for the 3 pm service. I was still allowed to go to Sunday school.

I wished Mum had come to the special Caleb afternoon because, although we all cried, it was very lovely. Lots of people got up and said nice things about him, including Dad. I was very worried about him talking to a big group about Caleb, but although his eyes filled with tears, and his voice caught a few times, he made it through and what he said was marvellous.

After the talks and a hymn, we sat in circles and each person had to say something they remembered about Caleb and thank God for giving him to us, even though it was for a very short time. I told them about the time Mum locked me in the laundry for being naughty, and Caleb pushed a lolly snake through the keyhole.

Ruthy wrote a lovely letter to God about him, and one of the Sunday school teachers read it out. It made everyone yowl and bawl it was so good. Dad was very proud of her and planned to frame the letter. I thought this was a great idea, although it would mean there would be Ruthy's letter for Caleb, and Ruthy's church exam prize and Ruthy's writing certificate on the wall, and nothing about being proud of me. But when I thought that thought, I realised it was selfish, and gave Ruthy an extra hug to say how glad I was for her.

School was done for the year, so Ruthy came over to play most days with me in Mr Driver's backyard. She often cried over little things, but always said it was just grief over Caleb, and that I wasn't to worry that it was anything to do with me. I thought this was especially kind and I felt closer to her over those weeks than I ever had before. When we got very sad, we sat on Mr Driver's sofa clinging to each other while he made us tea and biscuits.

Mr Driver arranged for Maynard to come to see me at least once every week. Maynard was very good at knowing when to talk about Caleb, and when to talk about something else completely. He caught me up on all the things that had happened at school while I was at Grange Primary, and often made them sound so entertaining he could make me laugh for a moment. Whenever I did laugh though, I immediately felt bad because it wasn't right to ever feel happy again because of what had happened.

One of the saddest days was when I heard a big noise in my old garden, and climbing onto Mr Driver's fence, I realised that Dad and Daniel were clearing away what was left of the old olive tree. Two men from Dad's work had come with a trailer and a chainsaw to help them, and it took them all day and lots of noise to finish the job. When they drove away, I almost fell off trying to stretch to see what my garden looked like now. All that was left was a sad, bare, burned sort of hole. With the tree gone, it seemed that there was too much light shining into our place. It looked like a desert. It felt like my heart.

Whenever I heard the creak of our back door, I'd rush to a little gap between the timber fence palings between the houses, hoping for a glimpse of Mum. It wasn't her very often. Ruthy said she largely stayed in bed or in the television room. Dad bought her ladies' magazines as a treat on his way home two nights a week. She had returned to eating almost nothing and was usually in bed when Dad got home from work. Ruthy said the only good thing about it all was that she often kept Dad and Daniel company in the evening, staying up quite late with them in the lounge room. There was no Cadbury's chocolate on Friday nights anymore.

One day, watching through the fence, I saw Mum come out of the house with Dad. She was in the same blue dress she was wearing when she walked off the plane, and she actually smiled at Dad when he opened the car door for her. I wanted to rush into my house to ask Daniel or Ruthy what was going on, but given what had happened, I was pretty sure I was cursed now, and if I stepped onto our place without permission, something else bad might happen.

Daniel came out to get something from the shed and saw me peering through the fence. He waved and turned back around to walk down the drive. He met me by Sixpence's grave. He told me Mum was going to see Dr Frayne, and that this was a very good thing. He said Mum had asked after me the night before and got cross when Dad told her he'd spilled oil on my prize night frock. She said she had chosen the material especially for me. I listened to those words and sort of hugged them to my chest when Daniel went home.

The next day, Mum stepped out into the back garden with a basket full of wet washing and started to hang it on the line. I tried not to breathe so she wouldn't notice I was watching her. But when she turned to go back inside, she looked over at Mr Driver's fence. I could tell she saw me, and she stopped halfway to the back stairs and then gave me a little wave.

Well, you'd have thought I'd been asked to throw the ball into Bozo the Clown's face on *The Channel Niners* show, I felt so happy.

Over the next few days, I spent most of my time during the day sitting on an old oil drum near the fence in case Mum came outside to the Hills Hoist. She used to wash every third day, but now that Daniel was home, I thought there was a chance she would wash a bit more often. Mr Driver tried to tempt me away from the fence, but when he realised how determined I was to stay on guard, he left me in peace, and sometimes pulled up a chair and read next to me for company.

After that first time, Mum stopped and waved every time she came outside. And then she would call out, 'Hello, Dorcas. Hope you are staying cool,' or something else that sounded like music to me. I noticed Mr Driver would shake his head and frown when she did this, but he didn't say anything to me because I think my face told him how happy it made me.

It wasn't long until Christmas Day, and I prayed and prayed that I could go home for Christmas, even though I loved Mr Driver very much and would miss him. I was too afraid to ask anyone in my family if this was a possibility. But I asked Mr Driver one night and he said we'd just have to wait to see.

CHAPTER 23

On the morning of Christmas Eve, I was eating toast and tea for breakfast at the table with Mr Driver when Dad walked through the door. I was so happy to see him that this time, as I rushed to hug him, my chair fell backwards to the floor and made a hell of a racket, but no one seemed to care. I threw my arms around his waist, and he just laughed a little laugh, righted my fallen chair and pulled up one for him next to it. Mr Driver stood up and limped to the sink to pour him a cuppa.

'Dorcas,' said Dad. 'There are some things I want to tell you about.' And when he said that, Mr Driver mumbled something about his shed needing a coat of paint and left us to it.

'Dorcas, I think half of you thinks what's happened is your fault, and the other half is my fault,' he said.

'No, Dad! I never thought it was any of your fault!' I said, shocked.

'Well, you should have, because it was all down to me. All of it. It's my fault because your mum gets very down and, when she does, I just tell her to pull up her socks and get on with it. I've made the mistake of thinking depression is something you can choose not to have. I know now I have been very wrong about that. Dr Frayne has wanted her to take a tablet for her sadness for a long time, but I kept thinking the power of prayer should fix it up, and I refused to let her have the tablets.

'When she was in Scotland, she went to a doctor who gave her medication and she started to feel better, but when she heard about Caleb, and thought about coming home to me, who would tell her off about the sadness thing, she got very down again and stopped taking them. I've thought a lot about it and decided these tablets for sadness are no different than Caleb's inhaler for asthma, or a Bex for a headache, and I went with her a couple of weeks ago to see Dr Frayne. He recommended another special kind of doctor who is good at helping with feelings, and he gave her some pills. They have been a big help to her, and she is starting to feel like her old self again. Maybe even happier than that.' Dad stopped for a moment and seemed to be making a close study of the hem of Mr Driver's kitchen tablecloth. 'I'm the reason she had to go to Scotland, and because she went home all you children were farmed out. None of this would have happened if I'd been a better dad and a better husband. I'm sorry, Dorcas. I really am.'

'No, Dad,' I said in the voice I get sometimes when I'm half talking and half crying. 'If I hadn't gone on and on about a guinea pig, and if I hadn't got cross with Caleb for being chesty, he wouldn't have believed you were going to be sacrificed. It's my fault, Dad. It's my fault.' I squeezed my arms around him so tight he had to loosen them a bit to breathe.

'No, my poor girl. No,' was all he could say but he hugged me and rocked me for a long time until I felt almost sleepy with sadness and relief.

'Your mum is missing you and she hopes to start being your proper mum again very soon. She knows that what happened was not your fault at all, but sometimes, even when you are a grown-up, you get very mixed up and put all your feelings onto one person so you can manage. And you were the person she put the feelings on because ... well ... you are both very alike in many ways, and the new doctor your mum is seeing says that parents often struggle with the child who is most like them,' said Dad.

'But I'm not like Mum at all, Dad. She is very well put together and always does the right thing and I am always messy and do the wrong thing.'

Dad laughed.

'Well, your mum has been telling me more about her life in Scotland growing up, and she was always getting into trouble. It's one of the reasons she got on the boat to come out here. She was always fighting with your grandma, and they both thought coming to live with her uncle out here would give her a good start and a bit of space.'

There was a lot of new information here, but the bit that stuck in my mind was the bit about punishing one person.

'Do you think she will ever love me again, Dad?' I asked.

'She never stopped loving you, Dorcas. But you can love people and hurt them at the same time, and that's what I've done to your mother without meaning to. We will always hurt about Caleb, but I'm hoping one day soon we can stop hurting each other. And then we'll have a new string on a tree with all the beads in a row instead of going up and down, and that will mean we are all equal – just different.'

I jumped back from him and just stared at his face. How did he know about the Wilson family string? I couldn't even ask him about it, I was so surprised.

After Dad left, Ruthy and Daniel came in to see me. They seemed very chirpy for some reason, and I hoped it was about me being able to have lunch with them on Christmas Day, but I was too scared to say anything in case I broke a good spell.

I asked Ruthy if she had told Dad about the Wilson string, but she said no, and Daniel asked us to explain what it meant. He was very impressed by the idea, although he looked a bit sad when we told him where his bead had landed. He said Dad always noticed things we thought he didn't, and that seemed to cheer him up a bit. We all agreed we didn't know what would happen next, but Daniel said Dad was back in charge of family things and would make it okay when he could.

Mr Driver had gone to the bakery while we were talking and bought us all a Kitchener bun to have after our sandwich, which was very kind of him, and made me think of Maynard who always shared his with me. One very good thing in the middle of the horribleness was that I knew I had a good friend forever in Maynard.

Daniel and Ruthy went back to our house. Mr Driver invited me into his shed and I helped him paint the wooden beams that held it up. He let me choose the paint colour from his set of sample tins, which he'd salvaged after the fire damage, and I painted the bottom while he painted the higher up bits that went to the roof. He said he approved of my choices, and it would never have occurred to him to paint every beam a different colour, but he liked it and said his favourites were purple, yellow and green. I liked the blue one, the red one and the pink one, and, if I'm honest, even the orange one in the middle.

I felt a bit excited with hope and a bit jittery with worry about whether Mum would ever be ready to see me again. Mr Driver seemed to know how I was feeling, and that it was calming to sit with my friend in his garden, so he brought out an old milk crate with his seat and made a kind of dinner table where we could eat our sausages and mash right next to Sixpence's house. I tried to be all cheerful for him because he'd made a special effort, but he just patted my back and said, 'Nothing wrong with sad at a time like this, Dorcas.' And so I let go of the effort and ate my tea in silence.

I waited and waited and hoped and hoped Mum would call me in to see her that night but she didn't. Mr Driver didn't make me go to bed and let me sit up with him by the television, but eventually I couldn't really keep my eyes open and he helped me climb into bed. He took off my shoes and socks and let me crawl in with my clothes on. He turned out the light but left the crack in the door for me, and I heard him return to his television chair that made a squeaking sound when he pulled the lever to make it a recliner.

I don't know how long I'd been asleep before I realised Daniel was shaking me awake. At first I was frightened about whether something else had gone wrong, but he had put the light on in my room and I could tell he was smiling, and so was Mr Driver standing behind him, who did a little clap of his hands which I guessed was happiness. I could see out the window it was morning, and that meant it was Christmas Day.

'Come on, sleepy head,' said Daniel, sounding very pleased. 'We're all waiting for you in Mum and Dad's room. Hurry up. Put your shoes on.'

I scrambled to find socks and shoes and together we raced out the back door and down our drive and into the house. My house! I was back in my house! I ran past the laminex table and chairs, past the bathroom door, and hurtled into Mum and Dad's room before coming to a sudden stop to check what I should do next. Mum and Dad were in bed in Mum's best floral cotton sheets. Ruthy was in between them, and Daniel took a seat on the bottom of their bed. I stood still, not quite sure what to do. I looked at Dad, who was smiling. I carefully looked at Mum, a bit scared of what her face might say to me. But she looked like my mum with the face she had when it was a Jesus day.

Everyone seemed to be smiling, which seemed a bit strange, but I guessed it was for Christmas.

My mum said, 'Dorcas, there seems to be something a bit smelly in the bottom of your wardrobe where you stash your hats when they are grubby. I'd like you to take it out and air it please.'

My stomach did a kind of somersault and ended up in my throat. Had she just let me in to tell me off for bad hat behaviour? I stayed still for a moment, but I noticed everyone was still smiling, so I felt very confused. Daniel made a shooing motion with his hand towards my bedroom, so I ran to the wardrobe to see what was what. Ruthy jumped out of Mum and Dad's bed and chased me in. She stood near the wardrobe door sort of shivering with excitement. This was proving to be a most bewildering morning.

I opened the door tentatively and on the bottom of it was a brown cardboard box. It was quite a big box and it was moving. I knelt down and pulled it out onto the carpet. Ruthy was looming over me, and I noticed that Mum, Dad and Daniel were all standing at the door. I looked up at Dad for reassurance, and he smiled and nodded for me to keep going.

When I opened the box, I gasped. There at the bottom was a tiny black puppy, squirming all over the place. I put my hand in to stroke it and it licked me on the fingers. I lifted it out. It was the most beautiful puppy I'd ever seen, with a shiny coat and big paws and floppy ears. It was like the puppy I imagined I'd have when I was a girl knight in Caramel Castle with my baby Arabella and my guinea pig called Thruppence. I turned to look at everyone grinning at me. I didn't know what to say.

Dad and Mum took a seat on the end of my bed, and Daniel leaned on the door lintel.

'She's the most beautiful dog I've ever seen. I love her.' The puppy was wriggling in my arms trying to get away, but I was possibly never going to let her go. 'Thank you so much, Dad. This is the best present ever.'

'It's not me you have to thank. This is your mother's doing, Dorcas. She rang the breeder and she chose this one for you.'

I looked at Mum with amazement. I needed to check her face to see if this could possibly be true. I handed my puppy to Ruthy and I stood up and walked towards Mum. She didn't reach out for me, but she didn't push me away either, which seemed like a very good thing.

'This is my present to you, Dorcas, to say I'm sorry because ...' But I didn't let her finish. I did something I wasn't expecting to do. I put my hand over her mouth to stop her saying more words. We stood looking at each other for a moment, and then she pulled me close to her. I could smell her rose soap and her skin all warm from bed, and it was an even better smell than my new puppy. After a moment she pulled back and looked at me with something more like her usual Mum face.

She said, 'All I ask is that it doesn't sleep on your bed and that you give it a bath every week. And Ruthy claims you'll want to call it Plops, and I'd prefer something nicer than that. This is your responsibility now, Dorcas. This is your dog, although I expect you to share her with Ruthy too.' It was almost a relief to hear something sort of usual coming out of her mouth, but she was still smiling, so I just nodded and nodded, probably about twenty times I think.

Suddenly there was another figure at the bedroom door. We hadn't heard Mr Driver come in, but I grabbed my puppy from Ruthy and ran to show him. He couldn't take her from me because he had a large tray in his hands.

'Well,' he said, 'I know it's breakfast time on Christmas Day, but I think a new puppy calls for chocolate self-saucing pudding whatever the time is.' And he pulled off the tea towel and let all the chocolatey smell and steam fill the room.

At that very moment I knew what I would call my new friend. 'Her name is Mona after your dead wife, Mr Driver,' I said. He looked startled and then laughed his head off. We all followed him into the kitchen where Mum took out bowls and Dad took out spoons and we had the best Christmas Day morning breakfast probably in the entire world.

After we'd all had pudding around the kitchen table, I cleared away the dishes and piled them up on the sink ready to wash. I filled the sink with hot water and carefully put one splodge of Sunlight liquid in ready to go. I started washing each bowl while my family laughed and chattered away behind me. It was a comforting kind of noise and I was back in my own house looking out of my own kitchen window.

I was up to the third bowl and about to lift it out of the water to lean up against the others on the drain board when an elegant hand with lovely pink nails took it from me.

'Sorry, Mum, I'll just check it's right,' I said, turning the bowl over to make sure I'd found every bit of sauce.

'It's perfectly fine, Dorcas. And thank you very much for doing the dishes. You're doing a lovely job. And, Dorcas, I thought after Christmas we'd go to the pet store and choose a nice collar for ... Mona. Just the two of us. They only had orange ones the day I picked her up, and I knew that wouldn't do.'

I just stared at her. My lovely mother. My mum who had chosen me a puppy and refused an orange collar because it was my least favourite colour, and she'd remembered. My mum who just thanked me for washing the dishes without being asked. My mum who didn't ask me to put the bowls back in the water and do them over again properly. And then she said: 'Close your mouth, Dorcas. You look like a guppy.' But she was smiling, and so I was smiling too.

I didn't know what would happen next. This day was a Jesus day for Mum, but the morrow could be a head day or a cross day. I didn't know if Mum would continue to spend her days in bed, or whether Dad would return to coming home for tea and Cadbury's on Friday nights. But I did know that although I'd lost my little Caleb, my big Daniel was home, and I knew Sixpence would be amazed when I introduced her to Mona.

And maybe, best of all, my mother and I were going shopping after Christmas. Just the two of us.

ACKNOWLEDGEMENTS

I've heard it said: *New York, New York, so nice they named it twice*. On that basis I must twice-name two people who are not only nice, but also talented and supportive, and without whom this book would not exist:

Samantha Sainsbury. Samantha Sainsbury.
Alex Craig. Alex Craig.

Expert editor that she is, Samantha helped me polish and develop an earlier version of this manuscript. I will remember with gratitude that it was children's editor Elise Jones who found Samantha for me.

Courageous and talented publisher that she is, Alex Craig read that version and offered publication with Ultimo, a senior publisher in a house that is so right for me on every level.

It's not true of many organisations that every staff member or contractor you meet under their brand is helpful, patient and passionate. But this has been my experience of Ultimo Press. Thanks to the whole team, including Robert Watkins, Brigid Mullane, Katherine Rajwar, and James Kellow. Thank you to Deonie Fiford for editing the final version, to Ronnie Scott for proofreading and to Christabella Designs for the cover, which my protagonist Dorcas says she 'love, love, loves'.

Thank you to author Fiona McIntosh, who stopped me falling into darkness before the book-contract dawn. And a shout-out also to literary agent Jacinta di Mase, who for several years gave me little shots in the arm to keep me going.

Special thanks to new writer friends who have shared their knowledge, and who so generously continue to encourage and celebrate with me. In particular I acknowledge the support of Tassie writer Rhonda McCoy, and the BookGang crew who welcomed me into their debut authors' group. Treasures, every one.

Thank you to all the friends, family and neighbours who for years practiced stifling a yawn when I felt the need to speak YET AGAIN about my ambitions to be published. In particular thanks to Dr David Waterford and Michael Lincoln, Brenda Kuhr and Nancy Wilson, Meg Barnett and Paul Arbon, and Taryn Schubert. I will always be grateful to the community with whom I have dinner once a month in the bucolic country hamlet we call home, and to so many of the clients of my management consulting firm who cheered me on tirelessly.

Thank you to my mother Margaret Palmer who is a natural story-teller.

And special thanks to the mysterious BeeMan, who makes me laugh every day.

Following the establishment of a career leading human services, Denise Picton retrained in business and established a management consulting firm that has worked across Australia and Asia for over thirty years. In her twenties she published short fiction in literary journals, and returned to writing to begin work on a series of novels in her fifties. This is her debut novel.